THE HOLLOW

A far-from-warm welcome greets Hercule Poirot as he arrives for lunch at Lucy Angkatell's country house. A man lies dying by the swimming pool, his blood dripping into the water — and his wife stands over him, holding a revolver. As Poirot investigates, he begins to realise that beneath the respectable surface lies a tangle of family secrets, and everyone becomes a suspect.

E r
resear eases.
E

MORTON

4\4   H2.   HAR 9/13   26 APR 2019

1 0 MAY 2011   1 0 JUN 2011

0 4 AUG 2014   -8 JUL 2011
22-2-16

-7 SEP 2011

Roy ists.

Th he
Great ldren,

1 1 JUL 2018   2 7 SEP 2012

You c ation
by m very
con ved
w :

ReeCml

BENTON HOLME   5/3

1 5 OCT 2013

TH N,
T ,

Agatha Christie is known throughout the world as the Queen of Crime. She is the most widely published author of all time and in any language, outsold only by the Bible and Shakespeare. She is the author of 80 crime novels and short story collections, 19 plays, and six novels written under the name of Mary Westmacott.

Agatha Christie's first novel, *The Mysterious Affair at Styles*, was written towards the end of the First World War, in which she served as a VAD. In it she created Hercule Poirot, the little Belgian detective who was destined to become the most popular detective in crime fiction since Sherlock Holmes.

Agatha Christie was made a Dame in 1971. She died in 1976.

AGATHA CHRISTIE

THE HOLLOW

Complete and Unabridged

ULVERSCROFT
Leicester

First published in Great Britain in 1946 by
Collins
London

First Large Print Edition
published 2011
by arrangement with
HarperCollins*Publishers*
London

British Library CIP Data

Christie, Agatha, *1890 – 1976.*
The hollow.
1. Poirot, Hercule (Fictitious character)- -Fiction.
2. Private investigators- -Belgium- -Fiction.
3. Detective and mystery stories. 4. Large type books.
I. Title
823.9′12–dc22

ISBN 978–1–44480–265–8

Published by
F. A. Thorpe (Publishing)
Anstey, Leicestershire
Set by Words & Graphics Ltd.
Anstey, Leicestershire
Printed and bound in Great Britain by
T. J. International Ltd., Padstow, Cornwall

This book is printed on acid-free paper

For Larry and Danae
With apologies for using their swimming
pool as the scene of a murder

1

At six thirteen am on a Friday morning Lucy Angkatell's big blue eyes opened upon another day and, as always, she was at once wide awake and began immediately to deal with the problems conjured up by her incredibly active mind. Feeling urgently the need of consultation and conversation, and selecting for the purpose her young cousin, Midge Hardcastle, who had arrived at The Hollow the night before, Lady Angkatell slipped quickly out of bed, threw a négligée round her still graceful shoulders, and went along the passage to Midge's room. Since she was a woman of disconcertingly rapid thought processes, Lady Angkatell, as was her invariable custom, commenced the conversation in her own mind, supplying Midge's answers out of her own fertile imagination.

The conversation was in full swing when Lady Angkatell flung open Midge's door.

' — And so, darling, you really must agree that the weekend *is* going to present difficulties!'

'Eh? Hwah!' Midge grunted inarticulately,

aroused thus abruptly from a satisfying and deep sleep.

Lady Angkatell crossed to the window, opening the shutters and jerking up the blind with a brisk movement, letting in the pale light of a September dawn.

'Birds!' she observed, peering with kindly pleasure through the pane. 'So sweet.'

'What?'

'Well, at any rate, the weather isn't going to present difficulties. It looks as though it has set in fine. That's something. Because if a lot of discordant personalities are boxed up indoors, I'm sure you will agree with me that it makes it ten times worse. Round games perhaps, and that would be like last year when I shall never forgive myself about poor Gerda. I said to Henry afterwards it was most thoughtless of me — and one *has* to have her, of course, because it would be so rude to ask John without her, but it really does make things difficult — and the worst of it is that she is so nice — really it seems odd sometimes that anyone so nice as Gerda is should be so devoid of any kind of intelligence, and if that is what they mean by the law of compensation I don't really think it is at all fair.'

'What *are* you talking about, Lucy?'

'The weekend, darling. The people who are

coming tomorrow. I have been thinking about it all night and I have been dreadfully bothered about it. So it really is a relief to talk it over with you, Midge. You are always so sensible and practical.'

'Lucy,' said Midge sternly. 'Do you know what time it is?'

'Not exactly, darling. I never do, you know.'

'It's quarter-past six.'

'Yes, dear,' said Lady Angkatell, with no signs of contrition.

Midge gazed sternly at her. How maddening, how absolutely impossible Lucy was! Really, thought Midge, I don't know why we put up with her!

Yet even as she voiced the thought to herself, she was aware of the answer. Lucy Angkatell was smiling, and as Midge looked at her, she felt the extraordinary pervasive charm that Lucy had wielded all her life and that even now, at over sixty, had not failed her. Because of it, people all over the world, foreign potentates, ADCs, Government officials, had endured inconvenience, annoyance and bewilderment. It was the childlike pleasure and delight in her own doings that disarmed and nullified criticism. Lucy had but to open those wide blue eyes and stretch out those fragile hands, and murmur, 'Oh!

but I'm so *sorry* . . . ' and resentment immediately vanished.

'Darling,' said Lady Angkatell, 'I'm so *sorry*. You should have told me!'

'I'm telling you now — but it's too late! I'm thoroughly awake.'

'What a shame! But you *will* help me, won't you?'

'About the weekend? Why? What's wrong with it?'

Lady Angkatell sat down on the edge of the bed. It was not, Midge thought, like anyone else sitting on your bed. It was as insubstantial as though a fairy had poised itself there for a minute.

Lady Angkatell stretched out fluttering white hands in a lovely, helpless gesture.

'All the wrong people coming — the wrong people to be *together*, I mean — not in themselves. They're all charming really.'

'Who *is* coming?'

Midge pushed thick wiry black hair back from her square forehead with a sturdy brown arm. Nothing insubstantial or fairylike about her.

'Well, John and Gerda. That's all right by itself. I mean, John is delightful — *most* attractive. And as for poor Gerda — well, I mean, we must all be very kind. Very, very kind.'

4

Moved by an obscure instinct of defence, Midge said:

'Oh, come now, she's not as bad as that.'

'Oh, darling, she's pathetic. Those *eyes*. And she never seems to understand a single word one says.'

'She doesn't,' said Midge. 'Not what you say — but I don't know that I blame her. Your mind, Lucy, goes so fast, that to keep pace with it your conversation takes the most amazing leaps. All the connecting links are left out.'

'Just like a monkey,' said Lady Angkatell vaguely.

'But who else is coming besides the Christows? Henrietta, I suppose?'

Lady Angkatell's face brightened.

'Yes — and I really do feel that she will be a tower of strength. She always is. Henrietta, you know, is really kind — kind all through, not just on top. She will help a lot with poor Gerda. She was simply wonderful last year. That was the time we played limericks, or word-making, or quotations — or one of those things, and we had all finished and were reading them out when we suddenly discovered that poor dear Gerda hadn't even begun. She wasn't even sure what the game was. It was dreadful, wasn't it, Midge?'

'Why anyone ever comes to stay with the

Angkatells, I don't know,' said Midge. 'What with the brainwork, and the round games, and your peculiar style of conversation, Lucy.'

'Yes, darling, we must be trying — and it must always be hateful for Gerda, and I often think that if she had any spirit she would stay away — but however, there it was, and the poor dear looked so bewildered and — well — mortified, you know. And John looked so dreadfully impatient. And I simply couldn't think of how to make things all right again — and it was then that I felt so grateful to Henrietta. She turned right round to Gerda and asked about the pullover she was wearing — really a dreadful affair in faded lettuce green — too depressing and jumble sale, darling — and Gerda brightened up at once, it seems that she had knitted it herself, and Henrietta asked her for the pattern, and Gerda looked so happy and proud. And that is what I mean about Henrietta. She can always *do* that sort of thing. It's a kind of knack.'

'She takes trouble,' said Midge slowly.

'Yes, and she knows what to say.'

'Ah,' said Midge. 'But it goes further than saying. Do you know, Lucy, that Henrietta actually knitted that pullover?'

'Oh, my dear.' Lady Angkatell looked grave. 'And wore it?'

'And wore it. Henrietta carries things through.'

'And was it very dreadful?'

'No. On Henrietta it looked very nice.'

'Well, of course it would. That's just the difference between Henrietta and Gerda. Everything Henrietta does she does well and it turns out right. She's clever about nearly everything, as well as in her own line. I must say, Midge, that if anyone carries us through this weekend, it will be Henrietta. She will be nice to Gerda and she will amuse Henry, and she'll keep John in a good temper and I'm sure she'll be most helpful with David.'

'David Angkatell?'

'Yes. He's just down from Oxford — or perhaps Cambridge. Boys of that age are so difficult — especially when they are intellectual. David is very intellectual. One wishes that they could put off being intellectual until they were rather older. As it is, they always glower at one so and bite their nails and seem to have so many spots and sometimes an Adam's apple as well. And they either won't speak at all, or else are very loud and contradictory. Still, as I say, I am trusting to Henrietta. She is very tactful and asks the right kind of questions, and being a sculptress they respect her, especially as she doesn't just carve animals or children's heads but does advanced things like that curious affair in metal and plaster that she exhibited at the New Artists last year. It looked rather like a Heath Robinson step-ladder. It was called Ascending Thought — or something like that. It is the kind of thing that would impress a boy like David . . . I thought myself it was just silly.'

'Dear Lucy!'

'But some of Henrietta's things I think are quite lovely. That Weeping Ash-tree figure, for instance.'

'Henrietta has a touch of real genius, I think. And she is a very lovely and satisfying person as well,' said Midge.

Lady Angkatell got up and drifted over to the window again. She played absent-mindedly with the blind cord.

'Why acorns, I wonder?' she murmured.

'Acorns?'

'On the blind cord. Like pineapples on gates. I mean, there must be a *reason*. Because it might just as easily be a fir-cone or a pear, but it's always an acorn. Mast, they call it in crosswords — you know, for pigs. So curious, I always think.'

'Don't ramble off, Lucy. You came in here to talk about the weekend and I can't see why you were so anxious about it. If you manage to keep off round games, and try to be coherent when you're talking to Gerda, and put Henrietta on to tame intellectual David, where is the difficulty?'

'Well, for one thing, darling, Edward is coming.'

'Oh, Edward.' Midge was silent for a moment after saying the name.

Then she asked quietly:

'What on earth made you ask Edward for this weekend?'

'I didn't, Midge. That's just it. He asked himself. Wired to know if we could have him. You know what Edward is. How sensitive. If I'd wired back 'No,' he'd probably never have asked himself again. He's like that.'

Midge nodded her head slowly.

Yes, she thought, Edward was like that. For an instant she saw his face clearly, that very dearly loved face. A face with something of Lucy's insubstantial charm; gentle, diffident, ironic . . .

'Dear Edward,' said Lucy, echoing the thought in Midge's mind.

She went on impatiently:

'If only Henrietta would make up her mind to marry him. She is really fond of him, I know she is. If they had been here some weekend without the Christows . . . As it is, John Christow has always the most unfortunate effect on Edward. John, if you know

9

what I mean, becomes so much *more* so and Edward becomes so much *less* so. You understand?'

Again Midge nodded.

'And I can't put the Christows off because this weekend was arranged long ago, but I do feel, Midge, that it is all going to be difficult, with David glowering and biting his nails, and with trying to keep Gerda from feeling out of it, and with John being so positive and dear Edward so negative — '

'The ingredients of the pudding are not promising,' murmured Midge.

Lucy smiled at her.

'Sometimes,' she said meditatively, 'things arrange themselves quite simply. I've asked the Crime man to lunch on Sunday. It will make a distraction, don't you think so?'

'Crime man?'

'Like an egg,' said Lady Angkatell. 'He was in Baghdad, solving something, when Henry was High Commissioner. Or perhaps it was afterwards? We had him to lunch with some other Duty people. He had on a white duck suit, I remember, and a pink flower in his buttonhole, and black patent-leather shoes. I don't remember much about it because I never think it's very interesting who killed who. I mean, once they are dead it doesn't seem to matter why, and to make a fuss about it all seems so silly . . . '

'But have you any crimes down here, Lucy?'

'Oh, no, darling. He's in one of those funny new cottages — you know, beams that bump your head and a lot of very good plumbing and quite the wrong kind of garden. London people like that sort of thing. There's an actress in the other, I believe. They don't live in them all the time like we do. Still,' Lady Angkatell moved vaguely across the room, 'I dare say it pleases them. Midge, darling, it's sweet of you to have been so helpful.'

'I don't think I have been so very helpful.'

'Oh, haven't you?' Lucy Angkatell looked surprised. 'Well, have a nice sleep now and don't get up to breakfast, and when you do get up, do be as rude as ever you like.'

'Rude?' Midge looked surprised. 'Why! Oh!' she laughed. 'I see! Penetrating of you, Lucy. Perhaps I'll take you at your word.'

Lady Angkatell smiled and went out. As she passed the open bathroom door and saw the kettle and gas-ring, an idea came to her.

People were fond of tea, she knew — and Midge wouldn't be called for hours. She would make Midge some tea. She put

11

the kettle on and then went on down the passage.

She paused at her husband's door and turned the handle, but Sir Henry Angkatell, that able administrator, knew his Lucy. He was extremely fond of her, but he liked his morning sleep undisturbed. The door was locked.

Lady Angkatell went on into her own room. She would have liked to have consulted Henry, but later would do. She stood by her open window, looked out for a moment or two, then she yawned. She got into bed, laid her head on the pillow and in two minutes was sleeping like a child.

In the bathroom the kettle came to the boil and went on boiling . . .

'Another kettle gone, Mr Gudgeon,' said Simmons, the housemaid.

Gudgeon, the butler, shook his grey head.

He took the burnt-out kettle from Simmons and, going into the pantry, produced another kettle from the bottom of the plate cupboard where he had a stock of half a dozen.

'There you are, Miss Simmons. Her ladyship will never know.'

'Does her ladyship often do this sort of thing?' asked Simmons.

Gudgeon sighed.

'Her ladyship,' he said, 'is at once kind-hearted and very forgetful, if you know what I mean. But in this house,' he continued, 'I see to it that everything possible is done to spare her ladyship annoyance or worry.'

2

Henrietta Savernake rolled up a little strip of clay and patted it into place. She was building up the clay head of a girl with swift practised skill.

In her ears, but penetrating only to the edge of her understanding, was the thin whine of a slightly common voice:

'And I do think, Miss Savernake, that I was quite right! 'Really,' I said, 'if *that*'s the line you're going to take!' Because I do think, Miss Savernake, that a girl owes it to herself to make a stand about these sort of things — if you know what I mean. 'I'm not accustomed,' I said, 'to having things like that said to me, and I can only say that you must have a very nasty imagination!' One does hate unpleasantness, but I do think I was right to make a stand, don't you, Miss Savernake?'

'Oh, absolutely,' said Henrietta with a fervour in her voice which might have led someone who knew her well to suspect that she had not been listening very closely.

' 'And if your wife says things of that kind,' I said, 'well, I'm sure *I* can't help it!' I don't know how it is, Miss Savernake, but it seems to be trouble wherever I go, and I'm sure it's not *my* fault. I mean, men are so susceptible, aren't they?' The model gave a coquettish little giggle.

'Frightfully,' said Henrietta, her eyes half-closed.

'Lovely,' she was thinking. 'Lovely that plane just below the eyelid — and the other plane coming up to meet it. That angle by the jaw's wrong . . . I must scrape off there and build up again. It's tricky.'

Aloud she said in her warm, sympathetic voice:

'It must have been *most* difficult for you.'

'I do think jealousy's so unfair, Miss Savernake, and so *narrow*, if you know what I mean. It's just envy, if I may say so, because someone's better-looking and younger than they are.'

Henrietta, working on the jaw, said absently: 'Yes, of course.'

She had learned the trick, years ago, of shutting her mind into watertight compartments. She could play a game of bridge, conduct an intelligent conversation, write a clearly constructed letter, all without giving more than a fraction of her essential mind to the task. She was now completely intent on seeing the head of Nausicaa build itself up under her fingers, and the thin, spiteful

15

stream of chatter issuing from those very lovely childish lips penetrated not at all into the deeper recesses of her mind. She kept the conversation going without effort. She was used to models who wanted to talk. Not so much the professional ones — it was the amateurs who, uneasy at their forced inactivity of limb, made up for it by bursting into garrulous self-revelation. So an inconspicuous part of Henrietta listened and replied, and, very far and remote, the real Henrietta commented, 'Common mean spiteful little piece — but what eyes . . . Lovely lovely lovely eyes . . . '

Whilst she was busy on the eyes, let the girl talk. She would ask her to keep silent when she got to the mouth. Funny when you came to think of it, that that thin stream of spite should come out through those perfect curves.

'Oh, damn,' thought Henrietta with sudden frenzy, 'I'm ruining that eyebrow arch! What the hell's the matter with it? I've over-emphasized the bone — it's sharp, not thick . . . '

She stood back again frowning from the clay to the flesh and blood sitting on the platform.

Doris Saunders went on:

' 'Well,' I said, 'I really don't see why your

husband shouldn't give me a present if he likes, and I don't think,' I said, 'you ought to make insinuations of that kind.' It was ever such a nice bracelet, Miss Savernake, reely quite lovely — and of course I dare say the poor fellow couldn't reely afford it, but I do think it was nice of him, and I certainly wasn't going to give it back!'

'No, no,' murmured Henrietta.

'And it's not as though there was anything between us — anything *nasty*, I mean — there was nothing of *that* kind.'

'No,' said Henrietta, 'I'm sure there wouldn't be . . .'

Her brow cleared. For the next half-hour she worked in a kind of fury. Clay smeared itself on her forehead, clung to her hair, as she pushed an impatient hand through it. Her eyes had a blind intense ferocity. It was coming . . . She was getting it . . .

Now, in a few hours, she would be out of her agony — the agony that had been growing upon her for the last ten days.

Nausicaa — she had been Nausicaa, she had got up with Nausicaa and had breakfast with Nausicaa and gone out with Nausicaa. She had tramped the streets in a nervous excitable restlessness, unable to fix her mind on anything but a beautiful blind face somewhere just beyond her mind's eye

17

— hovering there just not able to be clearly seen. She had interviewed models, hesitated over Greek types, felt profoundly dissatisfied . . .

She wanted something — something to give her the start — something that would bring her own already partially realized vision alive. She had walked long distances, getting physically tired out and welcoming the fact. And driving her, harrying her, was that urgent incessant longing — to see —

There was a blind look in her own eyes as she walked. She saw nothing of what was around her. She was straining — straining the whole time to make that face come nearer . . . She felt sick, ill, miserable . . .

And then, suddenly, her vision had cleared and with normal human eyes she had seen opposite her in the bus which she had boarded absent-mindedly and with no interest in its destination — she had seen — yes, *Nausicaa!* A foreshortened childish face, half-parted lips and eyes — lovely vacant, blind eyes.

The girl rang the bell and got out. Henrietta followed her.

She was now quite calm and businesslike. She had got what she wanted — the agony of baffled search was over.

'Excuse me speaking to you. I'm a

18

professional sculptor and to put it frankly, your head is just what I have been looking for.'

She was friendly, charming and compelling as she knew how to be when she wanted something.

Doris Saunders had been doubtful, alarmed, flattered.

'Well, I don't know, I'm sure. If it's just the *head*. Of course, I've never *done* that sort of thing!'

Suitable hesitations, delicate financial inquiry.

'Of course I should insist on your accepting the proper professional fee.'

And so here was Nausicaa, sitting on the platform, enjoying the idea of her attractions, being immortalized (though not liking very much the examples of Henrietta's work which she could see in the studio!) and enjoying also the revelation of her personality to a listener whose sympathy and attention seemed to be so complete.

On the table beside the model were her spectacles . . . the spectacles that she put on as seldom as possible owing to vanity, preferring to feel her way almost blindly sometimes, since she admitted to Henrietta that without them she was so shortsighted that she could hardly see a yard in front of her.

Henrietta had nodded comprehendingly. She understood now the physical reason for that blank and lovely stare.

Time went on. Henrietta suddenly laid down her modelling tools and stretched her arms widely.

'All right,' she said, 'I've finished. I hope you're not too tired?'

'Oh, no, thank you, Miss Savernake. It's been very interesting, I'm sure. Do you mean, it's really done — so soon?'

Henrietta laughed.

'Oh, no, it's not actually finished. I shall have to work on it quite a bit. But it's finished as far as you're concerned. I've got what I wanted — built up the planes.'

The girl came down slowly from the platform. She put on her spectacles and at once the blind innocence and vague confiding charm of the face vanished. There remained now an easy, cheap prettiness.

She came to stand by Henrietta and looked at the clay model.

'Oh,' she said doubtfully, disappointment in her voice. 'It's not very like me, is it?'

Henrietta smiled.

'Oh, no, it's not a portrait.'

There was, indeed, hardly a likeness at all. It was the setting of the eyes — the line of the cheekbones — that Henrietta had seen as the essential keynote of her conception of Nausicaa. This was not Doris Saunders, it was a blind girl about whom a poem could be made. The lips were parted as Doris's were parted, but they were not Doris's lips. They were lips that would speak another language and would utter thoughts that were not Doris's thoughts —

None of the features were clearly defined. It was Nausicaa remembered, not seen . . .

'Well,' said Miss Saunders doubtfully, 'I suppose it'll look better when you've got on with it a bit . . . And you reely don't want me any more?'

'No, thank you,' said Henrietta ('And thank God I don't!' said her inner mind). 'You've been simply splendid. I'm very grateful.'

She got rid of Doris expertly and returned to make herself some black coffee. She was tired — she was horribly tired. But happy — happy and at peace.

'Thank goodness,' she thought, 'now I can be a human being again.'

And at once her thoughts went to John.

'John,' she thought. Warmth crept into her cheeks, a sudden quick lifting of the heart made her spirits soar.

'Tomorrow,' she thought, 'I'm going to The Hollow . . . I shall see John . . .'

She sat quite still, sprawled back on the divan, drinking down the hot, strong liquid. She drank three cups of it. She felt vitality surging back.

It was nice, she thought, to be a human being again . . . and not that other thing. Nice to have stopped feeling restless and miserable and driven. Nice to be able to stop walking about the streets unhappily, looking for something, and feeling irritable and impatient because, really, you didn't know what you were looking for! Now, thank goodness, there would be only hard work — and who minded hard work?

She put down the empty cup and got up and strolled back to Nausicaa. She looked at it for some time, and slowly a little frown crept between her brows.

It wasn't — it wasn't quite —

What was it that was wrong? . . .

Blind eyes.

Blind eyes that were more beautiful than any eyes that could see . . . Blind eyes that tore at your heart because they were blind . . . Had she got that or hadn't she?

She'd got it, yes — but she'd got something else as well. Something that she hadn't meant or thought about . . . The structure was all right — yes, surely. But where did it come from — that faint, insidious suggestion? . . .

The suggestion, somewhere, of a common spiteful mind.

She hadn't been listening, not really listening. Yet somehow, in through her ears and out at her fingers, it had worked its way into the clay.

And she wouldn't, she knew she wouldn't, be able to get it out again . . .

Henrietta turned away sharply. Perhaps it was fancy. Yes, surely it was fancy. She would feel quite differently about it in the morning. She thought with dismay:

'How vulnerable one is . . . '

She walked, frowning, up to the end of the studio. She stopped in front of her figure of The Worshipper.

That was all right — a lovely bit of pearwood, graining just right. She'd saved it up for ages, hoarding it.

She looked at it critically. Yes, it was good. No doubt about that. The best thing she had done for a long time — it was for the International Group. Yes, quite a worthy exhibit.

She'd *got* it all right: the humility, the strength in the neck muscles, the bowed shoulders, the slightly upraised face — a featureless face, since worship drives out personality.

Yes, submission, adoration — and that final

devotion that is beyond, not this side, idolatry . . .

Henrietta sighed. If only, she thought, John had not been so angry.

It had startled her, that anger. It had told her something about him that he did not, she thought, know himself.

He had said flatly: 'You can't exhibit that!'

And she had said, as flatly: 'I shall.'

She went slowly back to Nausicaa. There was nothing there, she thought, that she couldn't put right. She sprayed it and wrapped it up in the damp cloths. It would have to stand over until Monday or Tuesday. There was no hurry now. The urgency had gone — all the essential planes were there. It only needed patience.

Ahead of her were three happy days with Lucy and Henry and Midge — and John!

She yawned, stretched herself like a cat stretches itself with relish and abandon, pulling out each muscle to its fullest extent. She knew suddenly how very tired she was.

She had a hot bath and went to bed. She lay on her back staring at a star or two through the skylight. Then from there her eyes went to the one light always left on, the small bulb that illuminated the glass mask that had been one of her earliest bits of work. Rather an obvious piece, she thought now.

Conventional in its suggestion.

Lucky, thought Henrietta, that one outgrew oneself . . .

And now, sleep! The strong black coffee that she had drunk did not bring wakefulness in its train unless she wished it to do so. Long ago she had taught herself the essential rhythm that could bring oblivion at call.

You took thoughts, choosing them out of your store, and then, not dwelling on them, you let them slip through the fingers of your mind, never clutching at them, never dwelling on them, no concentration . . . just letting them drift gently past.

Outside in the Mews a car was being revved up — somewhere there was hoarse shouting and laughing. She took the sounds into the stream of her semiconsciousness.

The car, she thought, was a tiger roaring . . . yellow and black . . . striped like the striped leaves — leaves and shadows — a hot jungle . . . and then down the river — a wide tropical river . . . to the sea and the liner starting . . . and hoarse voices calling goodbye — and John beside her on the deck . . . she and John starting — blue sea and down into the dining-saloon — smiling at him across the table — like dinner at the Maison Dorée — poor John, so angry! . . . out into the night air — and the car, the feeling of sliding in the gears — effortless, smooth, racing out of London . . . up over Shovel Down . . . the trees . . . tree worship . . . The Hollow . . . Lucy . . . John . . . John . . . Ridgeway's Disease . . . dear John . . .

Passing into unconsciousness now, into a happy beatitude.

And then some sharp discomfort, some haunting sense of guilt pulling her back. Something she ought to have done. Something that she had shirked.

Nausicaa?

Slowly, unwillingly, Henrietta got out of bed. She switched on the lights, went across to the stand and unwrapped the cloths.

She took a deep breath.

Not Nausicaa — Doris Saunders!

A pang went through Henrietta. She was pleading with herself: 'I can get it right — I can get it right . . . '

'Stupid,' she said to herself. 'You know quite well what you've got to do.'

Because if she didn't do it now, at once — tomorrow she wouldn't have the courage. It was like destroying your flesh and blood. It hurt — yes, it hurt.

Perhaps, thought Henrietta, cats feel like this when one of their kittens has something wrong with it and they kill it.

She took a quick, sharp breath, then she

seized the clay, twisting it off the armature, carrying it, a large heavy lump, to dump it in the clay bin.

She stood there breathing deeply, looking down at her clay-smeared hands, still feeling the wrench to her physical and mental self. She cleaned the clay off her hands slowly.

She went back to bed feeling a curious emptiness, yet a sense of peace.

Nausicaa, she thought sadly, would not come again. She had been born, had been contaminated and had died.

'Queer,' thought Henrietta, 'how things can seep into you without your knowing it.'

She hadn't been listening — not really listening — and yet knowledge of Doris's cheap, spiteful little mind had seeped into her mind and had, unconsciously, influenced her hands.

And now the thing that had been Nausicaa — Doris — was only clay — just the raw material that would, soon, be fashioned into something else.

Henrietta thought dreamily: 'Is that, then, what *death* is? Is what we call personality just the shaping of it — the impress of somebody's thought? Whose thought? God's?'

That was the idea, wasn't it, of Peer Gynt? Back into the Button Moulder's ladle.

'Where am I myself, the whole man, the true man? Where am I with God's mark upon my brow?'

Did John feel like that? He had been so tired the other night — so disheartened. Ridgeway's Disease . . . Not one of those books told you who Ridgeway was! Stupid, she thought, she would like to know . . . Ridgeway's Disease.

3

John Christow sat in his consulting-room, seeing his last patient but one for that morning. His eyes, sympathetic and encouraging, watched her as she described — explained — went into details. Now and then he nodded his head, understandingly. He asked questions, gave directions. A gentle glow pervaded the sufferer. Dr Christow was really wonderful! He was so interested — so truly concerned. Even talking to him made one feel stronger.

John Christow drew a sheet of paper towards him and began to write. Better give her a laxative, he supposed. That new American proprietary — nicely put up in cellophane and attractively coated in an unusual shade of salmon pink. Very expensive, too, and difficult to get — not every chemist stocked it. She'd probably have to go to that little place in Wardour Street. That would be all to the good — probably buck her up no end for a month or two, then he'd have to think of something else. There was nothing he could do for her. Poor physique and nothing to be done about it! Nothing to get your teeth into. Not like old mother Crabtree . . .

A boring morning. Profitable financially — but nothing else. God, he was tired! Tired of sickly women and their ailments. Palliation, alleviation — nothing to it but that. Sometimes he wondered if it was worth it. But always then he remembered St Christopher's, and the long row of beds in the Margaret Russell Ward, and Mrs Crabtree grinning up at him with her toothless smile.

He and she understood each other! She was a fighter, not like that limp slug of a woman in the next bed. She was on his side, she wanted to live — though God knew why, considering the slum she lived in, with a husband who drank and a brood of unruly children, and she herself obliged to work day in day out, scrubbing endless floors of endless offices. Hard unremitting drudgery and few pleasures! But she wanted to live — she enjoyed life — just as he, John Christow, enjoyed life! It wasn't the circumstances of life they enjoyed, it was life itself — the zest of existence. Curious — a thing one couldn't explain. He thought to himself that he must talk to Henrietta about that.

He got up to accompany his patient to the door. His hand took hers in a warm clasp, friendly, encouraging. His voice was encouraging too, full of interest and sympathy. She went away revived, almost happy. Dr Christow took such an interest!

As the door closed behind her, John Christow forgot her, he had really been hardly aware of her existence even when she had been there. He had just done his stuff. It was all automatic. Yet, though it had hardly ruffled the surface of his mind, he had given out strength. His had been the automatic response of the healer and he felt the sag of depleted energy.

'God,' he thought again, 'I'm tired.'

Only one more patient to see and then the clear space of the weekend. His mind dwelt on it gratefully. Golden leaves tinged with red and brown, the soft moist smell of autumn — the road down through the woods — the wood fires, Lucy, *most* unique and delightful of creatures — with her curious, elusive will-o'-the-wisp mind. He'd rather have Henry and Lucy than any host and hostess in England. And The Hollow was the most delightful house he knew. On Sunday he'd walk through the woods with Henrietta — up on to the crest of the hill and along the ridge. Walking with Henrietta he'd forget that there were any sick people in the world. Thank goodness, he thought, there's never anything the matter with Henrietta.

And then with a sudden, quick twist of humour:

'She'd never let on to me if there were!'

One more patient to see. He must press the bell on his desk. Yet, unaccountably, he delayed. Already he was late. Lunch would be ready upstairs in the dining-room. Gerda and the children would be waiting. He must get on.

Yet he sat there motionless. He was so tired — so very tired.

It had been growing on him lately, this tiredness. It was at the root of the constantly increasing irritability which he was aware of but could not check. Poor Gerda, he thought, she has a lot to put up with. If only she was not so submissive — so ready to admit herself in the wrong when, half the time, it was *he* who was to blame! There were days when everything that Gerda said or did conspired to irritate him, and mainly, he thought ruefully, it was her virtues that irritated him. It was her patience, her unselfishness, her subordination of her wishes to his, that aroused his ill-humour. And she never resented his quick bursts of temper, never stuck to her own opinion in preference to his, never attempted to strike out a line of her own.

(*Well, he thought, that's why you married*

32

her, isn't it? What are you complaining about? After that summer at San Miguel . . .)

Curious, when you came to think of it, that the very qualities that irritated him in Gerda were the qualities he wanted so badly to find in Henrietta. What irritated him in Henrietta (no, that was the wrong word — it was anger, not irritation, that she inspired) — what angered him there was Henrietta's unswerving rectitude where he was concerned. It was so at variance to her attitude to the world in general. He had said to her once:

'I think you are the greatest liar I know.'

'Perhaps.'

'You are always willing to say anything to people if only it pleases them.'

'That always seems to me more important.'

'More important than speaking the truth?'

'Much more.'

'Then why in God's name can't you lie a little more to *me*?'

'Do you want me to?'

'Yes.'

'I'm sorry, John, but I can't.'

'You must know so often what I want you to say.'

Come now, he mustn't start thinking of Henrietta. He'd be seeing her this very afternoon. The thing to do now was to get on with things! Ring the bell and see this last damned woman. Another sickly creature! One-tenth genuine ailment and nine-tenths hypochondria! Well, why shouldn't she enjoy ill-health if she cared to pay for it? It balanced the Mrs Crabtrees of this world.

But still he sat there motionless.

He was tired — he was so very tired. It seemed to him that he had been tired for a very long time. There was something he wanted — wanted badly.

And there shot into his mind the thought: '*I want to go home.*'

It astonished him. Where had that thought come from? And what did it mean? Home? He had never had a home. His parents had been Anglo-Indians, he had been brought up, bandied about from aunt to uncle, one set of holidays with each. The first permanent home he had had, he supposed, was this house in Harley Street.

Did he think of this house as home? He shook his head. He knew that he didn't.

But his medical curiosity was aroused. What had he meant by that phrase that had flashed out suddenly in his mind?

I want to go home.

There must be something — some image.

He half-closed his eyes — there must be some *background*.

And very clearly, before his mind's eye, he

saw the deep blue of the Mediterranean Sea, the palms, the cactus and the prickly pear; he smelt the hot summer dust, and remembered the cool feeling of the water after lying on the beach in the sun. *San Miguel!*

He was startled — a little disturbed. He hadn't thought of San Miguel for years. He certainly didn't want to go back there. All that belonged to a past chapter in his life.

That was twelve — fourteen — fifteen years ago. And he'd done the right thing! His judgment had been absolutely right! He'd been madly in love with Veronica but it wouldn't have done. Veronica would have swallowed him body and soul. She was the complete egoist and she had made no bones about admitting it! Veronica had grabbed most things that she wanted, but she hadn't been able to grab him! He'd escaped. He had, he supposed, treated her badly from the conventional point of view. In plain words, he had jilted her! But the truth was that he intended to live his own life, and that was a thing that Veronica would not have allowed him to do. She intended to live *her* life and carry John along as an extra.

She had been astonished when he had refused to come with her to Hollywood.

She had said disdainfully:

'If you really want to be a doctor you can

take a degree over there, I suppose, but it's quite unnecessary. You've got enough to live on, and *I* shall be making heaps of money.'

And he had replied vehemently:

'But I'm *keen* on my profession. I'm going to work with *Radley*.'

His voice — a young enthusiastic voice — was quite awed.

Veronica sniffed.

'That funny snuffy old man?'

'That funny snuffy old man,' John had said angrily, 'has done some of the most valuable research work on Pratt's Disease — '

She had interrupted: Who cared for Pratt's Disease? California, she said, was an enchanting climate. And it was fun to see the world. She added: 'I shall hate it without you. I want you, John — I *need* you.'

And then he had put forward the, to Veronica, amazing suggestion that she should turn down the Hollywood offer and marry him and settle down in London.

She was amused and quite firm. She was going to Hollywood, and she loved John, and John must marry her and come too. She had had no doubts of her beauty and of her power.

He had seen that there was only one thing to be done and he had done it. He had written to her breaking off the engagement.

36

He had suffered a good deal, but he had had no doubts as to the wisdom of the course he had taken. He'd come back to London and started work with Radley, and a year later he had married Gerda, who was as unlike Veronica in every way as it was possible to be . . .

The door opened and his secretary, Beryl Collins, came in.

'You've still got Mrs Forrester to see.'

He said shortly: 'I know.'

'I thought you might have forgotten.'

She crossed the room and went out at the farther door. Christow's eyes followed her calm withdrawal. A plain girl, Beryl, but damned efficient. He'd had her six years. She never made a mistake, she was never flurried or worried or hurried. She had black hair and a muddy complexion and a determined chin. Through strong glasses, her clear grey eyes surveyed him and the rest of the universe with the same dispassionate attention.

He had wanted a plain secretary with no nonsense about her, and he had got a plain secretary with no nonsense about her, but sometimes, illogically, John Christow felt aggrieved! By all the rules of stage and fiction, Beryl should have been hopelessly devoted to her employer. But he had always known that he cut no ice with Beryl. There was no devotion, no self-abnegation — Beryl regarded him as a definitely fallible human being. She remained unimpressed by his personality, uninfluenced by his charm. He doubted sometimes whether she even *liked* him.

He had heard her once speaking to a friend on the telephone.

'No,' she had been saying, 'I don't really think he is *much* more selfish than he was. Perhaps rather more thoughtless and inconsiderate.'

He had known that she was speaking of him, and for quite twenty-four hours he had been annoyed about it.

Although Gerda's indiscriminate enthusiasm irritated him, Beryl's cool appraisal irritated him too. In fact, he thought, nearly everything irritates me . . .

Something wrong there. Overwork? Perhaps. No, that was the excuse. This growing impatience, this irritable tiredness, it had some deeper significance. He thought: 'This won't do. I can't go on this way. What's the matter with me? If I could get away . . . '

There it was again — the blind idea rushing up to meet the formulated idea of escape.

I want to go home . . .

Damn it all, 404 Harley Street *was* his home!

And Mrs Forrester was sitting in the waiting-room. A tiresome woman, a woman with too much money and too much spare time to think about her ailments.

Someone had once said to him: 'You must get very tired of these rich patients always fancying themselves ill. It must be so satisfactory to get to the poor, who only come when there is something *really* the matter with them!' He had grinned. Funny the things people believed about the Poor with a capital P. They should have seen old Mrs Pearstock, on five different clinics, up every week, taking away bottles of medicine, liniments for her back, linctus for her cough, aperients, digestive mixtures. 'Fourteen years I've 'ad the brown medicine, Doctor, and it's the only thing does me any good. That young doctor last week writes me down a *white* medicine. No good at all! It stands to reason, doesn't it, Doctor? I mean, I've 'ad me brown medicine for fourteen years, and if I don't 'ave me liquid paraffin and them brown pills . . . '

He could hear the whining voice now — excellent physique, sound as a bell — even all the physic she took couldn't really do her any harm!

39

They were the same, sisters under the skin, Mrs Pearstock from Tottenham and Mrs Forrester of Park Lane Court. You listened and you wrote scratches with your pen on a piece of stiff expensive notepaper, or on a hospital card as the case might be . . .

God, he was tired of the whole business . . .

Blue sea, the faint sweet smell of mimosa, hot dust . . .

Fifteen years ago. All that was over and done with — yes, done with, thank heaven. He'd had the courage to break off the whole business.

Courage? said a little imp somewhere. Is *that* what you call it?

Well, he'd done the sensible thing, hadn't he? It had been a wrench. Damn it all, it had hurt like hell! But he'd gone through with it, cut loose, come home, and married Gerda.

He'd got a plain secretary and he'd married a plain wife. That was what he wanted, wasn't it? He'd had enough of beauty, hadn't he? He'd seen what someone like Veronica could do with her beauty — seen the effect it had on every male within range. After Veronica, he'd wanted safety. Safety and peace and devotion and the quiet, enduring things of life. He'd wanted, in fact, Gerda! He'd wanted someone who'd take her ideas of life from him, who would accept his decisions and who wouldn't have, for one moment, any ideas of her own . . .

Who was it who had said that the real tragedy of life was that you got what you wanted?

Angrily he pressed the buzzer on his desk. He'd deal with Mrs Forrester.

It took him a quarter of an hour to deal with Mrs Forrester. Once again it was easy money. Once again he listened, asked questions, reassured, sympathized, infused something of his own healing energy. Once more he wrote out a prescription for an expensive proprietary.

The sickly neurotic woman who had trailed into the room left it with a firmer step, with colour in her cheeks, with a feeling that life might possibly after all be worth while.

John Christow leant back in his chair. He was free now — free to go upstairs to join Gerda and the children — free from the preoccupations of illness and suffering for a whole weekend.

But he felt still that strange disinclination to move, that new queer lassitude of the will.

He was tired — tired — tired.

4

In the dining-room of the flat above the consulting room Gerda Christow was staring at a joint of mutton.

Should she or should she not send it back to the kitchen to be kept warm?

If John was going to be much longer it would be cold — congealed, and that would be dreadful.

But on the other hand the last patient had gone, John would be up in a moment, if she sent it back there would be delay — John was so impatient. 'But surely you knew I was just coming . . . ' There would be that tone of suppressed exasperation in his voice that she knew and dreaded. Besides, it would get over-cooked, dried up — John hated over-cooked meat.

But on the other hand he disliked cold food very much indeed.

At any rate the dish was nice and hot.

Her mind oscillated to and fro, and her sense of misery and anxiety deepened.

The whole world had shrunk to a leg of mutton getting cold on a dish.

On the other side of the table her son

Terence, aged twelve, said:

'Boracic salts burn with a green flame, sodium salts are yellow.'

Gerda looked distractedly across the table at his square, freckled face. She had no idea what he was talking about.

'Did you know that, Mother?'

'Know what, dear?'

'About salts.'

Gerda's eye flew distractedly to the salt-cellar. Yes, salt and pepper were on the table. That was all right. Last week Lewis had forgotten them and that had annoyed John. There was always something . . .

'It's one of the chemical tests,' said Terence in a dreamy voice. 'Jolly interesting. *I* think.'

Zena, aged nine, with a pretty, vacuous face, whimpered:

'I want my dinner. Can't we start, Mother?'

'In a minute, dear, we must wait for Father.'

'We could start,' said Terence. 'Father wouldn't mind. You know how fast he eats.'

Gerda shook her head.

Carve the mutton? But she never could remember which was the right side to plunge the knife in. Of course, perhaps Lewis had put it the right way on the dish — but sometimes she didn't — and John was always annoyed if it was done the wrong way. And,

Gerda reflected desperately, it always *was* the wrong way when she did it. Oh, dear, how cold the gravy was getting — a skin was forming on the top of it — and surely he would be coming now.

Her mind went round and round unhappily . . . like a trapped animal.

Sitting back in his consulting-room chair, tapping with one hand on the table in front of him, conscious that upstairs lunch must be ready, John Christow was nevertheless unable to force himself to get up.

San Miguel . . . blue sea . . . smell of mimosa . . . a scarlet tritoma upright against green leaves . . . the hot sun . . . the dust . . . that desperation of love and suffering . . .

He thought: 'Oh, God, not that. Never that again! That's over . . . '

He wished suddenly that he had never known Veronica, never married Gerda, never met Henrietta . . .

Mrs Crabtree, he thought, was worth the lot of them. That had been a bad afternoon last week. He'd been so pleased with the reactions. She could stand .005 by now. And then had come that alarming rise in toxicity and the DL reaction had been negative instead of positive.

The old bean had lain there, blue, gasping for breath — peering up at him with

44

malicious, indomitable eyes.

'Making a bit of a guinea pig out of me, ain't you, dearie? Experimenting — that kinder thing.'

'We want to get you well,' he had said, smiling down at her.

'Up to your tricks, yer mean!' She had grinned suddenly. 'I don't mind, bless yer. You carry on, Doctor! Someone's got to be first, that's it, ain't it? 'Ad me 'air permed, I did, when I was a kid. It wasn't 'alf a difficult business then. Looked like a nigger, I did. Couldn't get a comb through it. But there — I enjoyed the fun. You can 'ave yer fun with me. *I* can stand it.'

'Feel pretty bad, don't you?' His hand was on her pulse. Vitality passed from him to the panting old woman on the bed.

'Orful, I feel. You're about right! 'Asn't gone according to plan — that's it, isn't it? Never you mind. Don't you lose 'eart. I can stand a lot, I can!'

John Christow said appreciatively:

'You're fine. I wish all my patients were like you.'

'I wanter get well — that's why! I wanter get well. Mum, she lived to be eighty-eight — and old Grandma was ninety when she popped off. We're long-livers in our family, we are.'

45

He had come away miserable, racked with doubt and uncertainty. He'd been so sure he was on the right track. Where had he gone wrong? How to diminish the toxicity and keep up the hormone content and at the same time neutralize the pantratin? . . .

He'd been too cocksure — he'd taken it for granted that he'd circumvented all the snags.

And it was then, on the steps of St Christopher's, that a sudden desperate weariness had overcome him — a hatred of all this long, slow, wearisome clinical work, and he'd thought of Henrietta, thought of her suddenly not as herself, but of her beauty and her freshness, her health and her radiant vitality — and the faint smell of primroses that clung about her hair.

And he had gone to Henrietta straight away, sending a curt telephone message home about being called away. He had strode into the studio and taken Henrietta in his arms, holding her to him with a fierceness that was new in their relationship.

There had been a quick, startled wonder in her eyes. She had freed herself from his arms and had made him coffee. And as she moved about the studio she had thrown out desultory questions. Had he come, she asked, straight from the hospital?

He didn't want to talk about the hospital.

He wanted to make love to Henrietta and forget that the hospital and Mrs Crabtree and Ridgeway's Disease and all the rest of the caboodle existed.

But, at first unwillingly, then more fluently, he answered her questions. And presently he was striding up and down, pouring out a spate of technical explanations and surmises. Once or twice he paused, trying to simplify — to explain:

'You see, you have to get a reaction — '

Henrietta said quickly:

'Yes, yes, the DL reaction has to be positive. I understand that. Go on.'

He said sharply, 'How do *you* know about the DL reaction?'

'I got a book — '

'What book? Whose?'

She motioned towards the small book table. He snorted.

'Scobell? Scobell's no good. He's fundamentally unsound. Look here, if you want to read — don't — '

She interrupted him.

'I only want to understand some of the terms you use — enough so as to understand you without making you stop to explain everything the whole time. Go on. I'm following you all right.'

'Well,' he said doubtfully, 'remember

Scobell's unsound.' He went on talking. He talked for two hours and a half. Reviewing the setbacks, analysing the possibilities, outlining possible theories. He was hardly conscious of Henrietta's presence. And yet, more than once, as he hesitated, her quick intelligence took him a step on the way, seeing, almost before he did, what he was hesitating to advance. He was interested now, and his belief in himself was creeping back. He had been right — the main theory was correct — and there were ways, more ways than one, of combating the toxic symptoms.

And then, suddenly, he was tired out. He'd got it all clear now. He'd get on to it tomorrow morning. He'd ring up Neill, tell him to combine the two solutions and try that. Yes, try that. By God, he wasn't going to be beaten!

'I'm tired,' he said abruptly. 'My God, I'm tired.'

And he had flung himself down and slept — slept like the dead.

He had awoken to find Henrietta smiling at him in the morning light and making tea and he had smiled back at her.

'Not at all according to plan,' he said.

'Does it matter?'

'No. No. You are rather a nice person, Henrietta.' His eye went to the book table. 'If

48

you're interested in this sort of thing, I'll get you the proper stuff to read.'

'I'm not interested in this sort of thing. I'm interested in you, John.'

'You can't read Scobell.' He took up the offending volume. 'The man's a charlatan.'

And she had laughed. He could not understand why his strictures on Scobell amused her so.

But that was what, every now and then, startled him about Henrietta. The sudden revelation, disconcerting to him, that she was able to laugh at him.

He wasn't used to it. Gerda took him in deadly earnest. And Veronica had never thought about anything but herself. But Henrietta had a trick of throwing her head back, of looking at him through half-closed eyes, with a sudden tender half-mocking little smile, as though she were saying: 'Let me have a good look at this funny person called John . . . Let me get a long way away and look at him . . . '

It was, he thought, very much the same as the way she screwed up her eyes to look at her work — or a picture. It was — damn it all — it was *detached*. He didn't want Henrietta to be detached. He wanted Henrietta to think only of him, never to let her mind stray away from him.

('Just what you object to in Gerda, in fact,' said his private imp, bobbing up again.)

The truth of it was that he was completely illogical. He didn't know what he wanted.

('*I want to go home.*' What an absurd, what a ridiculous phrase. It didn't mean anything.)

In an hour or so at any rate he'd be driving out of London — forgetting about sick people with their faint sour 'wrong' smell . . . sniffing wood smoke and pines and soft wet autumn leaves . . . The very motion of the car would be soothing — that smooth, effortless increase of speed.

But it wouldn't, he reflected suddenly, be at all like that because owing to a slightly strained wrist, Gerda would have to drive, and Gerda, God help her, had never been able to begin to drive a car! Every time she changed gear he would be silent, grinding his teeth together, managing not to say anything because he knew, by bitter experience, that when he did say anything Gerda became immediately worse. Curious that no one had ever been able to teach Gerda to change gear — not even Henrietta. He'd turned her over to Henrietta, thinking that Henrietta's enthusiasm might do better than his own irritability.

For Henrietta loved cars. She spoke of cars with the lyrical intensity that other people gave to spring, or the first snow-drop.

'Isn't he a beauty, John? Doesn't he just purr along?' (For Henrietta's cars were always masculine.) 'He'll do Bale Hill in third — not straining at all — quite effortlessly. Listen to the even way he ticks over.'

Until he had burst out suddenly and furiously:

'Don't you think, Henrietta, you could pay *some* attention to me and forget the damned car for a minute or two!'

He was always ashamed of these outbursts.

He never knew when they would come upon him out of a blue sky.

It was the same thing over her work. He realized that her work was good. He admired it — and hated it — at the same time.

The most furious quarrel he had had with her had arisen over that.

Gerda had said to him one day:

'Henrietta has asked me to sit for her.'

'What?' His astonishment had not, if he came to think of it, been flattering. '*You?*'

'Yes, I'm going over to the studio tomorrow.'

'What on earth does she want you for?'

Yes, he hadn't been very polite about it. But luckily Gerda hadn't realized that fact. She had looked pleased about it. He suspected Henrietta of one of those insincere kindnesses of hers — Gerda, perhaps, had hinted that she would like to be modelled. Something of that kind.

Then, about ten days later, Gerda had shown him triumphantly a small plaster statuette.

It was a pretty thing — technically skilful like all Henrietta's work. It idealized Gerda — and Gerda herself was clearly pleased about it.

'I really think it's rather charming, John.'

'Is that Henrietta's work? It means nothing — nothing at all. I don't see how she came to do a thing like that.'

'It's different, of course, from her abstract work — but I think it's good, John, I really do.'

He had said no more — after all, he didn't want to spoil Gerda's pleasure. But he tackled Henrietta about it at the first opportunity.

'What did you want to make that silly thing of Gerda for? It's unworthy of you. After all, you usually turn out decent stuff.'

Henrietta said slowly:

'I didn't think it was bad. Gerda seemed quite pleased.'

'Gerda was delighted. She would be. Gerda doesn't know art from a coloured photograph.'

'It wasn't bad art, John. It was just a

52

portrait statuette — quite harmless and not at all pretentious.'

'You don't usually waste your time doing that kind of stuff — '

He broke off, staring at a wooden figure about five feet high.

'Hallo, what's this?'

'It's for the International Group. Pearwood. The Worshipper.'

She watched him. He stared and then — suddenly, his neck swelled and he turned on her furiously.

'So that's what you wanted Gerda for? How dare you?'

'I wondered if you'd see . . . '

'See it? Of course I see it. It's *here*.' He placed a finger on the broad heavy neck muscles.

Henrietta nodded.

'Yes, it's the neck and shoulders I wanted — and that heavy forward slant — the submission — that bowed look. It's wonderful!'

'Wonderful? Look here, Henrietta, I won't have it. You're to leave Gerda alone.'

'Gerda won't know. Nobody will know. You know Gerda would never recognize herself here — nobody else would either. And it *isn't* Gerda. It isn't *anybody*.'

'*I* recognized it, didn't I?'

'You're different, John. You — see things.'

'It's the damned cheek of it! I won't have it, Henrietta! I won't have it. Can't you see that it was an indefensible thing to do?'

'Was it?'

'Don't you know it was? Can't you *feel* it was? Where's your usual sensitiveness?'

Henrietta said slowly:

'You don't understand, John. I don't think I could ever make you understand . . . You don't know what it is to want something — to look at it day after day — that line of the neck — those muscles — the angle where the head goes forward — that heaviness round the jaw. I've been looking at them, wanting them — every time I saw Gerda . . . In the end I just had to have them!'

'Unscrupulous!'

'Yes, I suppose just that. But when you want things, in that way, you just have to take them.'

'You mean you don't care a damn about anybody else. You don't care about Gerda —'

'Don't be stupid, John. That's why I made that statuette thing. To please Gerda and make her happy. I'm not inhuman!'

'Inhuman is exactly what you are.'

'Do you think — honestly — that Gerda would ever recognize herself in this?'

John looked at it unwillingly. For the first

time his anger and resentment became subordinated to his interest. A strange submissive figure, a figure offering up worship to an unseen deity — the face raised — blind, dumb, devoted — terribly strong, terribly fanatical . . . He said:

'That's rather a terrifying thing that you have made, Henrietta!'

Henrietta shivered slightly.

She said, 'Yes — I thought that . . . '

John said sharply:

'What's she looking at — who is it? There in front of her?'

Henrietta hesitated. She said, and her voice had a queer note in it:

'I don't know. But I *think* — she might be looking at *you*, John.'

5

In the dining-room the child Terry made another scientific statement.

'Lead salts are more soluble in cold water than hot. If you add potassium iodide you get a yellow precipitate of lead iodide.'

He looked expectantly at his mother but without any real hope. Parents, in the opinion of young Terence, were sadly disappointing.

'Did you know that, Mother — '

'I don't know anything about chemistry, dear.'

'You could read about it in a book,' said Terence.

It was a simple statement of fact, but there was a certain wistfulness behind it.

Gerda did not hear the wistfulness. She was caught in the trap of her anxious misery. Round and round and round. She had been miserable ever since she woke up this morning and realized that at last this long-dreaded weekend with the Angkatells was upon her. Staying at The Hollow was always a nightmare to her. She always felt

56

bewildered and forlorn. Lucy Angkatell with her sentences that were never finished, her swift inconsequences, and her obvious attempts at kindliness, was the figure she dreaded most. But the others were nearly as bad. For Gerda it was two days of sheer martyrdom — to be endured for John's sake.

For John that morning as he stretched himself had remarked in tones of unmitigated pleasure:

'Splendid to think we'll be getting into the country this weekend. It will do you good, Gerda, just what you need.'

She had smiled mechanically and had said with unselfish fortitude: 'It will be delightful.'

Her unhappy eyes had wandered round the bedroom. The wallpaper, cream striped with a black mark just by the wardrobe, the mahogany dressing-table with the glass that swung too far forward, the cheerful bright blue carpet, the watercolours of the Lake District. All dear familiar things and she would not see them again until Monday.

Instead, tomorrow a housemaid who rustled would come into the strange bedroom and put down a little dainty tray of early tea by the bed and pull up the blinds, and would then rearrange and fold Gerda's clothes — a thing which made Gerda feel hot and uncomfortable all over. She would lie miserably, enduring these things, trying to comfort herself by thinking, 'Only one morning more.' Like being at school and counting the days.

Gerda had not been happy at school. At school there had been even less reassurance than elsewhere. Home had been better. But even home had not been very good. For they had all, of course, been quicker and cleverer than she was. Their comments, quick, impatient, not quite unkind, had whistled about her ears like a hailstorm. 'Oh, do be quick, Gerda.' 'Butter-fingers, give it to me!' 'Oh don't let Gerda do it, she'll be *ages*.' 'Gerda never takes in anything . . .'

Hadn't they seen, all of them, that that was the way to make her slower and stupider still? She'd got worse and worse, more clumsy with her fingers, more slow-witted, more inclined to stare vacantly at what was said to her.

Until, suddenly, she had reached the point where she had found a way out. Almost accidentally, really, she found her weapon of defence.

She had grown slower still, her puzzled stare had become even blanker. But now, when they said impatiently: 'Oh, Gerda, how stupid you are, don't you understand *that*?' she had been able, behind her blank expression, to hug herself a little in her secret knowledge . . . For she wasn't as stupid as they thought. Often, when she pretended not to understand, she *did* understand. And often, deliberately, she slowed down in her task of whatever it was, smiling to herself when someone's impatient fingers snatched it away from her.

For, warm and delightful, was a secret knowledge of superiority. She began to be, quite often, a little amused. Yes, it was amusing to know more than they thought you knew. To be able to do a thing, but not let anybody know that you could do it.

And it had the advantage, suddenly discovered, that people often did things for you. That, of course, saved you a lot of trouble. And, in the end, if people got into the habit of doing things for you, you didn't have to do them at all, and then people didn't know that you did them badly. And so, slowly, you came round again almost to where you started. To feeling that you could hold your own on equal terms with the world at large.

(But that wouldn't, Gerda feared, hold good with the Angkatells; the Angkatells were always so far ahead that you didn't feel even in the same street with them. How she hated the Angkatells! It was good for John — John liked it there. He came home less tired — and sometimes less irritable.)

Dear John, she thought. John was wonderful. Everyone thought so. Such a clever doctor, so terribly kind to his patients. Wearing himself out — and the interest he took in his hospital patients — all that side of his work that didn't pay at all. John was so *disinterested* — so truly noble.

She had always known, from the very first, that John was brilliant and was going to get to the top of the tree. And he had chosen her, when he might have married somebody far more brilliant. He had not minded her being slow and rather stupid and not very pretty. 'I'll look after you,' he had said. Nicely, rather masterfully. 'Don't worry about things, Gerda, I'll take care of you . . . '

Just what a man ought to be. Wonderful to think John should have chosen her.

He had said with that sudden, very attractive, half-pleading smile of his: 'I like my own way, you know, Gerda.'

Well, that was all right. She had always tried to give in to him in everything. Even lately when he had been so difficult and nervy — when nothing seemed to please him. When, somehow, nothing she did was right. One couldn't blame him. He was so busy, so unselfish —

Oh, dear, that mutton! She ought to have sent it back. Still no sign of John. Why couldn't she, sometimes, decide right? Again those dark waves of misery swept over her. The mutton! This awful weekend with the Angkatells. She felt a sharp pain through both temples. Oh, dear, now she was going to have one of her headaches. And it did so annoy John when she had headaches. He never would give her anything for them, when surely it would be so easy, being a doctor. Instead he always said: 'Don't think about it. No use poisoning yourself with drugs. Take a brisk walk.'

The mutton! Staring at it, Gerda felt the words repeating themselves in her aching head, 'The mutton, the MUTTON, THE MUTTON . . . '

Tears of self-pity sprang to her eyes. 'Why,' she thought, 'does nothing *ever* go right for me?'

Terence looked across the table at his mother and then at the joint. He thought: 'Why can't *we* have our dinner? How stupid grown-up people are. They haven't any sense!'

Aloud he said in a careful voice:

'Nicholson Minor and I are going to make nitroglycerine in his father's shrubbery. They live at Streatham.'

'Are you, dear? That will be very nice,' said Gerda.

There was still time. If she rang the bell and told Lewis to take the joint down now —

Terence looked at her with faint curiosity. He had felt instinctively that the manufacture of nitroglycerine was not the kind of occupation that would be encouraged by parents. With base opportunism he had selected a moment when he felt tolerably certain that he had a good chance of getting away with his statement. And his judgement had been justified. If, by any chance, there should be a fuss — if, that is, the properties of nitroglycerine should manifest themselves too evidently, he would be able to say in an injured voice, 'I *told* Mother.'

All the same, he felt vaguely disappointed.

'Even *Mother*,' he thought, 'ought to know about nitroglycerine.'

He sighed. There swept over him that intense sense of loneliness that only childhood can feel. His father was too impatient to listen, his mother was too inattentive. Zena was only a silly kid.

Pages of interesting chemical tests. And who cared about them? Nobody!

Bang! Gerda started. It was the door of John's consulting-room. It was John running upstairs.

John Christow burst into the room, bringing with him his own particular atmosphere of intense energy. He was good-humoured, hungry, impatient.

'God,' he exclaimed as he sat down and energetically sharpened the carving knife against the steel. 'How I hate sick people!'

'Oh, John.' Gerda was quickly reproachful. 'Don't say things like that. *They'll* think you mean it.'

She gestured slightly with her head towards the children.

'I do mean it,' said John Christow. 'Nobody ought to be ill.'

'Father's joking,' said Gerda quickly to Terence.

Terence examined his father with the dispassionate attention he gave to everything.

'I don't think he is,' he said.

'If you hated sick people, you wouldn't be a doctor, dear,' said Gerda, laughing gently.

'That's exactly the reason,' said John Christow. 'No doctors like sickness. Good God, this meat's stone cold. Why on earth didn't you have it sent down to keep hot?'

'Well, dear, I didn't know. You see, I thought you were just coming — '

John Christow pressed the bell, a long, irritated push. Lewis came promptly.

'Take this down and tell Cook to warm it up.'

He spoke curtly.

'Yes, sir.' Lewis, slightly impertinent, managed to convey in the two innocuous words exactly her opinion of a mistress who sat at the dining-table watching a joint of meat grow cold.

Gerda went on rather incoherently:

'I'm so sorry, dear, it's all my fault, but first, you see, I thought you were coming, and then I thought, well, if I did send it back . . . '

John interrupted her impatiently.

'Oh, what does it matter? It isn't important. Not worth making a song and dance about.'

Then he asked:

'Is the car here?'

'I think so. Collie ordered it.'

'Then we can get away as soon as lunch is over.'

Across Albert Bridge, he thought, and then over Clapham Common — the short-cut by the Crystal Palace — Croydon — Purley Way, then avoid the main road — take that right-hand fork up Metherly Hill — along Haverston Ridge — get suddenly right off the suburban belt, through Cormerton, and then up Shovel Down — trees golden red — woodland below one everywhere — the soft autumn smell, and down over the crest of the hill.

Lucy and Henry . . . Henrietta . . .

He hadn't seen Henrietta for four days. When he had last seen her, he'd been angry. She'd had that look in her eyes. Not abstracted, not inattentive — he couldn't quite describe it — that look of *seeing* something — something that wasn't there — something (and that was the crux of it) something that wasn't John Christow!

He said to himself: 'I know she's a sculptor. I know her work's good. But damn it all, can't she put it aside sometimes? Can't she sometimes think of me — and nothing else?'

He was unfair. He knew he was unfair. Henrietta seldom talked of her work — was indeed less obsessed by it than most artists he knew. It was only on very rare occasions that her absorption with some inner vision spoiled the completeness of her interest in him. But it always roused his furious anger.

Once he had said, his voice sharp and hard: 'Would you give all this up if I asked you to?'

'All — what?' Her warm voice held surprise.

'All — this.' He waved a comprehensive hand round the studio.

And immediately he thought to himself: 'Fool! Why did you ask her that?' And again: 'Let her say: 'Of course.' Let her lie to me! If she'll only say: 'Of course I will.' It doesn't matter if she means it or not! But let her say it. I *must* have peace.'

Instead she had said nothing for some time. Her eyes had gone dreamy and abstracted. She had frowned a little.

Then she had said slowly:

'I suppose so. If it was *necessary*.'

'Necessary? What do you mean by necessary?'

'I don't really know what I mean by it, John. Necessary, as an amputation might be necessary.'

'Nothing short of a surgical operation, in fact!'

'You are angry. What did you want me to say?'

'You know well enough. One word would have done. Yes. Why couldn't you say it? You say enough things to people to please them, without caring whether they're true or not. Why not to me? For God's sake, why not to me?'

And still very slowly she had answered:

'I don't know ... really, I don't know, John. I can't — that's all. I can't.'

He had walked up and down for a minute or two. Then he said:

'You will drive me mad, Henrietta. I never feel that I have any influence over you at all.'

'Why should you want to have?'

'I don't know. I do.'

66

He threw himself down on a chair.

'I want to come first.'

'You do, John.'

'No. If I were dead, the first thing you'd do, with the tears streaming down your face, would be to start modelling some damned mourning woman or some figure of grief.'

'I wonder. I believe — yes, perhaps I would. It's rather horrible.'

She had sat there looking at him with dismayed eyes.

II

The pudding was burnt. Christow raised his eyebrows over it and Gerda hurried into apologies.

'I'm sorry, dear. I can't think *why* that should happen. It's my fault. Give me the top and you take the underneath.'

The pudding was burnt because he, John Christow, had stayed sitting in his consulting-room for a quarter of an hour after he need, thinking about Henrietta and Mrs Crabtree and letting ridiculous nostalgic feelings about San Miguel sweep over him. The fault was his. It was idiotic of Gerda to try and take the blame, maddening of her to try and eat the burnt part herself. Why did she always have to make a martyr of herself? Why did Terence stare at him in that slow, interested way? Why, oh why, did Zena have to sniff so continually? Why were they all so damned irritating?

His wrath fell on Zena.

'Why on earth don't you blow your nose?'

'She's got a little cold, I think, dear.'

'No, she hasn't. You're always thinking they have colds! She's all right.'

Gerda sighed. She had never been able to understand why a doctor, who spent his time treating the ailments of others, could be so indifferent to the health of his own family. He always ridiculed any suggestions of illness.

'I sneezed eight times before lunch,' said Zena importantly.

'Heat sneeze!' said John.

'It's not hot,' said Terence. 'The thermometer in the hall is 55.'

John got up. 'Have we finished? Good, let's get on. Ready to start, Gerda?'

'In a minute, John. I've just a few things to put in.'

'Surely you could have done that *before*. What have you been doing all the morning?'

He went out of the dining-room fuming. Gerda had hurried off into her bedroom. Her anxiety to be quick would make her much slower. But why couldn't she have been ready? His own suitcase was packed and in the hall. Why on earth —

Zena was advancing on him, clasping some rather sticky cards.

'Can I tell your fortune, Daddy? I know how. I've told Mother's and Terry's and Lewis's and Jane's and Cook's.'

'All right.'

He wondered how long Gerda was going to be. He wanted to get away from this horrible house and this horrible street and this city full of ailing, sniffing, diseased people. He wanted to get to woods and wet leaves — and the graceful aloofness of Lucy Angkatell, who always gave you the impression she hadn't even got a body.

Zena was importantly dealing out cards.

'That's you in the middle, Father, the King of Hearts. The person whose fortune's told is always the King of Hearts. And then I deal the others face down. Two on the left of you and two on the right of you and one over your head — that has power over you, and one under your feet — you have power over it. And this one — covers you!

'Now.' Zena drew a deep breath. 'We turn them over. On the right of you is the Queen of Diamonds — quite close.'

'Henrietta,' he thought, momentarily diverted and amused by Zena's solemnity.

'And the next one is the knave of clubs

— he's some quiet young man.

'On the left of you is the eight of spades — that's a secret enemy. Have you got a secret enemy, Father?'

'Not that I know of.'

'And beyond is the Queen of Spades — that's a much older lady.'

'Lady Angkatell,' he said.

'Now this is what's over your head and has power over you — the Queen of Hearts.'

'Veronica,' he thought. 'Veronica!' And then, 'What a fool I am! Veronica doesn't mean a thing to me now.'

'And this is under your feet and you have power over it — the Queen of Clubs.'

Gerda hurried into the room.

'I'm quite ready now, John.'

'Oh, wait, Mother, wait, I'm telling Daddy's fortune. Just the last card, Daddy — the most important of all. The one that covers you.'

Zena's small sticky fingers turned it over. She gave a gasp.

'Oh — it's the Ace of Spades! That's usually a *death* — but — '

'Your mother,' said John, 'is going to run over someone on the way out of London. Come on, Gerda. Goodbye, you two. Try and behave.'

6

I

Midge Hardcastle came downstairs about eleven on Saturday morning. She had had breakfast in bed and had read a book and dozed a little and then got up.

It was nice lazing this way. About time she had a holiday! No doubt about it, Madame Alfrege's got on your nerves.

She came out of the front door into the pleasant autumn sunshine. Sir Henry Angkatell was sitting on a rustic seat reading *The Times*. He looked up and smiled. He was fond of Midge.

'Hallo, my dear.'

'Am I very late?'

'You haven't missed lunch,' said Sir Henry, smiling.

Midge sat down beside him and said with a sigh:

'It's nice being here.'

'You're looking rather peaked.'

'Oh, I'm all right. How delightful to be somewhere where no fat women are trying to get into clothes several sizes too small for them!'

'Must be dreadful!' Sir Henry paused and then said, glancing down at his wrist-watch: 'Edward's arriving by the 12.15.'

'Is he?' Midge paused, then said: 'I haven't seen Edward for a long time.'

'He's just the same,' said Sir Henry. 'Hardly ever comes up from Ainswick.'

'Ainswick,' thought Midge. 'Ainswick!' Her heart gave a sick pang. Those lovely days at Ainswick. Visits looked forward to for months! 'I'm going to Ainswick.' Lying awake for nights beforehand thinking about it. And at last — the day! The little country station at which the train — the big London express — had to stop if you gave notice to the guard! The Daimler waiting outside. The drive — the final turn in through the gate and up through the woods till you came out into the open and there the house was — big and white and welcoming. Old Uncle Geoffrey in his patchwork tweed coat.

'Now then, youngsters — enjoy yourselves.' And they had enjoyed themselves. Henrietta over from Ireland. Edward, home from Eton. She herself, from the North-country grimness of a manufacturing town. How like heaven it had been.

But always centring about Edward.

72

Edward, tall and gentle and diffident and always kind. But never, of course, noticing her very much because Henrietta was there.

Edward, always so retiring, so very much of a visitor so that she had been startled one day when Tremlet, the head gardener, had said:

'The place will be Mr Edward's some day.'

'But why, Tremlet? He's not Uncle Geoffrey's son.'

'He's the *heir*, Miss Midge. Entailed, that's what they call it. Miss Lucy, she's Mr Geoffrey's only child, but she can't inherit because she's a female, and Mr Henry, as she married, he's only a second cousin. Not so near as Mr Edward.'

And now Edward lived at Ainswick. Lived there alone and very seldom came away. Midge wondered, sometimes, if Lucy minded. Lucy always looked as though she never minded about anything.

Yet Ainswick had been her home, and Edward was only her first cousin once removed, and over twenty years younger than she was. Her father, old Geoffrey Angkatell, had been a great 'character' in the country. He had had considerable wealth as well, most of which had come to Lucy, so that Edward was a comparatively poor man, with enough to keep the place up, but not much over when that was done.

Not that Edward had expensive tastes. He had been in the diplomatic service for a time, but when he inherited Ainswick he had resigned and come to live on his property. He was of a bookish turn of mind, collected first editions, and occasionally wrote rather hesitating ironical little articles for obscure reviews. He had asked his second cousin, Henrietta Savernake, three times to marry him.

Midge sat in the autumn sunshine thinking of these things. She could not make up her mind whether she was glad she was going to see Edward or not. It was not as though she were what is called 'getting over it'. One simply did not get over any one like Edward. Edward of Ainswick was just as real to her as Edward rising to greet her from a restaurant table in London. She had loved Edward ever since she could remember . . .

Sir Henry's voice recalled her.

'How do you think Lucy is looking?'

'Very well. She's just the same as ever.' Midge smiled a little. 'More so.'

'Ye — es.' Sir Henry drew on his pipe. He said unexpectedly:

'Sometimes, you know, Midge, I get worried about Lucy.'

'Worried?' Midge looked at him in surprise. 'Why?'

Sir Henry shook his head.

'Lucy,' he said, 'doesn't realize that there are things that she can't do.'

Midge stared. He went on:

'She gets away with things. She always has.' He smiled. 'She's flouted the traditions of Government House — she's played merry hell with precedence at dinner parties (and that, Midge, is a black crime!). She's put deadly enemies next to each other at the dinner table, and run riot over the colour question! And instead of raising one big almighty row and setting everyone at loggerheads and bringing disgrace on the British Raj — I'm damned if she hasn't got away with it! That trick of hers — smiling at people and looking as though she couldn't help it! Servants are the same — she gives them any amount of trouble and they adore her.'

'I know what you mean,' said Midge thoughtfully. 'Things that you wouldn't stand from anyone else, you feel are all right if Lucy does them. What is it, I wonder? Charm? Magnetism?'

Sir Henry shrugged his shoulders.

'She's always been the same from a girl — only sometimes I feel it's growing on her. I mean that she doesn't realize that there *are* limits. Why, I really believe, Midge,' he said, amused, 'that Lucy would feel she could get away with murder!'

Henrietta got the Delage out from the garage in the Mews and, after a wholly technical conversation with her friend Albert, who looked after the Delage's health, she started off.

'Running a treat, miss,' said Albert.

Henrietta smiled. She shot away down the Mews, savouring the unfailing pleasure she always felt when setting off in the car alone. She much preferred to be alone when driving. In that way she could realize to the full the intimate personal enjoyment that driving a car brought to her.

She enjoyed her own skill in traffic, she enjoyed nosing out new short-cuts out of London. She had routes of her own and when driving in London itself had as intimate a knowledge of its streets as any taxi-driver.

She took now her own newly discovered way south-west, turning and twisting through intricate mazes of suburban streets.

When she came finally to the long ridge of Shovel Down it was half-past twelve.

Henrietta had always loved the view from that particular place. She paused now just at the point where the road began to descend. All around and below her were trees, trees whose leaves were turning from gold to brown. It was a world incredibly golden and splendid in the strong autumn sunlight.

Henrietta thought: 'I love autumn. It's so much richer than spring.'

And suddenly one of those moments of intense happiness came to her — a sense of the loveliness of the world — of her own intense enjoyment of that world.

She thought: 'I shall never be as happy again as I am now — never.'

She stayed there a minute, gazing out over that golden world that seemed to swim and dissolve into itself, hazy and blurred with its own beauty.

Then she came down over the crest of the hill, down through the woods, down the long steep road to The Hollow.

III

When Henrietta drove in, Midge was sitting on the low wall of the terrace, and waved to her cheerfully. Henrietta was pleased to see Midge, whom she liked.

Lady Angkatell came out of the house and said:

'Oh, there you are, Henrietta. When you've taken your car into the stables and given it a bran mash, lunch will be ready.'

'What a penetrating remark of Lucy's,' said Henrietta as she drove round the house, Midge accompanying her on the step. 'You know, I always prided myself on having completely escaped the horsy taint of my Irish forebears. When you've been brought up amongst people who talk nothing but horse, you go all superior about not caring for them. And now Lucy has just shown me that I treat my car exactly like a horse. It's quite true. I do.'

'I know,' said Midge. 'Lucy is quite devastating. She told me this morning that I was to be as rude as I liked whilst I was here.'

Henrietta considered this for a moment and then nodded.

'Of course,' she said. 'The *shop*!'

'Yes. When one has to spend every day of one's life in a damnable little box being polite to rude women, calling them Madam, pulling frocks over their heads, smiling and swallowing their damned cheek whatever they like to say to one — well, one does want to cuss! You know, Henrietta, I always wonder why people think it's so humiliating to go 'into service' and that it's grand and independent to be in a shop. One puts up with far more insolence in a shop than Gudgeon or Simmons or any decent domestic does.'

'It must be foul, darling. I wish you weren't so grand and proud and insistent on earning your own living.'

'Anyway, Lucy's an angel. I shall be gloriously rude to everyone this weekend.'

'Who's here?' said Henrietta as she got out of the car.

'The Christows are coming.' Midge paused and then went on, 'Edward's just arrived.'

'Edward? How nice. I haven't seen Edward for ages. Anybody else?'

'David Angkatell. That, according to Lucy, is where you are going to come in useful. You're going to stop him biting his nails.'

'It sounds very unlike me,' said Henrietta. 'I hate interfering with people, and I wouldn't dream of checking their personal habits. What did Lucy really say?'

'It amounted to that! He's got an Adam's apple, too!'

'I'm not expected to do anything about that, am I?' asked Henrietta, alarmed.

'And you're to be kind to Gerda.'

'How I should hate Lucy if I were Gerda!'

'And someone who solves crimes is coming to lunch tomorrow.'

'We're not going to play the Murder Game, are we?'

'I don't think so. I think it is just neighbourly hospitality.'

Midge's voice changed a little.

'Here's Edward coming out to meet us.'

'Dear Edward,' thought Henrietta with a sudden rush of warm affection.

Edward Angkatell was very tall and thin. He was smiling now as he came towards the two young women.

'Hallo, Henrietta, I haven't seen you for over a year.'

'Hallo, Edward.'

How nice Edward was! That gentle smile of his, the little creases at the corners of his eyes. And all his nice knobbly bones. 'I believe it's his *bones* I like so much,' thought Henrietta. The warmth of her affection for Edward startled her. She had forgotten that she liked Edward so much.

IV

After lunch Edward said: 'Come for a walk, Henrietta.'

It was Edward's kind of walk — a stroll.

They went up behind the house, taking a path that zigzagged up through the trees. Like the woods at Ainswick, thought Henrietta. Dear Ainswick, what fun they had had there! She began to talk to Edward about Ainswick. They revived old memories.

'Do you remember our squirrel? The one with the broken paw. And we kept it in a cage and it got well?'

'Of course. It had a ridiculous name — what was it now?'

'Cholmondeley-Marjoribanks!'

'That's it.'

The both laughed.

'And old Mrs Bondy, the housekeeper — she always *said* it would go up the chimney one day.'

'And we were so indignant.'

'And then it *did*.'

'She made it,' said Henrietta positively. 'She put the thought into the squirrel's head.'

She went on:

'Is it all the same, Edward? Or is it changed? I always imagine it just the same.'

'Why don't you come and see, Henrietta? It's a long long time since you've been there.'

'I know.'

Why, she thought, had she let so long a time go by? One got busy — interested — tangled up with people . . .

'You know you're always welcome there at any time.'

'How sweet you are, Edward!'

Dear Edward, she thought, with his *nice* bones.

He said presently:

'I'm glad you're fond of Ainswick, Henrietta.'

She said dreamily: 'Ainswick is the loveliest place in the world.'

A long-legged girl, with a mane of untidy brown hair . . . a happy girl with no idea at all of the things that life was going to do to her . . . a girl who loved trees . . .

To have been so happy and not to have known it! '*If I could go back*,' she thought.

And aloud she said suddenly:

'Is Ygdrasil still there?'

'It was struck by lightning.'

'Oh, no, not *Ygdrasil*!'

She was distressed. Ygdrasil — her own special name for the big oak tree. If the gods could strike down Ygdrasil, then nothing was safe! Better not go back.

'Do you remember your special sign, the Ygdrasil sign?'

'The funny tree like no tree that ever was I used to draw on bits of paper? I still do, Edward! On blotters, and on telephone books, and on bridge scores. I doodle it all the time. Give me a pencil.'

He handed her a pencil and notebook, and

laughing, she drew the ridiculous tree.

'Yes,' he said, 'that's Ygdrasil.'

They had come almost to the top of the path. Henrietta sat on a fallen tree-trunk. Edward sat down beside her.

She looked down through the trees.

'It's a little like Ainswick here — a kind of pocket Ainswick. I've sometimes wondered — Edward, do you think that that is why Lucy and Henry came here?'

'It's possible.'

'One never knows,' said Henrietta slowly, 'what goes on in Lucy's head.' Then she asked: 'What have you been doing with yourself, Edward, since I saw you last?'

'Nothing, Henrietta.'

'That sounds very peaceful.'

'I've never been very good at — doing things.'

She threw him a quick glance. There had been something in his tone. But he was smiling at her quietly.

And again she felt that rush of deep affection.

'Perhaps,' she said, 'you are wise.'

'Wise?'

'Not to do things.'

Edward said slowly, 'That's an odd thing for you to say, Henrietta. You, who've been so successful.'

'Do you think of me as successful? How funny.'

'But you are, my dear. You're an artist. You must be proud of yourself; you can't help being.'

'I know,' said Henrietta. 'A lot of people say that to me. They don't understand — they don't understand the first thing about it. *You* don't, Edward. Sculpture isn't a thing you set out to do and succeed in. It's a thing that gets *at* you, that nags at you — and haunts you — so that you've got, sooner or later, to make terms with it. And then, for a bit, you get some peace — until the whole thing starts over again.'

'Do you want to be peaceful, Henrietta?'

'Sometimes I think I want to be peaceful

more than anything in the world, Edward!'

'You could be peaceful at Ainswick. I think you could be happy there. Even — even if you had to put up with *me*. What about it, Henrietta? Won't you come to Ainswick and make it your home? It's always been there, you know, waiting for you.'

Henrietta turned her head slowly. She said in a low voice: 'I wish I wasn't so dreadfully fond of you, Edward. It makes it so very much harder to go on saying No.'

'It *is* No, then?'

'I'm sorry.'

'You've said No before — but this time — well, I thought it might be different. You've been happy this afternoon, Henrietta. You can't deny that.'

'I've been very happy.'

'Your face even — it's younger than it was this morning.'

'I know.'

'We've been happy together, talking about Ainswick, thinking about Ainswick. Don't you see what that means, Henrietta?'

'It's *you* who don't see what it means, Edward! We've been living all this afternoon in the past.'

'The past is sometimes a very good place to live.'

'One can't go back. That's the one thing

one can't do — go back.'

He was silent for a minute or two. Then he said in a quiet, pleasant and quite unemotional voice:

'What you really mean is that you won't marry me because of John Christow?'

Henrietta did not answer, and Edward went on:

'That's it, isn't it? If there were no John Christow in the world you would marry me.'

Henrietta said harshly, 'I can't imagine a world in which there was no John Christow! That's what *you've* got to understand.'

'If it's like that, why on earth doesn't the fellow get a divorce from his wife and then you could marry?'

'John doesn't want to get a divorce from his wife. And I don't know that I should want to marry John if he did. It isn't — it isn't in the least like you think.'

Edward said in a thoughtful, considering way:

'John Christow. There are too many John Christows in this world.'

'You're wrong,' said Henrietta. 'There are very few people like John.'

'If that's so — it's a good thing! At least, that's what I think!'

He got up. 'We'd better go back again.'

7

As they got into the car and Lewis shut the front door of the Harley Street house, Gerda felt the pang of exile go through her. That shut door was so final. She was barred out — this awful weekend was upon her. And there were things, quite a lot of things, that she ought to have done before leaving. Had she turned off that tap in the bathroom? And that note for the laundry — she'd put it — where had she put it? Would the children be all right with Mademoiselle? Mademoiselle was so — so — Would Terence, for instance, ever do anything that Mademoiselle told him to? French governesses never seemed to have any authority.

She got into the driving-seat, still bowed down by misery, and nervously pressed the starter. She pressed it again and again. John said: 'The car will start better, Gerda, if you switch on the engine.'

'Oh, dear, how stupid of me.' She shot a quick, alarmed glance at him. If John was going to become annoyed straight away — But to her relief he was smiling.

'That's because,' thought Gerda, with one

of her flashes of acumen, 'he's so pleased to be going to the Angkatells.'

Poor John, he worked so hard! His life was so unselfish, so completely devoted to others. No wonder he looked forward to this long weekend. And, her mind harking back to the conversation at lunch, she said, as she let in the clutch rather too suddenly so that the car leapt forward from the kerb:

'You know, John, you really shouldn't make jokes about hating sick people. It's wonderful of you to make light of all you do, and *I* understand. But the children don't. Terry, in particular, has such a very literal mind.'

'There are times,' said John Christow, 'when Terry seems to me almost human — not like Zena! How long do girls go on being a mass of affectation?'

Gerda gave a little quiet sweet laugh. John, she knew, was teasing her. She stuck to her point. Gerda had an adhesive mind.

'I really think, John, that it's *good* for children to realize the unselfishness and devotion of a doctor's life.'

'Oh God!' said Christow.

Gerda was momentarily deflected. The traffic lights she was approaching had been green for a long time. They were almost sure, she thought, to change before she got to them. She began to slow down. Still green.

John Christow forgot his resolutions of keeping silent about Gerda's driving and said, 'What are you stopping for?'

'I thought the lights might change — '

She pressed her foot on the accelerator, the car moved forward a little, just beyond the lights, then, unable to pick up, the engine stalled. The lights changed.

The cross-traffic hooted angrily.

John said, but quite pleasantly:

'You really are the worst driver in the world, Gerda!'

'I always find traffic lights so worrying. One doesn't know just when they are going to change.'

John cast a quick sideways look at Gerda's anxious unhappy face.

'Everything worries Gerda,' he thought, and tried to imagine what it must feel like to live in that state. But since he was not a man of much imagination, he could not picture it at all.

'You see,' Gerda stuck to her point, 'I've always impressed on the children just what a doctor's life is — the self-sacrifice, the dedication of oneself to helping pain and suffering — the desire to serve others. It's such a noble life — and I'm so proud of the way you give your time and energy and never spare yourself — '

John Christow interrupted her.

'Hasn't it ever occurred to you that I *like* doctoring — that it's a pleasure, not a sacrifice! — Don't you realize that the damned thing's *interesting*!'

But no, he thought, Gerda would never realize a thing like that! If he told her about Mrs Crabtree and the Margaret Russell Ward she would only see him as a kind of angelic helper of the Poor with a capital P.

'Drowning in treacle,' he said under his breath.

'What?' Gerda leaned towards him.

He shook his head.

If he were to tell Gerda that he was trying to 'find a cure for cancer', she would respond — she could understand a plain sentimental statement. But she would never understand the peculiar fascination of the intricacies of Ridgeway's Disease — he doubted if he could even make her understand what Ridgeway's Disease actually was. ('Particularly,' he thought with a grin, 'as we're not really quite sure ourselves! We don't really know *why* the cortex degenerates!')

But it occurred to him suddenly that Terence, child though he was, might be interested in Ridgeway's Disease. He had liked the way that Terence had eyed him appraisingly before stating: 'I think

90

Father does mean it.'

Terence had been out of favour the last few days for breaking the Cona coffee machine — some nonsense about trying to make ammonia. Ammonia? Funny kid, why should he want to make ammonia? Interesting in a way.

Gerda was relieved at John's silence. She could cope with driving better if she were not distracted by conversation. Besides, if John was absorbed in thought, he was not so likely to notice that jarring noise of her occasional forced changes of gear. (She never changed down if she could help it.)

There were times, Gerda knew, when she changed gear quite well (though never with confidence), but it never happened if John were in the car. Her nervous determination to do it right this time was almost disastrous, her hand fumbled, she accelerated too much or not enough, and then she pushed the gear lever quickly and clumsily so that it shrieked in protest.

'Stroke it in, Gerda, stroke it in,' Henrietta had pleaded once, years ago. Henrietta had demonstrated. 'Can't you feel the way it wants to go — it wants to slide in — keep your hand flat till you get the feeling of it — don't just push it anywhere — *feel* it.'

But Gerda had never been able to feel

91

anything about a gear lever. If she was pushing it more or less in the proper direction it ought to go in! Cars ought to be made so that you didn't have that horrible grinding noise.

On the whole, thought Gerda, as she began the ascent of Mersham Hill, this drive wasn't going too badly. John was still absorbed in thought — and he hadn't noticed rather a bad crashing of gears in Croydon. Optimistically, as the car gained speed, she changed up into third, and immediately the car slackened. John, as it were, woke up.

'What on earth's the point of changing up just when you're coming to a steep bit?'

Gerda set her jaw. Not very much farther now. Not that she wanted to get there. No, indeed, she'd much rather drive on for hours and hours, even if John *did* lose his temper with her!

But now they were driving along Shovel Down — flaming autumn woods all round them.

'Wonderful to get out of London into this,' exclaimed John. 'Think of it, Gerda, most afternoons we're stuck in that dingy drawing-room having tea — sometimes with the light on.'

The image of the somewhat dark drawing-room of the flat rose up before Gerda's eyes with the tantalizing delight of a mirage. Oh, if only she could be sitting there now.

'The country looks lovely,' she said heroically.

Down the steep hill — no escape now. That vague hope that something, she didn't know what, might intervene to save her from the nightmare, was unrealized. They were there.

She was a little comforted as she drove in to see Henrietta sitting on a wall with Midge and a tall thin man. She felt a certain reliance on Henrietta, who would sometimes unexpectedly come to the rescue if things were getting very bad.

John was glad to see Henrietta too. It seemed to him exactly the fitting journey's end to that lovely panorama of autumn, to drop down from the hilltop and find Henrietta waiting for him.

She had on the green tweed coat and the skirt he liked her in and which he thought suited her so much better than London clothes. Her long legs were stuck out in front of her, ending in well-polished brown brogues.

They exchanged a quick smile — a brief recognition of the fact that each was glad of the other's presence. John didn't want to talk to Henrietta now. He just enjoyed feeling that she was there — knowing that without her the weekend would be barren and empty.

Lady Angkatell came out from the house and greeted them. Her conscience made her more effusive to Gerda than she would have been normally to any guest.

'But how *very* nice to see you, Gerda! It's been such a *long* time. *And* John!'

The idea was clearly that Gerda was the eagerly awaited guest, and John the mere adjunct. It failed miserably of its object, making Gerda stiff and uncomfortable.

Lucy said: 'You know Edward? Edward Angkatell?'

John nodded to Edward and said: 'No, I don't think so.'

The afternoon sun lighted up the gold of John's hair and the blue of his eyes. So might a Viking look who had just come ashore on a conquering mission. His voice, warm and resonant, charmed the ear, and the magnetism of his whole personality took charge of the scene.

That warmth and that objectiveness did no damage to Lucy. It set off, indeed, that curious elfin elusiveness of hers. It was Edward who seemed, suddenly, by contrast with the other man, bloodless — a shadowy figure, stooping a little.

Henrietta suggested to Gerda that they should go and look at the kitchen garden.

94

'Lucy is sure to insist on showing us the rock garden and the autumn border,' she said as she led the way. 'But I always think kitchen gardens are nice and peaceful. One can sit on the cucumber frames, or go inside a greenhouse if it's cold, and nobody bothers one and sometimes there's something to eat.'

They found, indeed, some late peas, which Henrietta ate raw, but which Gerda did not much care for. She was glad to have got away from Lucy Angkatell, whom she had found more alarming than ever.

She began to talk to Henrietta with something like animation. The questions Henrietta asked always seemed to be questions to which Gerda knew the answers. After ten minutes Gerda felt very much better and began to think that perhaps the weekend wouldn't be so bad after all.

Zena was going to dancing class now and had just had a new frock. Gerda described it at length. Also she had found a very nice new leathercraft shop. Henrietta asked whether it would be difficult to make herself a handbag. Gerda must show her.

It was really very easy, she thought, to make Gerda look happy, and what an enormous difference it made to her when she did look happy!

'She only wants to be allowed to curl up

and purr,' thought Henrietta.

They sat happily on the corner of the cucumber frames where the sun, now low in the sky, gave an illusion of a summer day.

Then a silence fell. Gerda's face lost its expression of placidity. Her shoulders drooped. She sat there, the picture of misery. She jumped when Henrietta spoke.

'Why do you come,' said Henrietta, 'if you hate it so much?'

Gerda hurried into speech.

'Oh, I don't! I mean, I don't know why you should think — '

She paused, then went on:

'It is really delightful to get out of London, and Lady Angkatell is so *very* kind.'

'Lucy? She's not a bit kind.'

Gerda looked faintly shocked.

'Oh, but she *is*. She's so very nice to me always.'

'Lucy has got good manners and she can be gracious. But she is rather a cruel person. I think really because she isn't quite human — she doesn't know what it's like to feel and think like ordinary people. And you *are* hating being here, Gerda! You know you are. And why should you come if you feel like that?'

'Well, you see, John likes it — '

'Oh, John likes it all right. But you could let

96

him come by himself?'

'He wouldn't like that. He wouldn't enjoy it without me. John is so unselfish. He thinks it is good for me to get out into the country.'

'The country is all right,' said Henrietta. 'But there's no need to throw in the Angkatells.'

'I — I don't want you to feel that I'm ungrateful.'

'My dear Gerda, why should you like us? I always have thought the Angkatells were an odious family. We all like getting together and talking an extraordinary language of our own. I don't wonder outside people want to murder us.'

Then she added:

'I expect it's about teatime. Let's go back.'

She was watching Gerda's face as the latter got up and started to walk towards the house.

'It's interesting,' thought Henrietta, one portion of whose mind was always detached, 'to see exactly what a female Christian martyr's face looked like before she went into the arena.'

As they left the walled kitchen garden, they heard shots, and Henrietta remarked: 'Sounds as though the massacre of the Angkatells has begun!'

It turned out to be Sir Henry and Edward discussing firearms and illustrating their discussion by firing revolvers. Henry Angkatell's hobby was firearms and he had quite a collection of them.

He had brought out several revolvers and some target cards, and he and Edward were firing at them.

'Hallo, Henrietta, want to try if you could kill a burglar?'

Henrietta took the revolver from him.

'That's right — yes, so, aim like this.'

Bang!

'Missed him,' said Sir Henry.

'You try, Gerda.'

'Oh, I don't think I — '

'Come on, Mrs Christow. It's quite simple.'

Gerda fired the revolver, flinching, and shutting her eyes. The bullet went even wider than Henrietta's had done.

'Oh, I want to do it,' said Midge, strolling up.

'It's more difficult than you'd think,' she remarked after a couple of shots. 'But it's rather fun.'

Lucy came out from the house. Behind her came a tall, sulky young man with an Adam's apple.

'Here's David,' she announced.

She took the revolver from Midge, as her husband greeted David Angkatell, reloaded it, and without a word put three holes close to the centre of the target.

'Well done, Lucy,' exclaimed Midge. 'I didn't know shooting was one of your accomplishments.'

'Lucy,' said Sir Henry gravely, 'always kills her man!'

Then he added reminiscently, 'Came in useful once. Do you remember, my dear, those thugs that set upon us that day on the Asian side of the Bosphorus? I was rolling about with two of them on top of me feeling for my throat.'

'And what did Lucy do?' asked Midge.

'Fired two shots in the mêlée. I didn't even know she had the pistol with her. Got one bad man through the leg and the other in the shoulder. Nearest escape in the world *I've* ever had. I can't think how she didn't hit me.'

Lady Angkatell smiled at him.

'I think one always has to take some risk,' she said gently. 'And one should do it quickly and not think too much about it.'

'An admirable sentiment, my dear,' said Sir Henry. 'But I have always felt slightly aggrieved that *I* was the risk you took!'

8

I

After tea John said to Henrietta, 'Come for a walk,' and Lady Angkatell said that she *must* show Gerda the rock garden though of course it was quite the wrong time of year.

Walking with John, thought Henrietta, was as unlike walking with Edward as anything could be.

With Edward one seldom did more than potter. Edward, she thought, was a born potterer. Walking with John, it was all she could do to keep up, and by the time they got up to Shovel Down she said breathlessly: 'It's not a marathon, John!'

He slowed down and laughed.

'Am I walking you off your feet?'

'I can do it — but is there any need? We haven't got a train to catch. Why do you have this ferocious energy? Are you running away from yourself?'

He stopped dead. 'Why do you say that?'

Henrietta looked at him curiously.

'I didn't mean anything particular by it.'

John went on again, but walking more slowly.

'As a matter of fact,' he said, 'I'm tired. I'm very tired.'

She heard the lassitude in his voice.

'How's the Crabtree?'

'It's early days to say, but I think, Henrietta, that I've got the hang of things. If I'm right' — his footsteps began to quicken — 'a lot of our ideas will be revolutionized — we'll have to reconsider the whole question of hormone secretion — '

'You mean that there will be a cure for Ridgeway's Disease? That people won't die?'

'That, incidentally.'

What odd people doctors were, thought Henrietta. Incidentally!

'Scientifically, it opens up all sorts of possibilities!'

He drew a deep breath. 'But it's good to get down here — good to get some air into your lungs — good to see you.' He gave her one of his sudden quick smiles. 'And it will do Gerda good.'

'Gerda, of course, simply loves coming to The Hollow!'

'Of course she does. By the way, have I met Edward Angkatell before?'

'You've met him twice,' said Henrietta dryly.

'I couldn't remember. He's one of those vague, indefinite people.'

'Edward's a dear. I've always been very fond of him.'

'Well, don't let's waste time on Edward! None of these people count.'

Henrietta said in a low voice:

'Sometimes, John — I'm afraid for you!'

'Afraid for me — what do you mean?'

He turned an astonished face upon her.

'You are so oblivious — so — yes, *blind*.'

'Blind?'

'You don't know — you don't see — you're curiously insensitive! You don't know what other people are feeling and thinking.'

'I should have said just the opposite.'

'You see what you're looking *at*, yes. You're — you're like a searchlight. A powerful beam turned on to the one spot where your interest is, and behind it and each side of it, darkness!'

'Henrietta, my dear, what is all this?'

'It's *dangerous*, John. You assume that everyone likes you, that they mean well to you. People like Lucy, for instance.'

'Doesn't Lucy like me?' he said, surprised. 'I've always been extremely fond of her.'

'And so you assume that she likes you. But I'm not sure. And Gerda and Edward — oh, and Midge and Henry. How do you know what they feel towards you?'

'And Henrietta? Do I know how she feels?' He caught her hand for a moment. 'At least — I'm sure of you.'

She took her hand away.

'You can be sure of no one in this world, John.'

His face had grown grave.

'No, I won't believe that. I'm sure of you and I'm sure of myself. At least — ' His face changed.

'What is it, John?'

'Do you know what I found myself saying today? Something quite ridiculous. '*I want to go home.*' That's what I said and I hadn't the least idea what I meant by it.'

Henrietta said slowly: 'You must have had some picture in your mind.'

He said sharply: 'Nothing. Nothing at all!'

II

At dinner that night, Henrietta was put next to David, and from the end of the table Lucy's delicate eyebrows telegraphed not a command — Lucy never commanded — but an appeal.

Sir Henry was doing his best with Gerda and succeeding quite well. John, his face

103

amused, was following the leaps and bounds of Lucy's discursive mind. Midge talked in rather a stilted way to Edward, who seemed more absent-minded than usual.

David was glowering and crumbling his bread with a nervous hand.

David had come to The Hollow in a spirit of considerable unwillingness. Until now, he had never met either Sir Henry or Lady Angkatell, and disapproving of the Empire generally, he was prepared to disapprove of these relatives of his. Edward, whom he did not know, he despised as a dilettante. The remaining four guests he examined with a critical eye. Relations, he thought, were pretty awful, and one was expected to talk to people, a thing which he hated doing.

Midge and Henrietta he discounted as empty-headed. This Dr Christow was just one of these Harley Street charlatans — all manner and social success — his wife obviously did not count.

David shifted his neck in his collar and wished fervently that all these people could know how little he thought of them! They were really all quite negligible.

When he had repeated that three times to himself he felt rather better. He still glowered but he was able to leave his bread alone.

Henrietta, though responding loyally to the

eyebrows, had some difficulty in making headway. David's curt rejoinders were snubbing in the extreme. In the end she had recourse to a method she had employed before with the tongue-tied young.

She made, deliberately, a dogmatic and quite unjustifiable pronouncement on a modern composer, knowing that David had much technical and musical knowledge.

To her amusement the plan worked. David drew himself up from his slouching position where he had been more or less reclining on his spine. His voice was no longer low and mumbling. He stopped crumbling his bread.

'That,' he said in loud, clear tones, fixing a cold eye on Henrietta, 'shows that you don't know the first thing about the subject!'

From then on until the end of dinner he lectured her in clear and biting accents, and Henrietta subsided into the proper meekness of one instructed.

Lucy Angkatell sent a benignant glance down the table, and Midge grinned to herself.

'So clever of you, darling,' muttered Lady Angkatell as she slipped an arm through Henrietta's on the way to the drawing-room. 'What an awful thought it is that if people had less in their heads they would know better what to do with their hands! Do you think Hearts or Bridge or Rummy or something terribly terribly simple like Animal Grab?'

'I think David would be rather insulted by Animal Grab.'

'Perhaps you are right. Bridge, then. I am sure he will feel that Bridge is rather worthless, and then he can have a nice glow of contempt for us.'

They made up two tables. Henrietta played with Gerda against John and Edward. It was not her idea of the best grouping. She had wanted to segregate Gerda from Lucy and if possible from John also — but John had shown determination. And Edward had then forestalled Midge.

The atmosphere was not, Henrietta thought, quite comfortable, but she did not quite know from whence the discomfort arose. Anyway, if the cards gave them anything like a break, she intended that Gerda should win. Gerda was not really a bad Bridge player — away from John she was quite average — but she was a nervous player with bad judgment and with no real knowledge of the value of her hand. John was a good, if slightly over-confident player. Edward was a very good player indeed.

The evening wore on, and at Henrietta's table they were still playing the same rubber.

The scores rose above the line on either side. A curious tensity had come into the play of which only one person was unaware.

To Gerda this was just a rubber of Bridge which she happened for once to be quite enjoying. She felt indeed a pleasurable excitement. Difficult decisions had been unexpectedly eased by Henrietta's over-calling her own bids and playing the hand.

Those moments when John, unable to refrain from that critical attitude which did more to undermine Gerda's self-confidence than he could possibly have imagined, exclaimed: 'Why on earth did you lead that club, Gerda?' were countered almost immediately by Henrietta's swift, 'Nonsense, John, of course she had to lead the club! It was the only possible thing to do.'

Finally, with a sigh, Henrietta drew the score towards her.

'Game and rubber, but I don't think we shall make much out of it, Gerda.'

John said: 'A lucky finesse,' in a cheerful voice.

Henrietta looked up sharply. She knew his tone. She met his eyes and her own dropped.

She got up and went to the mantelpiece, and John followed her. He said conversationally: 'You don't *always* look deliberately into people's hands, do you?'

107

Henrietta said calmly: 'Perhaps I was a little obvious. How despicable it is to want to win at games!'

'You wanted Gerda to win the rubber, you mean. In your desire to give pleasure to people, you don't draw the line at cheating.'

'How horribly you put things! And you are always quite right.'

'Your wishes seemed to be shared by my partner.'

So he *had* noticed, thought Henrietta. She had wondered herself, if she had been mistaken. Edward was so skilful — there was nothing you could have taken hold of. A failure, once, to call the game. A lead that had been sound and obvious — but when a less obvious lead would have assured success.

It worried Henrietta. Edward, she knew, would never play his cards in order that she, Henrietta, might win. He was far too imbued with English sportsmanship for that. No, she thought, it was just one more success for John Christow that he was unable to endure.

She felt suddenly keyed up, alert. She didn't like this party of Lucy's.

And then dramatically, unexpectedly — with the unreality of a stage entrance, Veronica Cray came through the window.

The french windows had been pushed to, not closed, for the evening was warm.

Veronica pushed them wide, came through them and stood there framed against the night, smiling, a little rueful, wholly charming, waiting just that infinitesimal moment before speaking so that she might be sure of her audience.

'You must forgive me — bursting in upon you this way. I'm your neighbour, Lady Angkatell — from that ridiculous cottage Dovecotes — and the most frightful catastrophe has occurred!'

Her smile broadened — became more humorous.

'Not a match! Not a single match in the house! And Saturday evening. So stupid of me. But what could I do? I came along here to beg help from my only neighbour within miles.'

Nobody spoke for a moment, for Veronica had rather that effect. She was lovely — not quietly lovely, not even dazzlingly lovely — but so efficiently lovely that it made you gasp! The waves of pale shimmering hair, the curving mouth — the platinum foxes that swathed her shoulders and the long sweep of white velvet underneath them.

She was looking from one to the other of them, humorous, charming!

'And I smoke,' she said, 'like a chimney! And my lighter won't work! And besides there's breakfast — gas stoves — ' She thrust out her hands. 'I do feel such a complete fool.'

Lucy came forward, gracious, faintly amused.

'Why, of course — ' she began, but Veronica Cray interrupted.

She was looking at John Christow. An expression of utter amazement, of incredulous delight, was spreading over her face. She took a step towards him, hands outstretched.

'Why, surely — *John*! It's John Christow! Now isn't that too extraordinary? I haven't seen you for years and years and years! And suddenly — to find you *here*!'

She had his hands in hers by now. She was all warmth and simple eagerness. She half-turned her head to Lady Angkatell.

'This is just the most wonderful surprise. John's an old old friend of mine. Why, John's the first man I ever loved! I was crazy about you, John.'

She was half-laughing now — a woman moved by the ridiculous remembrance of first love.

'I always thought John was just wonderful!'

Sir Henry, courteous and polished, had moved forward to her.

She must have a drink. He manoeuvred glasses. Lady Angkatell said:

'Midge, dear, ring the bell.'

When Gudgeon came, Lucy said:

'A box of matches, Gudgeon — at least, has Cook got plenty?'

'A new dozen came in today, m'lady.'

'Then bring in half a dozen, Gudgeon.'

'Oh, no, Lady Angkatell — just one!'

Veronica protested, laughing. She had her drink now and was smiling round at everyone. John Christow said:

'This is my wife, Veronica.'

'Oh, but how lovely to meet you.' Veronica beamed upon Gerda's air of bewilderment.

Gudgeon brought in the matches, stacked on a silver salver.

Lady Angkatell indicated Veronica Cray with a gesture and he brought the salver to her.

'Oh, dear Lady Angkatell, not all these!'

Lucy's gesture was negligently royal.

'It's so tiresome only having one of a thing. We can spare them quite easily.'

Sir Henry was saying pleasantly:

'And how do you like living at Dovecotes?'

'I adore it. It's wonderful here, near London, and yet one feels so beautifully isolated.'

Veronica put down her glass. She drew the platinum foxes a little closer round her. She smiled on them all.

'Thank you *so* much! You've been so kind.' The words floated between Sir Henry, Lady Angkatell, and for some reason, Edward. 'I shall now carry home the spoils. John,' she gave him an artless, friendly smile, 'you must see me safely back, because I want dreadfully to hear all you've been doing in the years and years since I've seen you. It makes me feel, of course, dreadfully *old*.'

She moved to the window, and John Christow followed her. She flung a last brilliant smile at them all.

'I'm so dreadfully sorry to have bothered you in this stupid way. Thank you *so* much, Lady Angkatell.'

She went out with John. Sir Henry stood by the window looking after them.

'Quite a fine warm night,' he said.

Lady Angkatell yawned.

'Oh, dear,' she murmured, 'we must go to bed. Henry, we must go and see one of her pictures. I'm sure, from tonight, she must give a lovely performance.'

They went upstairs. Midge, saying goodnight, asked Lucy:

'A lovely performance?'

'Didn't you think so, darling?'

'I gather, Lucy, that you think it's just possible she may have had some matches in Dovecotes all the time.'

112

'Dozens of boxes, I expect, darling. But we mustn't be uncharitable. And it *was* a lovely performance!'

Doors were shutting all down the corridor, voices were murmuring goodnights. Sir Henry said: 'I'll leave the window for Christow.' His own door shut.

Henrietta said to Gerda: 'What fun actresses are. They make such marvellous entrances and exits!' She yawned and added: 'I'm frightfully sleepy.'

Veronica Cray moved swiftly along the narrow path through the chestnut woods.

She came out from the woods to the open space by the swimming pool. There was a small pavilion here where the Angkatells sat on days that were sunny but when there was a cold wind.

Veronica Cray stood still. She turned and faced John Christow.

Then she laughed. With her hand she gestured towards the leaf-strewn surface of the swimming pool.

'Not quite like the Mediterranean, is it, John?' she said.

He knew then what he had been waiting for — knew that in all those fifteen years of separation from Veronica she had still been with him. *The blue sea, the scent of mimosa, the hot dust* — pushed down, thrust out of sight, but never really forgotten. They all meant one thing — Veronica. He was a young man of twenty-four, desperately and agonizingly in love, and this time he was not going to run away.

9

John Christow came out from the chestnut woods on to the green slope by the house. There was a moon and the house basked in the moonlight with a strange innocence in its curtained windows. He looked down at the wrist-watch he wore.

It was three o'clock. He drew a deep breath and his face was anxious. He was no longer, even remotely, a young man of twenty-four in love. He was a shrewd, practical man of just on forty, and his mind was clear and level-headed.

He'd been a fool, of course, a complete damned fool, but he didn't regret that! For he was, he now realized, completely master of himself. It was as though, for years, he had dragged a weight upon his leg — and now the weight was gone. He was free.

He was free and himself, John Christow — and he knew that to John Christow, successful Harley Street specialist, Veronica Cray meant nothing whatsoever. All that had been in the past — and because that conflict had never been resolved, because he had always suffered humiliatingly from the fear that he had, in plain language, 'run away', so Veronica's image had never completely left him. She had come to him tonight out of a dream, and he had accepted the dream, and now, thank God, he was delivered from it for ever. He was back in the present — and it was 3 am, and it was just possible that he had mucked up things rather badly.

He'd been with Veronica for three hours. She had sailed in like a frigate, and cut him out of the circle and carried him off as her prize, and he wondered now what on earth everybody had thought about it.

What, for instance, would Gerda think?

And Henrietta? (But he didn't care quite so much about Henrietta. He could, he felt, at a pinch explain to Henrietta. He could never explain to Gerda.)

And he didn't, definitely he didn't want to lose anything.

All his life he had been a man who took a justifiable number of risks. Risks with patients, risks with treatment, risks with investments. Never a fantastic risk — only the kind of risk that was just beyond the margin of safety.

If Gerda guessed — if Gerda had the least suspicion . . .

But would she have? How much did he really know about Gerda? Normally, Gerda would believe white was black if he told her so. But over a thing like this . . .

What had he looked like when he followed Veronica's tall, triumphant figure out of that window? What had he shown in his face? Had they seen a boy's dazed, lovesick face? Or had they only observed a man doing a polite duty? He didn't know. He hadn't the least idea.

But he was afraid — afraid for the ease and order and safety of his life. He'd been mad — quite mad, he thought with exasperation — and then took comfort in that very thought. Nobody would believe, surely, he could have been as mad as that?

Everybody was in bed and asleep, that was clear. The french window of the drawing-room stood half-open, left for his return. He looked up again at the innocent, sleeping house. It looked, somehow, too innocent.

Suddenly he started. He had heard, or he had imagined he heard, the faint closing of a door.

He turned his head sharply. If someone had come down to the pool, following him there. If someone had waited and followed him back that someone could have taken a higher path and so gained entrance to the house again by the side garden door, and the soft closing of the garden door would have made just the sound that he had heard.

He looked up sharply at the windows. Was that curtain moving, had it been pushed aside for someone to look out, and then allowed to fall? Henrietta's room.

Henrietta! Not Henrietta, his heart cried in a sudden panic. I can't lose Henrietta!

He wanted suddenly to fling up a handful of pebbles at her window, to cry out to her.

'Come out, my dear love. Come out to me now and walk with me up through the woods to Shovel Down and there listen — listen to everything that I now know about myself and that you must know, too, if you do not know it already.'

He wanted to say to Henrietta:

'I am starting again. A new life begins from today. The things that crippled and hindered me from living have fallen away. You were right this afternoon when you asked me if I was running away from myself. That is what I have been doing for years. Because I never knew whether it was strength or weakness that took me away from Veronica. I have been afraid of myself, afraid of life, afraid of you.'

If he were to wake Henrietta and make her come out with him now — up through the woods to where they could watch, together, the sun come up over the rim of the world.

'You're mad,' he said to himself. He shivered. It was cold now, late September after all. 'What the devil is the matter with you?' he asked himself. 'You've behaved quite insanely enough for one night. If you get away with it as it is, you're damned lucky!' What on earth would Gerda think if he stayed out all night and came home with the milk?

What, for the matter of that, would the Angkatells think?

But that did not worry him for a moment. The Angkatells took Greenwich time, as it were, from Lucy Angkatell. And to Lucy Angkatell, the unusual always appeared perfectly reasonable.

But Gerda, unfortunately, was not an Angkatell.

Gerda would have to be dealt with, and he'd better go in and deal with Gerda as soon as possible.

Supposing it had been Gerda who had followed him tonight?

No good saying people didn't do such things. As a doctor, he knew only too well what people, high-minded, sensitive, fastidious, honourable people, constantly did. They listened at doors, and opened letters and spied and snooped — not because for one moment they approved of such conduct, but because before the sheer necessity of human anguish they were rendered desperate.

Poor devils, he thought, poor suffering

human devils. John Christow knew a good deal about human suffering. He had not very much pity for weakness, but he had for suffering, for it was, he knew, the strong who suffer.

If Gerda knew —

Nonsense, he said to himself, why should she? She's gone up to bed and she's fast asleep. She's no imagination, never has had.

He went in through the french windows, switched on a lamp, closed and locked the windows. Then, switching off the light, he left the room, found the switch in the hall, went quickly and lightly up the stairs. A second switch turned off the hall light. He stood for a moment by the bedroom door, his hand on the door-knob, then he turned it and went in.

The room was dark and he could hear Gerda's even breathing. She stirred as he came in and closed the door. Her voice came to him, blurred and indistinct with sleep.

'Is that you, John?'

'Yes.'

'Aren't you very late? What time is it?'

He said easily:

'I've no idea. Sorry I woke you up. I had to go in with the woman and have a drink.'

He made his voice sound bored and sleepy.

Gerda murmured: 'Oh? Goodnight, John.'

There was a rustle as she turned over in bed.

It was all right! As usual, he'd been lucky. As *usual* — just for a moment it sobered him, the thought of how often his luck had held! Time and again there had been a moment when he'd held his breath and said, 'If *this* goes wrong.' And it hadn't gone wrong! But some day, surely, his luck would change.

He undressed quickly and got into bed. Funny that kid's fortune. *'And this one is over your head and has power over you . . .'* Veronica! And she *had* had power over him all right.

'But not any more, my girl,' he thought with a kind of savage satisfaction. 'All that's over. I'm quit of you now!'

10

It was ten o'clock the next morning when John came down. Breakfast was on the sideboard. Gerda had had her breakfast sent up to her in bed and had been rather perturbed since perhaps she might be 'giving trouble'.

Nonsense, John had said. People like the Angkatells who still managed to have butlers and servants might just as well give them something to do.

He felt very kindly towards Gerda this morning. All that nervous irritation that had so fretted him of late seemed to have died down and disappeared.

Sir Henry and Edward had gone out shooting, Lady Angkatell told him. She herself was busy with a gardening basket and gardening gloves. He stayed talking to her for a while until Gudgeon approached him with a letter on a salver.

'This has just come by hand, sir.'

He took it with slightly raised eyebrows.

Veronica!

He strolled into the library, tearing it open.

Please come over this morning. I must see you. Veronica.

Imperious as ever, he thought. He'd a good mind not to go. Then he thought he might as well and get it over. He'd go at once.

He took the path opposite the library window, passed by the swimming pool which was a kind of nucleus with paths radiating from it in every direction, one up the hill to the woods proper, one from the flower walk above the house, one from the farm and the one that led on to the lane which he took now. A few yards up the lane was the cottage called Dovecotes.

Veronica was waiting for him. She spoke from the window of the pretentious half-timbered building.

'Come inside, John. It's cold this morning.'

There was a fire lit in the sitting-room, which was furnished in off-white with pale cyclamen cushions.

Looking at her this morning with an appraising eye, he saw the differences there were from the girl he remembered, as he had not been able to see them last night.

Strictly speaking, he thought, she was more beautiful now than then. She understood her beauty better, and she cared for it and enhanced it in every way. Her hair, which had been deep golden, was now a silvery platinum colour. Her eyebrows were different, giving much more poignancy to her expression.

Hers had never been a mindless beauty. Veronica, he remembered, had qualified as one of our 'intellectual actresses'. She had a university degree and had views on Strindberg and on Shakespeare.

He was struck now with what had only been dimly apparent to him in the past — that she was a woman whose egoism was quite abnormal. Veronica was accustomed to getting her own way, and beneath the smooth beautiful contours of flesh he seemed to sense an ugly iron determination.

'I sent for you,' said Veronica, as she handed him a box of cigarettes, 'because we've got to talk. We've got to make arrangements. For our future, I mean.'

He took a cigarette and lighted it. Then he said quite pleasantly:

'But have we a future?'

She gave him a sharp glance.

'What do you mean, John? Of course we have got a future. We've wasted fifteen years. There's no need to waste any more time.'

He sat down.

'I'm sorry, Veronica. But I'm afraid you've got all this taped out wrong. I've — enjoyed meeting you again very much. But your life and mine don't touch anywhere. They are quite divergent.'

'Nonsense, John. I love you and you love me. We've always loved each other. You were incredibly obstinate in the past! But never mind that now. Our lives needn't clash. I don't mean to go back to the States. When I've finished this picture I'm working on now, I'm going to play a straight play on the London stage. I've got a wonderful play — Elderton's written it for me. It will be a terrific success.'

'I'm sure it will,' he said politely.

'And you can go on being a doctor.' Her voice was kind and condescending. 'You're quite well known, they tell me.'

'My dear girl, I'm married. I've got children.'

'I'm married myself at the moment,' said Veronica. 'But all these things are easily arranged. A good lawyer can fix up everything.' She smiled at him dazzlingly. 'I always did mean to marry you, darling. I can't think why I have this terrible passion for you, but there it is!'

'I'm sorry, Veronica, but no good lawyer is going to fix up anything. Your life and mine have nothing to do with each other.'

'Not after last night?'

'You're not a child, Veronica. You've had a

couple of husbands, and by all accounts several lovers. What does last night mean actually? Nothing at all, and you know it.'

'Oh, my dear John.' She was still amused, indulgent. 'If you'd seen your face — there in that stuffy drawing-room! You might have been in San Miguel again.'

John sighed. He said:

'I *was* in San Miguel. Try to understand, Veronica. You came to me out of the past. Last night, I, too, was in the past, but today — today's different. I'm a man fifteen years older. A man you don't even know — and whom I dare say you wouldn't like much if you did know.'

'You prefer your wife and children to me?' She was genuinely amazed.

'Odd as it may seem to you, I do.'

'Nonsense, John, you love me.'

'I'm sorry, Veronica.'

She said incredulously:

'You don't love me?'

'It's better to be quite clear about these things. You are an extraordinarily beautiful woman, Veronica, but I don't love you.'

She sat so still that she might have been a waxwork. That stillness of hers made him just a little uneasy.

When she spoke it was with such venom that he recoiled.

'Who is she?'

'She? Who do you mean?'

'That woman by the mantelpiece last night?'

Henrietta! he thought. How the devil did she get on to Henrietta? Aloud he said:

'Who are you talking about? Midge Hardcastle?'

'Midge? That's the square, dark girl, isn't it? No, I don't mean her. And I don't mean your wife. I mean that insolent devil who was leaning against the mantelpiece! It's because of *her* that you're turning me down! Oh, don't pretend to be so moral about your wife and children. It's that other woman.'

She got up and came towards him.

'Don't you understand, John, that ever since I came back to England, eighteen months ago, I've been thinking about you? Why do you imagine I took this idiotic place here? Simply because I found out that you often came down for weekends with the Angkatells!'

'So last night was all planned, Veronica?'

'You *belong* to me, John. You always have!'

'I don't belong to anyone, Veronica. Hasn't life taught you even now that you can't own other human beings body and soul? I loved you when I was a young man. I wanted you to share my life. You wouldn't do it!'

'*My* life and career were much more important than *yours*. Anyone can be a doctor!'

He lost his temper a little.

'Are you *quite* as wonderful as you think you are?'

'You mean that I haven't got to the top of the tree. I shall! *I shall*!'

John Christow looked at her with a sudden, quite dispassionate interest.

'I don't believe, you know, that you will. There's a *lack* in you, Veronica. You're all grab and snatch — no real generosity — I think that's it.'

Veronica got up. She said in a quiet voice:

'You turned me down fifteen years ago. You've turned me down again today. I'll make you sorry for this.'

John got up and went to the door.

'I'm sorry, Veronica, if I've hurt you. You're very lovely, my dear, and I once loved you very much. Can't we leave it at that?'

'Goodbye, John. We're not leaving it at that. You'll find that out all right. I think — I think I hate you more than I believed I could hate anyone.'

He shrugged his shoulders:

'I'm sorry. Goodbye.'

John walked back slowly through the wood. When he got to the swimming pool he sat down on the bench there. He had no regrets for his treatment of Veronica. Veronica, he thought dispassionately, was a nasty bit of work. She always had been a nasty bit of work, and the best thing he had ever done was to get clear of her in time. God alone knew what would have happened to him by now if he hadn't!

As it was, he had that extraordinary sensation of starting a new life, unfettered and unhampered by the past. He must have been extremely difficult to live with for the last year or two. Poor Gerda, he thought, with her unselfishness and her continual anxiety to please him. He would be kinder in future.

And perhaps now he would be able to stop trying to bully Henrietta. Not that one could really bully Henrietta — she wasn't made that way. Storms broke over her and she stood there, meditative, her eyes looking at you from very far away.

He thought: 'I shall go to Henrietta and tell her.'

He looked up sharply, disturbed by some small unexpected sound. There had been shots in the woods higher up, and there had been the usual small noises of woodlands, birds, and the faint melancholy dropping of leaves. But this was another noise — a very faint businesslike click.

And suddenly, John was acutely conscious of danger. How long had he been sitting here? Half an hour? An hour? There was someone watching him. Someone —

And that click was — of course it was —

He turned sharply, a man very quick in his reactions. But he was not quick enough. His eyes widened in surprise, but there was no time for him to make a sound.

The shot rang out and he fell, awkwardly, sprawled out by the edge of the swimming pool.

A dark stain welled up slowly on his left side and trickled slowly on to the concrete of the pool edge; and from there dripped red into the blue water.

11

I

Hercule Poirot flicked a last speck of dust from his shoes. He had dressed carefully for his luncheon party and he was satisfied with the result.

He knew well enough the kind of clothes that were worn in the country on a Sunday in England, but he did not choose to conform to English ideas. He preferred his own standards of urban smartness. He was not an English country gentleman. He was Hercule Poirot!

He did not, he confessed it to himself, really like the country. The weekend cottage — so many of his friends had extolled it — he had allowed himself to succumb, and had purchased Resthaven, though the only thing he had liked about it was its shape, which was quite square like a box. The surrounding landscape he did not care for though it was, he knew, supposed to be a beauty spot. It was, however, too wildly asymmetrical to appeal to him. He did not care much for trees at any time — they had that untidy habit of shedding their leaves. He could endure poplars and he approved of a monkey puzzle — but this riot of beech and oak left him unmoved. Such a landscape was best enjoyed from a car on a fine afternoon. You exclaimed, 'Quel beau paysage!' and drove back to a good hotel.

The best thing about Resthaven, he considered, was the small vegetable garden neatly laid out in rows by his Belgian gardener Victor. Meanwhile Françoise, Victor's wife, devoted herself with tenderness to the care of her employer's stomach.

Hercule Poirot passed through the gate, sighed, glanced down once more at his shining black shoes, adjusted his pale grey Homburg hat, and looked up and down the road.

He shivered slightly at the aspect of Dovecotes. Dovecotes and Resthaven had been erected by rival builders, both of whom had acquired a small piece of land. Further enterprise on their part had been swiftly curtailed by a National Trust for preserving the beauties of the countryside. The two houses remained representative of two schools of thought. Resthaven was a box with a roof, severely modern and a little dull. Dovecotes was a riot of half-timbering and Olde Worlde packed into as small a space as possible.

Hercule Poirot debated within himself as to how he should approach The Hollow. There was, he knew, a little higher up the lane, a small gate and a path. This, the unofficial way, would save a half-mile *détour* by the road. Nevertheless Hercule Poirot, a stickler for etiquette, decided to take the longer way round and approach the house correctly by the front entrance.

This was his first visit to Sir Henry and Lady Angkatell. One should not, he considered, take short-cuts uninvited, especially when one was the guest of people of social importance. He was, it must be admitted, pleased by their invitation.

'*Je suis un peu snob*,' he murmured to himself.

He had retained an agreeable impression of the Angkatells from the time in Baghdad, particularly of Lady Angkatell. '*Une originale!*' he thought to himself.

His estimation of the time required for walking to The Hollow by road was accurate. It was exactly one minute to one when he rang the front-door bell. He was glad to have arrived and felt slightly tired. He was not fond of walking.

The door was opened by the magnificent Gudgeon, of whom Poirot approved. His reception, however, was not quite as he had hoped. 'Her ladyship is in the pavilion by the swimming pool, sir. Will you come this way?'

The passion of the English for sitting out of doors irritated Hercule Poirot. Though one had to put up with this whimsy in the height of summer, surely, Poirot thought, one should be safe from it by the end of September! The day was mild, certainly, but it had, as autumn days always had, a certain dampness. How infinitely pleasanter to have been ushered into a comfortable drawing-room with, perhaps, a small fire in the grate. But no, here he was being led out through french windows across a slope of lawn, past a rockery and then through a small gate and along a narrow track between closely planted young chestnuts.

It was the habit of the Angkatells to invite guests for one o'clock, and on fine days they had cocktails and sherry in the small pavilion by the swimming pool. Lunch itself was scheduled for one-thirty, by which time the most unpunctual of guests should have managed to arrive, which permitted Lady Angkatell's excellent cook to embark on soufflés and such accurately timed delicacies without too much trepidation.

To Hercule Poirot, the plan did not commend itself.

'In a little minute,' he thought, 'I shall be almost back where I started.'

With an increasing awareness of his feet in his shoes, he followed Gudgeon's tall figure.

It was at that moment from just ahead of him that he heard a little cry. It increased, somehow, his dissatisfaction. It was incongruous, in some way unfitting. He did not classify it, nor indeed think about it. When he thought about it afterwards he was hard put to it to remember just what emotions it had seemed to convey. Dismay? Surprise? Horror? He could only say that it suggested, very definitely, the unexpected.

Gudgeon stepped out from the chestnuts. He was moving to one side, deferentially, to allow Poirot to pass and at the same time clearing his throat preparatory to murmuring, 'M. Poirot, my lady' in the proper subdued and respectful tones when his suppleness became suddenly rigid. He gasped. It was an unbutlerlike noise.

Hercule Poirot stepped out on to the open space surrounding the swimming pool, and immediately he, too, stiffened, but with annoyance.

It was too much — it was really too much! He had not suspected such cheapness of the Angkatells. The long walk by the road, the disappointment at the house — and now *this*! The misplaced sense of humour of the English!

He was annoyed and he was bored — oh, how he was bored. Death was not, to him, amusing. And here they had arranged for him, by way of a joke, a set-piece.

For what he was looking at was a highly artificial murder scene. By the side of the pool was the body, artistically arranged with an outflung arm and even some red paint dripping gently over the edge of the concrete into the pool. It was a spectacular body, that of a handsome fair-haired man. Standing over the body, revolver in hand, was a woman, a short, powerfully built, middle-aged woman with a curiously blank expression.

And there were three other actors. On the far side of the pool was a tall young woman whose hair matched the autumn leaves in its rich brown; she had a basket in her hand full of dahlia heads. A little farther off was a man, a tall, inconspicuous man in a shooting-coat, carrying a gun. And immediately on his left, with a basket of eggs in her hand, was his hostess, Lady Angkatell.

It was clear to Hercule Poirot that several different paths converged here at the swimming pool and that these people had each arrived by a different path.

It was all very mathematical and artificial.

He sighed. *Enfin*, what did they expect him to do? Was he to pretend to believe in this 'crime'? Was he to register dismay — alarm? Or was he to bow, to congratulate his hostess: 'Ah, but it is very charming, what you arrange for me here'?

Really, the whole thing was very stupid — not *spirituel* at all! Was it not Queen Victoria who had said: 'We are not amused'? He felt very inclined to say the same: 'I, Hercule Poirot, am not amused.'

Lady Angkatell had walked towards the body. He followed, conscious of Gudgeon, still breathing hard, behind him. 'He is not in the secret, that one,' Hercule Poirot thought to himself. From the other side of the pool, the other two people joined them. They were all quite close now, looking down on that spectacular sprawling figure by the pool's edge.

And suddenly, with a terrific shock, with that feeling as of blurring on a cinematograph screen before the picture comes into focus, Hercule Poirot realized that this artificially set scene had a point of reality.

For what he was looking down at was, if not a dead, at least a dying man.

It was not red paint dripping off the edge of the concrete, it was blood. This man had been shot, and shot a very short time ago.

He darted a quick glance at the woman who stood there, revolver in hand. Her face

137

was quite blank, without feeling of any kind. She looked dazed and rather stupid.

'Curious,' he thought.

Had she, he wondered, drained herself of all emotion, all feeling, in the firing of the shot? Was she now all passion spent, nothing but an exhausted shell? It might be so, he thought.

Then he looked down on the shot man, and he started. For the dying man's eyes were open. They were intensely blue eyes and they held an expression that Poirot could not read but which he described to himself as a kind of intense awareness.

And suddenly, or so it felt to Poirot, there seemed to be in all this group of people only one person who was really alive — the man who was at the point of death.

Poirot had never received so strong an impression of vivid and intense vitality. The others were pale shadowy figures, actors in a remote drama, but this man was *real.*

John Christow opened his mouth and spoke. His voice was strong, unsurprised and urgent.

'*Henrietta —* ' he said.

Then his eyelids dropped, his head jerked sideways.

Hercule Poirot knelt down, made sure, then rose to his feet, mechanically dusting the knees of his trousers.

'Yes,' he said. 'He is dead.'

II

The picture broke up, wavered, refocused itself. There were individual reactions now — trivial happenings. Poirot was conscious of himself as a kind of magnified eyes and ears — recording. Just that, *recording*.

He was aware of Lady Angkatell's hand relaxing its grip on her basket and Gudgeon springing forward, quickly taking it from her.

'Allow me, my lady.'

Mechanically, quite naturally, Lady Angkatell murmured:

'Thank you, Gudgeon.'

And then, hesitantly, she said:

'Gerda — '

The woman holding the revolver stirred for the first time. She looked round at them all. When she spoke, her voice held what seemed to be pure bewilderment.

'John's dead,' she said. 'John's *dead*.'

With a kind of swift authority, the tall young woman with the leaf-brown hair came swiftly to her.

'Give that to me, Gerda,' she said.

And dexterously, before Poirot could

139

protest or intervene, she had taken the revolver out of Gerda Christow's hand.

Poirot took a quick step forward.

'You should not do that, Mademoiselle — '

The young woman started nervously at the sound of his voice. The revolver slipped through her fingers. She was standing by the edge of the pool and the revolver fell with a splash into the water.

Her mouth opened and she uttered an 'Oh' of consternation, turning her head to look at Poirot apologetically.

'What a fool I am,' she said. 'I'm sorry.'

Poirot did not speak for a moment. He was staring into a pair of clear hazel eyes. They met his quite steadily and he wondered if his momentary suspicion had been unjust.

He said quietly:

'Things should be handled as little as possible. Everything must be left exactly as it is for the police to see.'

There was a little stir then — very faint, just a ripple of uneasiness.

Lady Angkatell murmured distastefully: 'Of course. I suppose — yes, the police — '

In a quiet, pleasant voice, tinged with fastidious repulsion, the man in the shooting-coat said: 'I'm afraid, Lucy, it's inevitable.'

Into that moment of silence and realization there came the sound of footsteps and voices, assured, brisk footsteps and cheerful, incongruous voices.

Along the path from the house came Sir Henry Angkatell and Midge Hardcastle, talking and laughing together.

At the sight of the group round the pool, Sir Henry stopped short, and exclaimed in astonishment:

'What's the matter? What's happened?'

His wife answered: 'Gerda has — ' She broke off sharply. 'I mean — John is — '

Gerda said in her flat, bewildered voice:

'John has been shot. He's dead.'

They all looked away from her, embarrassed.

Then Lady Angkatell said quickly:

'My dear, I think you'd better go and — and lie down. Perhaps we had better all go back to the house? Henry, you and M. Poirot can stay here and — and wait for the police.'

'That will be the best plan, I think,' said Sir Henry. He turned to Gudgeon. 'Will you ring up the police station, Gudgeon? Just state exactly what has occurred. When the police arrive, bring them straight out here.'

Gudgeon bent his head a little and said: 'Yes, Sir Henry.' He was looking a little white about the gills, but he was still the perfect servant.

The tall young woman said: 'Come,

Gerda,' and putting her hand through the other woman's arm, she led her unresistingly away and along the path towards the house. Gerda walked as though in a dream. Gudgeon stood back a little to let them pass, and then followed carrying the basket of eggs.

Sir Henry turned sharply to his wife. 'Now, Lucy, what is all this? What happened exactly?'

Lady Angkatell stretched out vague hands, a lovely helpless gesture. Hercule Poirot felt the charm of it and the appeal.

'My dear, I hardly know. I was down by the hens. I heard a shot that seemed very near, but I didn't really think anything about it. After all,' she appealed to them all, 'one doesn't! And then I came up the path to the pool and there was John lying there and Gerda standing over him with the revolver. Henrietta and Edward arrived almost at the same moment — from over there.'

She nodded towards the farther side of the pool, where two paths ran into the woods.

Hercule Poirot cleared his throat.

'Who are they, this John and this Gerda? If I may know,' he added apologetically.

'Oh, of course.' Lady Angkatell turned to him in quick apology. 'One forgets — but then one doesn't exactly *introduce* people — not when somebody has just been killed.

142

John is John Christow, Dr Christow. Gerda Christow is his wife.'

'And the lady who went with Mrs Christow to the house?'

'My cousin, Henrietta Savernake.'

There was a movement, a very faint movement from the man on Poirot's left.

'*Henrietta* Savernake,' thought Poirot, 'and he does not like that she should say it — but it is, after all, inevitable that I should know . . .'

('*Henrietta!*' the dying man had said. He had said it in a very curious way. A way that reminded Poirot of something — of some incident . . . now, what was it? No matter, it would come to him.)

Lady Angkatell was going on, determined now on fulfilling her social duties.

'And this is another cousin of ours, Edward Angkatell. And Miss Hardcastle.'

Poirot acknowledged the introductions with polite bows. Midge felt suddenly that she wanted to laugh hysterically; she controlled herself with an effort.

'And now, my dear,' said Sir Henry, 'I think that, as you suggested, you had better go back to the house. I will have a word or two here with M. Poirot.'

Lady Angkatell looked thoughtfully at them.

'I do hope,' she said, 'that Gerda *is* lying down. Was that the right thing to suggest? I really couldn't think what to say. I mean, one has no *precedent*. What *does* one say to a woman who has just killed her husband?'

She looked at them as though hoping that some authoritative answer might be given to her question.

Then she went along the path towards the house. Midge followed her. Edward brought up the rear.

Poirot was left with his host.

Sir Henry cleared his throat. He seemed a little uncertain what to say.

'Christow,' he observed at last, 'was a very able fellow — a *very* able fellow.'

Poirot's eyes rested once more on the dead man. He still had the curious impression that the dead man was more alive than the living.

He wondered what gave him that impression.

He responded politely to Sir Henry.

'Such a tragedy as this is very unfortunate,' he said.

'This sort of thing is more your line than mine,' said Sir Henry. 'I don't think I have ever been at close quarters with a murder before. I hope I've done the right thing so far?'

'The procedure has been quite correct,'

said Poirot. 'You have summoned the police, and until they arrive and take charge there is nothing for us to do — except to make sure that nobody disturbs the body or tampers with the evidence.'

As he said the last word he looked down into the pool where he could see the revolver lying on the concrete bottom, slightly distorted by the blue water.

The evidence, he thought, had perhaps already been tampered with before he, Hercule Poirot, had been able to prevent it.

But no — that had been an accident.

Sir Henry murmured distastefully:

'Think we've got to stand about? A bit chilly. It would be all right, I should think, if we went inside the pavilion?'

Poirot, who had been conscious of damp feet and a disposition to shiver, acquiesced gladly. The pavilion was at the side of the pool farthest from the house, and through its open door they commanded a view of the pool and the body and the path to the house along which the police would come.

The pavilion was luxuriously furnished with comfortable settees and gay native rugs. On a painted iron table a tray was set with glasses and a decanter of sherry.

'I'd offer you a drink,' said Sir Henry, 'but I suppose I'd better not touch anything until the police come — not, I should imagine, that there's anything to interest them in here. Still, it is better to be on the safe side. Gudgeon hadn't brought out the cocktails yet, I see. He was waiting for you to arrive.'

The two sat down rather gingerly in two wicker chairs near the door so that they could watch the path from the house.

A constraint settled over them. It was an occasion on which it was difficult to make small talk.

Poirot glanced round the pavilion, noting anything that struck him as unusual. An expensive cape of platinum fox had been flung carelessly across the back of one of the chairs. He wondered whose it was. Its rather ostentatious magnificence did not harmonize with any of the people he had seen up to now. He could not, for instance, imagine it round Lady Angkatell's shoulders.

It worried him. It breathed a mixture of opulence and self-advertisement — and those characteristics were lacking in anyone he had seen so far.

'I suppose we can smoke,' said Sir Henry, offering his case to Poirot.

Before taking the cigarette, Poirot sniffed the air.

French perfume — an expensive French perfume.

Only a trace of it lingered, but it was there, and again the scent was not the scent that associated itself in his mind with any of the occupants of The Hollow.

As he leaned forward to light his cigarette at Sir Henry's lighter, Poirot's glance fell on a little pile of matchboxes — six of them — stacked on a small table near one of the settees.

It was a detail that struck him as definitely odd.

12

I

'Half-past two,' said Lady Angkatell.

She was in the drawing-room, with Midge and Edward. From behind the closed door of Sir Henry's study came the murmur of voices. Hercule Poirot, Sir Henry and Inspector Grange were in there.

Lady Angkatell sighed:

'You know, Midge, I still feel one ought to do something about lunch. It seems, of course, quite heartless to sit down round the table as though nothing had happened. But after all, M. Poirot was asked to lunch — and he is probably hungry. And it can't be upsetting to *him* that poor John Christow has been killed like it is to us. And I must say that though I really do not feel like eating myself, Henry and Edward must be extremely hungry after being out shooting all the morning.'

Edward Angkatell said: 'Don't worry on my account, Lucy, dear.'

'You are always considerate, Edward. And then there is David — I noticed that he ate a great deal at dinner last night. Intellectual people always seem to need a good deal of food. Where *is* David, by the way?'

'He went up to his room,' said Midge, 'after he had heard what had happened.'

'Yes — well, that was rather tactful of him. I dare say it made him feel awkward. Of course, say what you like, a murder is an awkward thing — it upsets the servants and puts the general routine out — we were having ducks for lunch — fortunately they are quite nice eaten cold. What does one do about Gerda, do you think? Something on a tray? A little strong soup, perhaps?'

'Really,' thought Midge, 'Lucy is inhuman!' And then with a qualm she reflected that it was perhaps because Lucy was too human that it shocked one so! Wasn't it the plain unvarnished truth that all catastrophes were hedged round with these little trivial wonderings and surmises? Lucy merely gave utterance to the thoughts which most people did not acknowledge. One did remember the servants, and worry about meals. And one did, even, feel hungry. She felt hungry herself at this very moment! Hungry, she thought, and at the same time, rather sick. A curious mixture.

And there was, undoubtedly, just plain awkward embarrassment in not knowing how to react to a quiet, commonplace woman whom one had referred to, only yesterday, as 'poor Gerda' and who was now, presumably, shortly to be standing in the dock accused of murder.

'These things happen to other people,' thought Midge. 'They can't happen to *us*.'

She looked across the room at Edward. 'They oughtn't,' she thought, 'to happen to people like Edward. People who are so very unviolent.' She took comfort in looking at Edward. Edward, so quiet, so reasonable, so kind and calm.

Gudgeon entered, inclined himself confidentially and spoke in a suitably muted voice.

'I have placed sandwiches and some coffee in the dining-room, my lady.'

'Oh, *thank* you, Gudgeon!'

'Really,' said Lady Angkatell as Gudgeon left the room. 'Gudgeon is wonderful: I don't know what I should do without Gudgeon. He always knows the right thing to do. Some really substantial sandwiches are as good as lunch — and nothing *heartless* about them, if you know what I mean!'

'Oh, Lucy, *don't*.'

Midge suddenly felt warm tears running down her cheek. Lady Angkatell looked surprised, murmured:

'Poor darling. It's all been too much for you.'

Edward crossed to the sofa and sat down by Midge. He put his arm round her.

'Don't worry, little Midge,' he said.

Midge buried her face on his shoulder and sobbed there comfortably. She remembered how nice Edward had been to her when her rabbit had died at Ainswick one Easter holidays.

Edward said gently: 'It's been a shock. Can I get her some brandy, Lucy?'

'On the sideboard in the dining-room. I don't think — '

She broke off as Henrietta came into the room. Midge sat up. She felt Edward stiffen and sit very still.

What, thought Midge, does Henrietta feel? She felt almost reluctant to look at her cousin — but there was nothing to see. Henrietta looked, if anything, belligerent. She had come in with her chin up, her colour high, and with a certain swiftness.

'Oh, there you are, Henrietta,' cried Lady Angkatell. 'I have been wondering. The police are with Henry and M. Poirot. What have you given Gerda? Brandy? Or tea and aspirin?'

'I gave her some brandy — and a hot-water bottle.'

'Quite right,' said Lady Angkatell approvingly. 'That's what they tell you in First Aid classes — the hot-water bottle, I mean, for shock — *not* the brandy; there is a reaction nowadays against stimulants. But I think that is only a fashion. We always gave brandy for shock when I was a girl at Ainswick. Though, really, I suppose, it can't be exactly *shock* with Gerda. I don't know really *what* one would feel if one had killed one's husband — it's the sort of thing one just can't begin to imagine — but it wouldn't exactly give one a *shock*. I mean, there wouldn't be any element of *surprise*.'

Henrietta's voice, icy cold, cut into the placid atmosphere.

She said: 'Why are you all so sure that Gerda killed John?'

There was a moment's pause — and Midge felt a curious shifting in the atmosphere. There was confusion, strain and, finally, a kind of slow watchfulness.

Then Lady Angkatell said, her voice quite devoid of any inflection:

'It seemed — self-evident. What else do you suggest?'

'Isn't it possible that Gerda came along to the pool, that she found John lying there, and that she had just picked up the revolver when — when we came upon the scene?'

Again there was that silence. Then Lady Angkatell asked:

'Is that what Gerda says?'

'Yes.'

It was not a simple assent. It had force behind it. It came out like a revolver shot.

Lady Angkatell raised her eyebrows, then she said with apparent irrelevancy:

'There are sandwiches and coffee in the dining-room.'

She broke off with a little gasp as Gerda Christow came through the open door. She said hurriedly and apologetically:

'I — I really didn't feel I could lie down any longer. One is — one is so terribly restless.'

Lady Angkatell cried:

'You must sit down — you must sit down at once.'

She displaced Midge from the sofa, settled Gerda there, put a cushion at her back.

'You poor dear,' said Lady Angkatell.

She spoke with emphasis, but the words seemed quite meaningless.

Edward walked to the window and stood there looking out.

Gerda pushed back the untidy hair from her forehead. She spoke in a worried, bewildered tone.

'I — I really am only just beginning to

153

realize it. You know I haven't been able to feel — I still can't feel — that it's *real* — that John — is *dead*.' She began to shake a little. 'Who can have killed him? Who can possibly have killed him?'

Lady Angkatell drew a deep breath — then she turned her head sharply. Sir Henry's door had opened. He came in accompanied by Inspector Grange, who was a large, heavily built man with a down-drooping, pessimistic moustache.

'This is my wife — Inspector Grange.'

Grange bowed and said:

'I was wondering, Lady Angkatell, if I could have a few words with Mrs Christow — '

He broke off as Lady Angkatell indicated the figure on the sofa.

'Mrs Christow?'

Gerda said eagerly:

'Yes, I am Mrs Christow.'

'I don't want to distress you, Mrs Christow, but I would like to ask you a few questions. You can, of course, have your solicitor present if you prefer it — '

Sir Henry put in:

'It is sometimes wiser, Gerda — '

She interrupted:

'A solicitor? Why a solicitor? Why should a solicitor know anything about John's death?'

Inspector Grange coughed. Sir Henry seemed about to speak. Henrietta put in:

'The inspector only wants to know just what happened this morning.'

Gerda turned to him. She spoke in a wondering voice:

'It seems all like a bad dream — not real. I — I haven't been able to cry or anything. One just doesn't feel anything at all.'

Grange said soothingly:

'That's the shock, Mrs Christow.'

'Yes, yes — I suppose it is. But you see it was all so *sudden*. I went out from the house and along the path to the swimming pool — '

'At what time, Mrs Christow?'

'It was just before one o'clock — about two minutes to one. I know because I looked at that clock. And when I got there — there was John, lying there — and blood on the edge of the concrete.'

'Did you hear a shot, Mrs Christow?'

'Yes, — no — I don't know. I knew Sir Henry and Mr Angkatell were out shooting. I — I just saw John — '

'Yes, Mrs Christow?'

'John — and blood — and a revolver. I picked up the revolver — '

'Why?'

'I beg your pardon?'

'Why did you pick up the revolver, Mrs Christow?'

'I — I don't know.'

'You shouldn't have touched it, you know.'

'Shouldn't I?' Gerda was vague, her face vacant. 'But I did. I held it in my hands.'

She looked down now at her hands as though she was, in fancy, seeing the revolver lying in them.

She turned sharply to the inspector. Her voice was suddenly sharp — anguished.

'Who could have killed John? Nobody could have wanted to kill him. He was — he was the best of men. So kind, so unselfish — he did everything for other people. Everybody loved him, Inspector. He was a wonderful doctor. The best and kindest of husbands. It must have been an accident — it must — it *must!*'

She flung out a hand to the room.

'Ask anyone, Inspector. Nobody could have wanted to kill John, could they?'

She appealed to them all.

Inspector Grange closed up his notebook.

'Thank you, Mrs Christow,' he said in an unemotional voice. 'That will be all for the present.'

Hercule Poirot and Inspector Grange went together through the chestnut woods to the swimming pool. The thing that had been John

Christow but which was now 'the body' had been photographed and measured and written about and examined by the police surgeon, and had now been taken away to the mortuary. The swimming pool, Poirot thought, looked curiously innocent. Everything about today, he thought, had been strangely fluid. Except John Christow — he had not been fluid. Even in death he had been purposeful and objective. The swimming pool was not now pre-eminently a swimming pool, it was the place where John Christow's body had lain and where his life-blood had welled away over concrete into artificially blue water.

Artificial — for a moment Poirot grasped at the word. Yes, there had been something artificial about it all. As though —

A man in a bathing suit came up to the inspector.

'Here's the revolver, sir,' he said.

Grange took the dripping object gingerly.

'No hope of fingerprints now,' he remarked, 'but luckily it doesn't matter in this case. Mrs Christow was actually holding the revolver when you arrived, wasn't she, M. Poirot?'

'Yes.'

'Identification of the revolver is the next thing,' said Grange. 'I should imagine Sir

Henry will be able to do that for us. She got it from his study, I should say.'

He cast a glance round the pool.

'Now, let's have that again to be quite clear. The path below the pool comes up from the farm and that's the way Lady Angkatell came. The other two, Mr Edward Angkatell and Miss Savernake, came down from the woods — but not together. He came by the left-hand path, and she by the right-hand one which leads out of the long flower walk above the house. But they were both standing on the far side of the pool when you arrived?'

'Yes.'

'And this path here, beside the pavilion, leads on to Podder's Lane. Right — we'll go along it.'

As they walked, Grange spoke, without excitement, just with knowledge and quiet pessimism.

'Never like these cases much,' he said. 'Had one last year — down near Ashridge. Retired military man, he was — distinguished career. Wife was the nice quiet, old-fashioned kind, sixty-five, grey hair — rather pretty hair with a wave in it. Did a lot of gardening. One day she goes up to his room, gets out his service revolver, and walks out into the garden and shoots him. Just like that! A good deal behind it, of course, that one had to dig out.

Sometimes they think up some fool story about a tramp! We pretend to accept it, of course, keep things quiet whilst we're making inquiries, but we know what's what.'

'You mean,' said Poirot, 'that you have decided that Mrs Christow shot her husband.'

Grange gave him a look of surprise.

'Well, don't you think so?'

Poirot said slowly: 'It could all have happened as she said.'

Inspector Grange shrugged his shoulders.

'It *could* have — yes. But it's a thin story. And *they* all think she killed him! They know something we don't.' He looked curiously at his companion. 'You thought she'd done it all right, didn't you, when you arrived on the scene?'

Poirot half-closed his eyes. Coming along the path . . . Gudgeon stepping . . . Gerda Christow standing over her husband with the revolver in her hand and that blank look on her face. Yes, as Grange had said, he *had* thought she had done it . . . had thought, at least, that that was the impression he was meant to have.

Yes, but that was not the same thing.

A scene staged — set to deceive.

Had Gerda Christow looked like a woman who had just shot her husband? That was what Inspector Grange wanted to know.

And with a sudden shock of surprise, Hercule Poirot realized that in all his long experience of deeds of violence he had never actually come face to face with a woman who had just killed her husband. What would a woman look like in such circumstances? Triumphant, horrified, satisfied, dazed, incredulous, empty?

Any one of these things, he thought.

Inspector Grange was talking. Poirot caught the end of his speech.

' — Once you get all the facts behind the case, and you can usually get all that from the servants.'

'Mrs Christow is going back to London?'

'Yes. There's a couple of kids there. Have to let her go. Of course, we keep a sharp eye on her, but she won't know that. She thinks she's got away with it all right. Looks rather a stupid kind of woman to me . . . '

Did Gerda Christow realize, Poirot wondered, what the police thought — and what the Angkatells thought? She had looked as though she did not realize anything at all. She had looked like a woman whose reactions were slow and who was completely dazed and heartbroken by her husband's death.

They had come out into the lane.

Poirot stopped by his gate. Grange said:

'This your little place? Nice and snug. Well, goodbye for the present, M. Poirot. Thanks for your cooperation. I'll drop in some time and give you the lowdown on how we're getting on.'

His eye travelled up the lane.

'Who's your neighbour? That's not where our new celebrity hangs out, is it?'

'Miss Veronica Cray, the actress, comes there for weekends, I believe.'

'Of course. Dovecotes. I liked her in *Lady Rides on Tiger*, but she's a bit high-brow for my taste. Give me Hedy Lamarr.'

He turned away.

'Well, I must get back to the job. So long, M. Poirot.'

II

'You recognize this, Sir Henry?'

Inspector Grange laid the revolver on the desk in front of Sir Henry and looked at him expectantly.

'I can handle it?' Sir Henry's hand hesitated over the revolver as he asked the question.

Grange nodded. 'It's been in the pool. Destroyed whatever fingerprints there were on it. A pity, if I may say so, that Miss Savernake let it slip out of her hand.'

161

'Yes, yes — but of course it was a very tense moment for all of us. Women are apt to get flustered and — er — drop things.'

Again Inspector Grange nodded. He said:

'Miss Savernake seems a cool, capable young lady on the whole.'

The words were devoid of emphasis, yet something in them made Sir Henry look up sharply. Grange went on:

'Now, do you recognize it, sir?'

Sir Henry picked up the revolver and examined it. He noted the number and compared it with a list in a small leather-bound book. Then, closing the book with a sigh, he said:

'Yes, Inspector, this comes from my collection here.'

'When did you see it last?'

'Yesterday afternoon. We were doing some shooting in the garden with a target, and this was one of the firearms we were using.'

'Who actually fired this revolver on that occasion?'

'I think everybody had at least one shot with it.'

'Including Mrs Christow?'

'Including Mrs Christow.'

'And after you had finished shooting?'

'I put the revolver away in its usual place. Here.'

He pulled out the drawer of a big bureau. It was half-full of guns.

'You've got a big collection of firearms, Sir Henry.'

'It's been a hobby of mine for many years.'

Inspector Grange's eyes rested thoughtfully on the ex-Governor of the Hollowene Islands. A good-looking, distinguished man, the kind of man he would be quite pleased to serve under himself — in fact, a man he would much prefer to his own present Chief Constable. Inspector Grange did not think much of the Chief Constable of Wealdshire — a fussy despot and a tuft-hunter. He brought his mind back to the job in hand.

'The revolver was not, of course, loaded when you put it away, Sir Henry?'

'Certainly not.'

'And you keep your ammunition — where?'

'Here.' Sir Henry took a key from a pigeon-hole and unlocked one of the lower drawers of the desk.

'Simple enough,' thought Grange. The Christow woman had seen where it was kept. She'd only got to come along and help herself. Jealousy, he thought, plays the dickens with women. He'd lay ten to one it *was* jealousy. The thing would come clear enough when he'd finished the routine here and got on to the Harley Street end. But you'd got to do things in their proper order.

He got up and said:

'Well, thank you, Sir Henry. I'll let you know about the inquest.'

13

They had the cold ducks for supper. After the ducks there was a caramel custard which, Lady Angkatell said, showed just the right feeling on the part of Mrs Medway.

Cooking, she said, really gave great scope to delicacy of feeling.

'We are only, as she knows, moderately fond of caramel custard. There would be something very gross, just after the death of a friend, in eating one's favourite pudding. But caramel custard is so easy — slippery if you know what I mean — and then one leaves a little on one's plate.'

She sighed and said that she hoped they had done right in letting Gerda go back to London.

'But quite correct of Henry to go with her.'

For Sir Henry had insisted on driving Gerda to Harley Street.

'She will come back here for the inquest, of course,' went on Lady Angkatell, meditatively eating caramel custard. 'But naturally she wanted to break it to the children — they might see it in the papers and only a Frenchwoman in the house — one knows

how excitable — a *crise de nerfs*, possibly.
But Henry will deal with her, and I really
think Gerda will be quite all right. She will
probably send for some relations — sisters
perhaps. Gerda is the sort of person who is
sure to have sisters — three or four, I should
think, probably living at Tunbridge Wells.'

'What extraordinary things you do say,
Lucy,' said Midge.

'Well, darling, Torquay if you prefer it
— no, not Torquay. They would be at least
sixty-five if they were living at Torquay.
Eastbourne, perhaps, or St Leonards.'

Lady Angkatell looked at the last spoonful
of caramel custard, seemed to condole with
it, and laid it down very gently uneaten.

David, who only liked savouries, looked
down gloomily at his empty plate.

Lady Angkatell got up.

'I think we shall all want to go to bed early
tonight,' she said. 'So much has happened,
hasn't it? One has no idea from reading about
these things in the paper how *tiring* they are.
I feel, you know, as though I had walked
about fifteen miles. Instead of actually having
done nothing but sit down — but that is
tiring, too, because one does not like to read
a book or a newspaper, it looks so heartless.
Though I think perhaps the leading article in
The Observer would have been all right

— but *not* the *News of the World*. Don't you agree with me, David? I like to know what the young people think, it keeps one from losing touch.'

David said in a gruff voice that he never read the *News of the World*.

'I always do,' said Lady Angkatell. 'We pretend we get it for the servants, but Gudgeon is very understanding and never takes it out until after tea. It is a most interesting paper, all about women who put their heads in gas ovens — an incredible number of them!'

'What will they do in the houses of the future which are all electric?' asked Edward Angkatell with a faint smile.

'I suppose they will just have to decide to make the best of things — so much more sensible.'

'I disagree with you, sir,' said David, 'about the houses of the future being all electric. There can be communal heating laid on from a central supply. Every working-class house should be completely labour-saving.'

Edward Angkatell said hastily that he was afraid that was a subject he was not very well up in. David's lip curled with scorn.

Gudgeon brought in coffee on a tray, moving a little slower than usual to convey a sense of mourning.

'Oh, Gudgeon,' said Lady Angkatell, 'about those eggs. I meant to write the date in pencil on them as usual. Will you ask Mrs Medway to see to it?'

'I think you will find, my lady, that everything has been attended to quite satisfactorily.' He cleared his throat. 'I have seen to things myself.'

'Oh, thank you, Gudgeon.'

As Gudgeon went out she murmured: 'Really, Gudgeon is wonderful. The servants are all being marvellous. And one does so sympathize with them having the police here — it must be dreadful for them. By the way, are there any left?'

'Police, do you mean?' asked Midge.

'Yes. Don't they usually leave one standing in the hall? Or perhaps he's watching the front door from the shrubbery outside.'

'Why should he watch the front door?'

'I don't know, I'm sure. They do in books. And then somebody else is murdered in the night.'

'Oh, Lucy, don't,' said Midge.

Lady Angkatell looked at her curiously.

'Darling, I am so sorry. Stupid of me. And of course nobody else could be murdered. Gerda's gone home — I mean — Oh, Henrietta dear, I am sorry. I didn't mean to say *that*.'

But Henrietta did not answer. She was standing by the round table staring down at the bridge score she had kept last night.

She said, rousing herself, 'Sorry, Lucy, what did you say?'

'I wondered if there were any police left over.'

'Like remnants in a sale? I don't think so. They've all gone back to the police station, to write out what we said in proper police language.'

'What are you looking at, Henrietta?'

'Nothing.'

Henrietta moved across to the mantelpiece.

'What do you think Veronica Cray is doing tonight?' she asked.

A look of dismay crossed Lady Angkatell's face.

'My dear! You don't think she might come over here again? She must have heard by now.'

'Yes,' said Henrietta thoughtfully. 'I suppose she's heard.'

'Which reminds me,' said Lady Angkatell. 'I really must telephone to the Careys. We can't have them coming to lunch tomorrow just as though nothing had happened.'

She left the room.

David, hating his relations, murmured that he wanted to look up something in the

Encyclopædia Britannica. The library, he thought, would be a peaceful place.

Henrietta went to the french windows, opened them, and passed through. After a moment's hesitation Edward followed her.

He found her standing outside looking up at the sky. She said:

'Not so warm as last night, is it?'

In his pleasant voice, Edward said: 'No, distinctly chilly.'

She was standing looking up at the house. Her eyes were running along the windows. Then she turned and looked towards the woods. He had no clue to what was in her mind.

He made a movement towards the open window.

'Better come in. It's cold.'

She shook her head.

'I'm going for a stroll. To the swimming pool.'

'Oh, my dear.' He took a quick step towards her. 'I'll come with you.'

'No, thank you, Edward.' Her voice cut sharply through the chill of the air. 'I want to be alone with my dead.'

'Henrietta! My dear — I haven't said anything. But you do know how — how sorry I am.'

'Sorry? That John Christow is dead?'

There was still the brittle sharpness in her tone.

'I meant — sorry for you, Henrietta. I know it must have been a — a great shock.'

'Shock? Oh, but I'm very tough, Edward. I can stand shocks. Was it a shock to you? What did you feel when you saw him lying there? Glad, I suppose. You didn't like John Christow.'

Edward murmured: 'He and I — hadn't much in common.'

'How nicely you put things! In such a restrained way. But as a matter of fact you did have one thing in common. Me! You were both fond of me, weren't you? Only that didn't make a bond between you — quite the opposite.'

The moon came fitfully through a cloud and he was startled as he suddenly saw her face looking at him. Unconsciously he always saw Henrietta as a projection of the Henrietta he had known at Ainswick. She was always to him a laughing girl, with dancing eyes full of eager expectation. The woman he saw now seemed to him a stranger, with eyes that were brilliant but cold and which seemed to look at him inimically.

He said earnestly:

'Henrietta, dearest, do believe this — that I do sympathize with you — in — in

171

your grief, your loss.'

'*Is* it grief?'

The question startled him. She seemed to be asking it, not of him, but of herself.

She said in a low voice:

'So quick — it can happen so quickly. One moment living, breathing, and the next — dead — gone — emptiness. Oh, the emptiness! And here we are, all of us, eating caramel custard and calling ourselves alive — and John, who was more alive than any of us, is dead. I say the word, you know, over and over again to myself. Dead — dead — dead — dead — *dead*. And soon it hasn't got any meaning — not any meaning at all. It's just a funny little word like the breaking off of a rotten branch. *Dead — dead — dead — dead*. It's like a tom-tom, isn't it, beating in the jungle. Dead — dead — dead — dead — dead — '

'Henrietta, stop! For God's sake, stop!'

She looked at him curiously.

'Didn't you know I'd feel like this? What did you think? That I'd sit gently crying into a nice little pocket handkerchief while you held my hand? That it would all be a great shock but that presently I'd begin to get over it? And that you'd comfort me very nicely? You *are* nice, Edward. You're very nice, but you're so — so inadequate.'

He drew back. His face stiffened. He said in a dry voice:

'Yes, I've always known that.'

She went on fiercely:

'What do you think it's been like all the evening, sitting round, with John dead and nobody caring but me and Gerda! With you glad, and David embarrassed and Midge distressed and Lucy delicately enjoying the *News of the World* come from print into real life! Can't you see how like a fantastic nightmare it all is?'

Edward said nothing. He stepped back a pace, into shadows.

Looking at him, Henrietta said:

'Tonight — nothing seems real to me, nobody *is* real — but John!'

Edward said quietly: 'I know . . . I am not very real.'

'What a brute I am, Edward. But I can't help it. I can't help resenting that John, who was so alive, is dead.'

'And that I who am half-dead, am alive.'

'I didn't mean that, Edward.'

'I think you did, Henrietta. I think, perhaps, you are right.'

But she was saying, thoughtfully, harking back to an earlier thought:

'But it is not grief. Perhaps I cannot feel grief. Perhaps I never shall. And yet — I would like to grieve for John.'

Her words seemed to him fantastic. Yet he was even more startled when she added suddenly, in an almost businesslike voice:

'I must go to the swimming pool.'

She glided away through the trees.

Walking stiffly, Edward went through the open window.

Midge looked up as Edward came through the window with unseeing eyes. His face was grey and pinched. It looked bloodless.

He did not hear the little gasp that Midge stifled immediately.

Almost mechanically he walked to a chair and sat down. Aware of something expected of him, he said:

'It's cold.'

'Are you very cold, Edward? Shall we — shall I — light a fire?'

'What?'

Midge took a box of matches from the mantelpiece. She knelt down and set a match to the fire. She looked cautiously sideways at Edward. He was quite oblivious, she thought, of everything.

She said: 'A fire is nice. It warms one.'

'How cold he looks,' she thought. 'But it can't be as cold as that outside? It's Henrietta! What has she said to him?'

'Bring your chair nearer, Edward. Come close to the fire.'

'What?'

'Oh, it was nothing. Just the fire.'

She was talking to him now loudly and slowly, as though to a deaf person.

And suddenly, so suddenly that her heart turned over with relief, Edward, the real Edward, was there again. Smiling at her gently:

'Have you been talking to me, Midge? I'm sorry. I'm afraid I was thinking — thinking of something.'

'Oh, it was nothing. Just the fire.'

The sticks were crackling and some fir-cones were burning with a bright, clean flame. Edward looked at them. He said:

'It's a nice fire.'

He stretched out his long, thin hands to the blaze, aware of relief from tension.

Midge said: 'We always had fir-cones at Ainswick.'

'I still do. A basket of them is brought every day and put by the grate.'

Edward at Ainswick. Midge half-closed her eyes, picturing it. He would sit, she thought, in the library, on the west side of the house. There was a magnolia that almost covered one window and which filled the room with a golden green light in the afternoons. Through the other window you looked out on the lawn and a tall Wellingtonia stood up like a sentinel. And to the right was the big copper beech.

Oh, Ainswick — Ainswick.

She could smell the soft air that drifted in from the magnolia which would still, in September, have some great white sweet-smelling waxy flowers on it. And the pine-cones on the fire. And a faintly musty smell from the kind of book that Edward was sure to be reading. He would be sitting in the saddle-back chair, and occasionally, perhaps, his eyes would go from the book to the fire, and he would think, just for a minute, of Henrietta.

Midge stirred and asked:

'Where is Henrietta?'

'She went to the swimming pool.'

Midge stared. 'Why?'

Her voice, abrupt and deep, roused Edward a little.

'My dear Midge, surely you knew — oh, well — guessed. She knew Christow pretty well.'

'Oh, of course one knew *that*. But I don't see why she should go mooning off to where he was shot. That's not at all like Henrietta. She's never melodramatic.'

'Do any of us know what anyone else is

like? Henrietta, for instance.'

Midge frowned. She said:

'After all, Edward, you and I have known Henrietta all our lives.'

'She has changed.'

'Not really. I don't think one changes.'

'Henrietta has changed.'

Midge looked at him curiously.

'More than we have, you and I?'

'Oh, I have stood still, I know that well enough. And you — '

His eyes, suddenly focusing, looked at her where she knelt by the fender. It was as though he was looking at her from a long way away, taking in the square chin, the dark eyes, the resolute mouth. He said:

'I wish I saw you more often, Midge, my dear.'

She smiled up at him. She said:

'I know. It isn't easy, these days, to keep in touch.'

There was a sound outside and Edward got up.

'Lucy was right,' he said. 'It has been a tiring day — one's first introduction to murder. I shall go to bed. Goodnight.'

He had left the room when Henrietta came through the window.

Midge turned on her.

'What have you done to Edward?'

'Edward?' Henrietta was vague. Her forehead was puckered. She seemed to be thinking of something a long way away.

'Yes, Edward. He came in looking dreadful — so cold and grey.'

'If you care about Edward so much, Midge, why don't you do something about him?'

'Do something? What do you mean?'

'I don't know. Stand on a chair and shout! Draw attention to yourself. Don't you know that's the only hope with a man like Edward?'

'Edward will never care about anyone but you, Henrietta. He never has.'

'Then it's very unintelligent of him.' She threw a quick glance at Midge's white face. 'I've hurt you. I'm sorry. But I hate Edward tonight.'

'Hate Edward? You *can't*.'

'Oh, yes, I can! You don't know — '

'What?'

Henrietta said slowly:

'He reminds me of such a lot of things I would like to forget.'

'What things?'

'Well, Ainswick, for instance.'

'Ainswick? You want to forget Ainswick?' Midge's tone was incredulous.

'Yes, yes, *yes*! I was happy there. I can't stand, just now, being reminded of happiness. Don't you understand? A time when one

178

didn't know what was coming. When one said confidently, everything is going to be lovely! Some people are wise — they never expect to be happy. I did.'

She said abruptly:

'I shall never go back to Ainswick.'

Midge said slowly:

'I wonder.'

14

Midge woke up abruptly on Monday morning.

For a moment she lay there bemused, her eyes going confusedly towards the door, for she half-expected Lady Angkatell to appear. What was it Lucy had said when she came drifting in that first morning?

A difficult weekend? She had been worried — had thought that something unpleasant might happen.

Yes, and something unpleasant had happened — something that was lying now upon Midge's heart and spirits like a thick black cloud. Something that she didn't want to think about — didn't want to remember. Something, surely, that *frightened* her. Something to do with Edward.

Memory came with a rush. One ugly stark word — *Murder!*

'Oh, no,' thought Midge, 'it can't be true. It's a dream I've been having. John Christow, murdered, shot — lying there by the pool. Blood and blue water — like a jacket of a detective story. Fantastic, unreal. The sort of thing that doesn't happen to oneself. If we were at Ainswick now. It couldn't have happened at Ainswick.'

The black weight moved from her forehead. It settled in the pit of her stomach, making her feel slightly sick.

It was not a dream. It was a real happening — a *News of the World* happening — and she and Edward and Lucy and Henry and Henrietta were all mixed up with it.

Unfair — surely unfair — since it was nothing to do with them if Gerda had shot her husband.

Midge stirred uneasily.

Quiet, stupid, slightly pathetic Gerda — you couldn't associate Gerda with melodrama — with violence.

Gerda, surely, couldn't shoot *anybody*.

Again that inward uneasiness rose. No, no, one mustn't think like that. Because who else *could* have shot John? And Gerda had been standing there by his body with the revolver in her hand. The revolver she had taken from Henry's study.

Gerda had said that she had found John dead and picked up the revolver. Well, what else could she say? She'd have to say *something*, poor thing.

All very well for Henrietta to defend her — to say that Gerda's story was perfectly possible. Henrietta hadn't considered the

181

impossible alternatives.

Henrietta had been very odd last night.

But that, of course, had been the shock of John Christow's death.

Poor Henrietta — who had cared so terribly for John.

But she would get over it in time — one got over everything. And then she would marry Edward and live at Ainswick — and Edward would be happy at last.

Henrietta had always loved Edward very dearly. It was only the aggressive, dominant personality of John Christow that had come in the way. He had made Edward look so — so *pale* by comparison.

It struck Midge when she came down to breakfast that morning that already Edward's personality, freed from John Christow's dominance, had begun to assert itself. He seemed more sure of himself, less hesitant and retiring.

He was talking pleasantly to the glowering and unresponsive David.

'You must come more often to Ainswick, David. I'd like you to feel at home there and to get to know all about the place.'

Helping himself to marmalade, David said coldly:

'These big estates are completely farcical. They should be split up.'

'That won't happen in my time, I hope,' said Edward, smiling. 'My tenants are a contented lot.'

'They shouldn't be,' said David. 'Nobody should be contented.'

'If apes had been content with tails — ' murmured Lady Angkatell from where she was standing by the sideboard looking vaguely at a dish of kidneys. 'That's a poem I learnt in the nursery, but I simply can't remember how it goes on. I must have a talk with you, David, and learn all the new ideas. As far as I can see, one must hate everybody, but at the same time give them free medical attention and a lot of extra education (poor things, all those helpless little children herded into schoolhouses every day) — and cod-liver oil forced down babies' throats whether they like it or not — such nasty-smelling stuff.'

Lucy, Midge thought, was behaving very much as usual.

And Gudgeon, when she passed him in the hall, also looked just as usual. Life at The Hollow seemed to have resumed its normal course. With the departure of Gerda, the whole business seemed like a dream.

Then there was a scrunch of wheels on the gravel outside, and Sir Henry drew up in his car. He had stayed the night at his club and driven down early.

'Well, dear,' said Lucy, 'was everything all right?'

'Yes. The secretary was there — competent sort of girl. She took charge of things. There's a sister, it seems. The secretary telegraphed to her.'

'I knew there would be,' said Lady Angkatell. 'At Tunbridge Wells?'

'Bexhill, I think,' said Sir Henry, looking puzzled.

'I dare say' — Lucy considered Bexhill. 'Yes — quite probably.'

Gudgeon approached.

'Inspector Grange telephoned, Sir Henry. The inquest will be at eleven o'clock on Wednesday.'

Sir Henry nodded. Lady Angkatell said:

'Midge, you'd better ring up your shop.'

Midge went slowly to the telephone.

Her life had always been so entirely normal and commonplace that she felt she lacked the phraseology to explain to her employers that after four days' holiday she was unable to return to work owing to the fact that she was mixed up in a murder case.

It did not sound credible. It did not even feel credible.

And Madame Alfrege was not a very easy person to explain things to at any time.

Midge set her chin resolutely and picked up the receiver.

It was all just as unpleasant as she had imagined it would be. The raucous voice of the vitriolic little Jewess came angrily over the wires.

'What wath that, Mith Hardcathle? A death? A funeral? Do you not know very well I am short-handed? Do you think I am going to stand for these excutheth? Oh, yeth, you are having a good time, I dare thay!'

Midge interrupted, speaking sharply and distinctly.

'The poleeth? The poleeth, you thay?' It was almost a scream. 'You are mixed up with the poleeth?'

Setting her teeth, Midge continued to explain. Strange how sordid that woman at the other end made the whole thing seem. A vulgar police case. What alchemy there was in human beings!

Edward opened the door and came in, then seeing that Midge was telephoning, he was about to go out. She stopped him.

'Do stay, Edward. Please. Oh, I want you to.'

The presence of Edward in the room gave her strength — counteracted the poison.

She took her hand from where she had laid it over the mouthpiece.

'What? Yes. I am sorry, Madame. But after all, it is hardly my fault — '

The ugly raucous voice was screaming angrily.

'Who are thethe friendth of yourth? What thort of people are they to have the poleeth there and a man shot? I've a good mind not to have you back at all! I can't have the tone of my ethablishment lowered.'

Midge made a few submissive non-committal replies. She replaced the receiver at last, with a sigh of relief. She felt sick and shaken.

'It's the place I work,' she explained. 'I had to let them know that I wouldn't be back until Thursday because of the inquest and the — the police.'

'I hope they were decent about it? What is it like, this dress shop of yours? Is the woman who runs it pleasant and sympathetic to work for?'

'I should hardly describe her as that! She's a Whitechapel Jewess with dyed hair and a voice like a corncrake.'

'But my dear Midge — '

Edward's face of consternation almost made Midge laugh. He was so concerned.

'But my dear child — you can't put up with that sort of thing. If you must have a job, you must take one where the surroundings

186

are harmonious and where you like the people you are working with.'

Midge looked at him for a moment without answering.

How explain, she thought, to a person like Edward? What did Edward know of the labour market, of jobs?

And suddenly a tide of bitterness rose in her. Lucy, Henry, Edward — yes, even Henrietta — they were all divided from her by an impassable gulf — the gulf that separates the leisured from the working.

They had no conception of the difficulties of getting a job, and once you had got it, of keeping it! One might say, perhaps, that there was no need, actually, for her to earn her living. Lucy and Henry would gladly give her a home — they would with equal gladness have made her an allowance. Edward would also willingly have done the latter.

But something in Midge rebelled against the acceptance of ease offered her by her well-to-do relations. To come on rare occasions and sink into the well-ordered luxury of Lucy's life was delightful. She could revel in that. But some sturdy independence of spirit held her back from accepting that life as a gift. The same feeling had prevented her from starting a business on her own with money borrowed from relations and friends.

187

She had seen too much of that.

She would borrow no money — use no influence. She had found a job for herself at four pounds a week, and if she had actually been given the job because Madame Alfrege hoped that Midge would bring her 'smart' friends to buy, Madame Alfrege was disappointed. Midge discouraged any such notion sternly on the part of her friends.

She had no particular illusions about working. She disliked the shop, she disliked Madame Alfrege, she disliked the eternal subservience to ill-tempered and impolite customers, but she doubted very much whether she could obtain any other job which she would like better since she had none of the necessary qualifications.

Edward's assumption that a wide range of choice was open to her was simply unbearably irritating this morning. What right had Edward to live in a world so divorced from reality?

They were Angkatells, all of them. And she — was only half an Angkatell! And sometimes, like this morning, she did not feel like an Angkatell at all! She was all her father's daughter.

She thought of her father with the usual pang of love and compunction, a grey-haired, middle-aged man with a tired face. A man who had struggled for years running a small family business that was bound, for all his care and efforts, to go slowly down the hill. It was not incapacity on his part — it was the march of progress.

Strangely enough, it was not to her brilliant Angkatell mother but to her quiet, tired father that Midge's devotion had always been given. Each time, when she came back from those visits to Ainswick, which were the wild delight of her life, she would answer the faint deprecating questions in her father's tired face by flinging her arms round his neck and saying: 'I'm *glad* to be home — I'm glad to be *home.*'

Her mother had died when Midge was thirteen. Sometimes Midge realized that she knew very little about her mother. She had been vague, charming, gay. Had she regretted her marriage, the marriage that had taken her outside the circle of the Angkatell clan? Midge had no idea. Her father had grown greyer and quieter after his wife's death. His struggles against the extinction of his business had grown more unavailing. He had died quietly and inconspicuously when Midge was eighteen.

Midge had stayed with various Angkatell relations, had accepted presents from the Angkatells, had had good times with the

Angkatells, but she had refused to be financially dependent on their goodwill. And much as she loved them, there were times, such as these, when she felt suddenly and violently divergent from them.

She thought with rancour: 'They don't know *anything!*'

Edward, sensitive as always, was looking at her with a puzzled face. He asked gently:

'I've upset you? Why?'

Lucy drifted into the room. She was in the middle of one of her conversations.

' — you see, one doesn't really know whether she'd *prefer* the White Hart to us or not?'

Midge looked at her blankly — then at Edward.

'It's no use looking at Edward,' said Lady Angkatell. 'Edward simply wouldn't know; you, Midge, are always so practical.'

'I don't know what you are talking about, Lucy.'

Lucy looked surprised.

'The *inquest*, darling. Gerda has to come down for it. Should she stay here? Or go to the White Hart? The associations here are painful, of course — but then at the White Hart there will be people who will stare and quantities of reporters. Wednesday, you know, at eleven, or is it eleven-thirty?' A smile lit up

Lady Angkatell's face. 'I have never been to an inquest! I thought my grey — and a hat, of course, like church — but *not* gloves.

'You know,' went on Lady Angkatell, crossing the room and picking up the telephone receiver and gazing down at it earnestly, 'I don't believe I've *got* any gloves except gardening gloves nowadays! And of course lots of long evening ones put away from the Government House days. Gloves are rather stupid, don't you think so?'

'The only use is to avoid fingerprints in crimes,' said Edward, smiling.

'Now, it's very interesting that you should say that, Edward — very interesting. What am I doing with this thing?' Lady Angkatell looked at the telephone receiver with faint distaste.

'Were you going to ring up someone?'

'I don't think so.' Lady Angkatell shook her head vaguely and put the receiver back on its stand very gingerly.

She looked from Edward to Midge.

'I don't think, Edward, that you ought to upset Midge. Midge minds sudden deaths more than we do.'

'My dear Lucy,' exclaimed Edward. 'I was only worrying about this place where Midge works. It sounds all wrong to me.'

'Edward thinks I ought to have a delightful

sympathetic employer who would appreciate me,' said Midge dryly.

'Dear Edward,' said Lucy with complete appreciation.

She smiled at Midge and went out again.

'Seriously, Midge,' said Edward, 'I am worried.'

She interrupted him:

'The damned woman pays me four pounds a week. That's all that matters.'

She brushed past him and went out into the garden.

Sir Henry was sitting in his usual place on the low wall, but Midge turned away and walked up towards the flower walk.

Her relations were charming, but she had no use for their charm this morning.

David Angkatell was sitting on the seat at the top of the path.

There was no overdone charm about David, and Midge made straight for him and sat down by him, noting with malicious pleasure his look of dismay.

How extraordinarily difficult it was, thought David, to get away from people.

He had been driven from his bedroom by the brisk incursion of housemaids, purposeful with mops and dusters.

The library (and the *Encyclopædia Britannica*) had not been the sanctuary he had hoped optimistically it might be. Twice Lady Angkatell had drifted in and out, addressing him kindly with remarks to which there seemed no possible intelligent reply.

He had come out here to brood upon his position. The mere weekend to which he had unwillingly committed himself had now lengthened out owing to the exigencies connected with sudden and violent death.

David, who preferred the contemplation of an Academic past or the earnest discussion of a Left Wing future, had no aptitude for dealing with a violent and realistic present. As he had told Lady Angkatell, he did not read the *News of the World*. But now the *News of the World* seemed to have come to The Hollow.

Murder! David shuddered distastefully. What would his friends think? How did one, so to speak, *take* murder? What was one's attitude? Bored? Disgusted? Lightly amused?

Trying to settle these problems in his mind, he was by no means pleased to be disturbed by Midge. He looked at her uneasily as she sat beside him.

He was rather startled by the defiant stare with which she returned his look. A disagreeable girl of no intellectual value.

She said, 'How do you like your relations?'

David shrugged his shoulders. He said:

'Does one really *think* about relations?'
Midge said:
'Does one really think about anything?'
Doubtless, David thought, *she* didn't. He said almost graciously:
'I was analysing my reactions to murder.'
'It is certainly odd,' said Midge, 'to be *in* one.'
David sighed and said:
'Wearisome.' That was quite the best attitude. 'All the clichés that one thought only existed in the pages of detective fiction!'
'You must be sorry you came,' said Midge.
David sighed.
'Yes, I might have been staying with a friend of mine in London.' He added, 'He keeps a Left Wing bookshop.'
'I expect it's more comfortable here,' said Midge.
'Does one really care about being comfortable?' David asked scornfully.
'There are times,' said Midge, 'when I feel I don't care about anything else.'
'The pampered attitude to life,' said David. 'If you were a worker — '
Midge interrupted him.
'I *am* a worker. That's just why being comfortable is so attractive. Box beds, down pillows — early-morning tea softly deposited beside the bed — a porcelain bath with

194

lashings of hot water — and delicious bath salts. The kind of easy-chair you really sink into . . . '

Midge paused in her catalogue.

'The workers,' said David, 'should have all these things.'

But he was a little doubtful about the softly deposited early-morning tea, which sounded impossibly sybaritic for an earnestly organized world.

'I couldn't agree with you more,' said Midge heartily.

15

Hercule Poirot, enjoying a mid-morning cup of chocolate, was interrupted by the ringing of the telephone. He got up and lifted the receiver.

'*'Allo?*'

'M. Poirot?'

'Lady Angkatell?'

'How nice of you to know my voice! Am I disturbing you?'

'But not at all. You are, I hope, none the worse for the distressing events of yesterday?'

'No, indeed. Distressing, as you say, but one feels, I find, quite *detached*. I rang you up to know if you could possibly come over — an imposition, I know, but I am really in great distress.'

'But certainly, Lady Angkatell. Did you mean now?'

'Well, yes, I did mean now. As quickly as you can. That's very sweet of you.'

'Not at all. I will come by the woods, then?'

'Oh, of course — the shortest way. Thank you so much, dear M. Poirot.'

Pausing only to brush a few specks of dust off the lapels of his coat and to slip on a thin overcoat, Poirot crossed the lane and hurried along the path through the chestnuts. The swimming pool was deserted — the police had finished their work and gone. It looked innocent and peaceful in the soft misty autumn light.

Poirot took a quick look into the pavilion. The platinum fox cape, he noted, had been removed. But the six boxes of matches still stood upon the table by the settee. He wondered more than ever about those matches.

'It is not a place to keep matches — here in the damp. One box, for convenience, perhaps — but not six.'

He frowned down on the painted iron table. The tray of glasses had been removed. Someone had scrawled with a pencil on the table — a rough design of a nightmarish tree. It pained Hercule Poirot. It offended his tidy mind.

He clicked his tongue, shook his head, and hurried on towards the house, wondering at the reason for this urgent summons.

Lady Angkatell was waiting for him at the french windows and swept him into the empty drawing-room.

'It was nice of you to come, M. Poirot.'

She clasped his hand warmly.

'Madame, I am at your service.'

Lady Angkatell's hands floated out expressively. Her wide, beautiful eyes opened.

'You see, it's all so difficult. The inspector person is interviewing — no, questioning — taking a statement — what *is* the term they use? — *Gudgeon*. And really our whole life here depends on Gudgeon, and one does so sympathize with him. Because naturally it is terrible for him to be questioned by the police — even Inspector Grange, who I do feel is really nice and probably a family man — boys, I think, and he helps them with Meccano in the evenings — and a wife who has everything spotless but a little overcrowded . . . '

Hercule Poirot blinked as Lady Angkatell developed her imaginary sketch of Inspector Grange's home life.

'By the way his moustache droops,' went on Lady Angkatell, 'I think that a home that is too spotless might be sometimes depressing — like soap on hospital nurses' faces. Quite a *shine*! But that is more in the country where things lag behind — in London nursing homes they have lots of powder and really *vivid* lipstick. But I was saying, M. Poirot, that you really must come to lunch *properly* when all this ridiculous business is over.'

'You are very kind.'

'I do not mind the police myself,' said Lady

Angkatell. 'I really find it all quite interesting. 'Do let me help you in any way I can,' I said to Inspector Grange. He seems rather a bewildered sort of person, but methodical.

'Motive seems so important to policemen,' she went on. 'Talking of hospital nurses just now, I believe that John Christow — a nurse with red hair and an upturned nose — quite attractive. But of course it was a long time ago and the police might not be interested. One doesn't really know how much poor Gerda had to put up with. She is the loyal type, don't you think? Or possibly she believes what is told her. I think if one has not a great deal of intelligence, it is wise to do that.'

Quite suddenly, Lady Angkatell flung open the study door and ushered Poirot in, crying brightly, 'Here is M. Poirot.' She swept round him and out, shutting the door. Inspector Grange and Gudgeon were sitting by the desk. A young man with a notebook was in a corner. Gudgeon rose respectfully to his feet.

Poirot hastened into apologies.

'I retire immediately. I assure you I had no idea that Lady Angkatell — '

'No, no, you wouldn't have.' Grange's moustache looked more pessimistic than ever this morning. 'Perhaps,' thought Poirot, fascinated by Lady Angkatell's recent sketch of Grange, 'there has been too much cleaning or perhaps a Benares brass table has been purchased so that the good inspector he really cannot have space to move.'

Angrily he dismissed these thoughts. Inspector Grange's clean but overcrowded home, his wife, his boys and their addiction to Meccano were all figments of Lady Angkatell's busy brain.

But the vividness with which they assumed concrete reality interested him. It was quite an accomplishment.

'Sit down, M. Poirot,' said Grange. 'There's something I want to ask you about, and I've nearly finished here.'

He turned his attention back to Gudgeon, who deferentially and almost under protest resumed his seat and turned an expressionless face towards his interlocutor.

'And that's all you can remember?'

'Yes, sir. Everything, sir, was very much as usual. There was no unpleasantness of any kind.'

'There's a fur cape thing — out in that summer-house by the pool. Which of the ladies *did* it belong to?'

'Are you referring, sir, to a cape of platinum fox? I noticed it yesterday when I took out the glasses to the pavilion. But it is not the property of anyone in this house, sir.'

'Whose is it, then?'

'It might possibly belong to Miss Cray, sir. Miss Veronica Cray, the motion-picture actress. She was wearing something of the kind.'

'When?'

'When she was here the night before last, sir.'

'You didn't mention her as having been a guest here?'

'She was not a guest, sir. Miss Cray lives at Dovecotes, the — er — cottage up the lane, and she came over after dinner, having run out of matches, to borrow some.'

'Did she take away six boxes?' asked Poirot.

Gudgeon turned to him.

'That is correct, sir. Her ladyship, after having inquired if we had plenty, insisted on Miss Cray's taking half a dozen boxes.'

'Which she left in the pavilion,' said Poirot.

'Yes, sir, I observed them there yesterday morning.'

'There is not much that that man does not observe,' remarked Poirot as Gudgeon departed, closing the door softly and deferentially behind him.

Inspector Grange merely remarked that servants were the devil!

'However,' he said with a little renewed cheerfulness, 'there's always the kitchenmaid.

Kitchenmaids *talk* — not like these stuck-up upper servants.

'I've put a man on to make inquiries at Harley Street,' he went on. 'And I shall be there myself later in the day. We ought to get something there. Dare say, you know, that wife of Christow's had a good bit to put up with. Some of these fashionable doctors and their lady patients — well, you'd be surprised! And I gather from Lady Angkatell that there was some trouble over a hospital nurse. Of course, she was very vague about it.'

'Yes,' Poirot agreed. 'She would be vague.'

A skilfully built-up picture . . . John Christow and amorous intrigues with hospital nurses . . . the opportunities of a doctor's life . . . plenty of reasons for Gerda Christow's jealousy which had culminated at last in murder.

Yes, a skilfully suggested picture, drawing attention to a Harley Street background — away from The Hollow — away from the moment when Henrietta Savernake, stepping forward, had taken the revolver from Gerda Christow's unresisting hand . . . Away from that other moment when John Christow, dying, had said '*Henrietta*'.

Suddenly opening his eyes, which had been half-closed, Hercule Poirot demanded with irresistible curiosity:

'Do your boys play with Meccano?'

'Eh, what?' Inspector Grange came back from a frowning reverie to stare at Poirot. 'Why, what on earth? As a matter of fact, they're a bit young — but I was thinking of giving Teddy a Meccano set for Christmas. What made you ask?'

Poirot shook his head.

What made Lady Angkatell dangerous, he thought, was the fact that those intuitive, wild guesses of hers might be often right. With a careless (seemingly careless?) word she built up a picture — and if part of the picture was right, wouldn't you, in spite of yourself, believe in the other half of the picture? . . .

Inspector Grange was speaking.

'There's a point I want to put to you, M. Poirot. This Miss Cray, the actress — she traipses over here borrowing matches. If she wanted to borrow matches, why didn't she come to your place, only a step or two away? Why come about half a mile?'

Hercule Poirot shrugged his shoulders.

'There might be reasons. Snob reasons, shall we say? My little cottage, it is small, unimportant. I am only a weekender, but Sir Henry and Lady Angkatell are important — they live here — they are what is called in the country. This Miss Veronica Cray, she may have wanted to get to know them — and after all, this was a way.'

Inspector Grange got up.

'Yes,' he said, 'that's perfectly possible, of course, but one doesn't want to overlook anything. Still, I've no doubt that everything's going to be plain sailing. Sir Henry has identified the gun as one of his collection. It seems they were actually practising with it the afternoon before. All Mrs Christow had to do was to go into the study and get it from where she'd seen Sir Henry put it and the ammunition away. It's all quite simple.'

'Yes,' Poirot murmured. 'It seems all quite simple.'

Just so, he thought, would a woman like Gerda Christow commit a crime. Without subterfuge or complexity — driven suddenly to violence by the bitter anguish of a narrow but deeply loving nature.

And yet surely — *surely*, she would have had *some* sense of self-preservation. Or had she acted in that blindness — that darkness of the spirit — when reason is entirely laid aside?

He recalled her blank, dazed face.

He did not know — he simply did not know.

But he felt that he ought to know.

16

Gerda Christow pulled the black dress up over her head and let it fall on a chair.

Her eyes were piteous with uncertainty.

She said: 'I don't know — I really don't know. Nothing seems to matter.'

'I know, dear, I know.' Mrs Patterson was kind but firm. She knew exactly how to treat people who had had a bereavement. 'Elsie is *wonderful* in a crisis,' her family said of her.

At the present moment she was sitting in her sister Gerda's bedroom in Harley Street being wonderful. Elsie Patterson was tall and spare with an energetic manner. She was looking now at Gerda with a mixture of irritation and compassion.

Poor dear Gerda — tragic for her to lose her husband in such an awful way. And really, even now, she didn't seem to take in the — well, the *implications*, properly. Of course, Mrs Patterson reflected, Gerda always was terribly slow. And there was shock, too, to take into account.

She said in a brisk voice: 'I think I should decide on that black marocain at twelve guineas.'

One always did have to make up Gerda's mind for her.

Gerda stood motionless, her brow puckered. She said hesitantly:

'I don't really know if John liked mourning. I think I once heard him say he didn't.'

'John,' she thought. 'If only John were here to tell me what to do.'

But John would never be there again. Never — never — never . . . Mutton getting cold — congealing on the table . . . the bang of the consulting-room door, John running up two steps at a time, always in a hurry, so vital, so alive . . .

Alive.

Lying on his back by the swimming pool . . . the slow drip of blood over the edge . . . the feel of the revolver in her hand . . .

A nightmare, a bad dream, presently she would wake up and none of it would be true.

Her sister's crisp voice came cutting through her nebulous thoughts.

'You *must* have something black for the inquest. It would look most odd if you turned up in bright blue.'

Gerda said: 'That awful inquest!' and half-shut her eyes.

'Terrible for you, darling,' said Elsie Patterson quickly. 'But after it is all over you will come straight down to us and we shall take great care of you.'

The nebulous blur of Gerda Christow's thoughts hardened. She said, and her voice was frightened, almost panic-stricken:

'What am I going to do without John?'

Elsie Patterson knew the answer to that one. 'You've got your children. You've got to live for *them*.'

Zena, sobbing and crying, 'My Daddy's dead!' Throwing herself on her bed. Terry, pale, inquiring, shedding no tears.

An accident with a revolver, she had told them — poor Daddy has had an accident.

Beryl Collins (so thoughtful of her) had confiscated the morning papers so that the children should not see them. She had warned the servants too. Really, Beryl had been most kind and thoughtful.

Terence coming to his mother in the dim drawing-room, his lips pursed close together, his face almost greenish in its odd pallor.

'Why was Father shot?'

'An accident, dear. I — I can't talk about it.'

'It wasn't an accident. Why do you say what isn't true? Father was killed. It was murder. The paper says so.'

'Terry, how did you get hold of a paper? I told Miss Collins — '

He had nodded — queer repeated nods

like a very old man.

'I went out and bought one, of course. I knew there must be something in them that you weren't telling us, or else why did Miss Collins hide them?'

It was never any good hiding truth from Terence. That queer, detached, scientific curiosity of his had always to be satisfied.

'*Why* was he killed, Mother?'

She had broken down then, becoming hysterical.

'Don't ask me about it — don't talk about it — I can't talk about it . . . it's all too dreadful.'

'But they'll find out, won't they? I mean, they have to find out. It's necessary.'

So reasonable, so detached. It made Gerda want to scream and laugh and cry. She thought: 'He doesn't care — he can't care — he just goes on asking questions. Why, he hasn't cried, even.'

Terence had gone away, evading his Aunt Elsie's ministrations, a lonely little boy with a stiff, pinched face. He had always felt alone. But it hadn't mattered until today.

Today, he thought, was different. If only there was someone who would answer questions reasonably and intelligently.

Tomorrow, Tuesday, he and Nicholson Minor were going to make nitroglycerine. He had been looking forward to it with a thrill. The thrill had gone. He didn't care if he never made nitroglycerine.

Terence felt almost shocked at himself. Not to care any more about scientific experiment. But when a chap's father had been murdered . . . He thought: 'My father — murdered.'

And something stirred — took root — grew . . . a slow anger.

Beryl Collins tapped on the bedroom door and came in. She was pale, composed, efficient. She said:

'Inspector Grange is here.' And as Gerda gasped and looked at her piteously, Beryl went on quickly: 'He said there was no need for him to worry you. He'll have a word with you before he goes, but it is just routine questions about Dr Christow's practice and I can tell him everything he wants to know.'

'Oh thank you, Collie.'

Beryl made a rapid exit and Gerda sighed out:

'Collie is such a help. She's so practical.'

'Yes, indeed,' said Mrs Patterson. 'An excellent secretary, I'm sure. Very plain, poor girl, isn't she? Oh, well, I always think that's just as well. Especially with an attractive man like John.'

Gerda flamed out at her:

'What do you mean, Elsie? John would

never — he never — you talk as though John would have flirted or something horrid if he had had a pretty secretary. John wasn't like that at all.'

'Of course not, darling,' said Mrs Patterson. 'But after all, one knows what men are like!'

In the consulting-room Inspector Grange faced the cool, belligerent glance of Beryl Collins. It *was* belligerent, he noted that. Well, perhaps that was only natural.

'Plain bit of goods,' he thought. 'Nothing between her and the doctor, I shouldn't think. *She* may have been sweet on *him*, though. It works that way sometimes.'

But not this time, he came to the conclusion, when he leaned back in his chair a quarter of an hour later. Beryl Collins's answers to his questions had been models of clearness. She replied promptly, and obviously had every detail of the doctor's practice at her fingertips. He shifted his ground and began to probe gently into the relations existing between John Christow and his wife.

They had been, Beryl said, on excellent terms.

'I suppose they quarrelled every now and then like most married couples?' The inspector sounded easy and confidential.

'I do not remember any quarrels. Mrs

Christow was quite devoted to her husband — really quite slavishly so.'

There was a faint edge of contempt in her voice. Inspector Grange heard it.

'Bit of a feminist, this girl,' he thought.

Aloud he said:

'Didn't stand up for herself at all?'

'No. Everything revolved round Dr Christow.'

'Tyrannical, eh?'

Beryl considered.

'No, I wouldn't say that. But he was what I should call a very selfish man. He took it for granted that Mrs Christow would always fall in with *his* ideas.'

'Any difficulties with patients — women, I mean? You needn't think about being frank, Miss Collins. One knows doctors have their difficulties in that line.'

'Oh, that sort of thing!' Beryl's voice was scornful. 'Dr Christow was quite equal to dealing with any difficulties in *that* line. He had an excellent manner with patients.' She added, 'He was really a wonderful doctor.'

There was an almost grudging admiration in her voice.

Grange said: 'Was he tangled up with any woman? Don't be loyal, Miss Collins, it's important that we should know.'

'Yes, I can appreciate that. Not to my knowledge.'

A little too brusque, he thought. She doesn't know, but perhaps she guesses.

He said sharply, 'What about Miss Henrietta Savernake?'

Beryl's lips closed tightly.

'She was a close friend of the family's.'

'No — trouble between Dr and Mrs Christow on her account?'

'Certainly not.'

The answer was emphatic. (Over-emphatic?)

The inspector shifted his ground.

'What about Miss Veronica Cray?'

'Veronica Cray?'

There was pure astonishment in Beryl's voice.

'She was a friend of Dr Christow's, was she not?'

'I never heard of her. At least, I seem to know the *name* — '

'The motion-picture actress.'

Beryl's brow cleared.

'Of course! I wondered why the name was familiar. But I didn't even know that Dr Christow knew her.'

She seemed so positive on the point that the inspector abandoned it at once. He went on to question her about Dr Christow's manner on the preceding Saturday. And here, for the first time, the confidence of Beryl's replies wavered. She said slowly:

'His manner *wasn't* quite as usual.'

'What was the difference?'

'He seemed distrait. There was quite a long gap before he rang for his last patient — and yet normally he was always in a hurry to get through when he was going away. I thought — yes, I definitely thought he had something on his mind.'

But she could not be more definite.

Inspector Grange was not very satisfied with his investigations. He'd come nowhere near establishing motive — and motive had to be established before there was a case to go to the Public Prosecutor.

He was quite certain in his own mind that Gerda Christow had shot her husband. He suspected jealousy as the motive — but so far he had found nothing to go on. Sergeant Coombes had been working on the maids but they all told the same story. Mrs Christow worshipped the ground her husband walked on.

Whatever happened, he thought, must have happened down at The Hollow. And remembering The Hollow he felt a vague disquietude. They were an odd lot down there.

The telephone on the desk rang and Miss Collins picked up the receiver.

She said: 'It's for you, Inspector,' and passed the instrument to him.

'Hallo, Grange here. What's that?' Beryl heard the alteration in his tone and looked at him curiously. The wooden-looking face was impassive as ever. He was grunting — listening.

'Yes . . . yes, I've got that. That's absolutely certain, is it? No margin of error. Yes . . . yes . . . yes, I'll be down. I've about finished here. Yes.'

He put the receiver back and sat for a moment motionless. Beryl looked at him curiously.

He pulled himself together and asked in a voice that was quite different from the voice of his previous questions:

'You've no ideas of your own, I suppose, Miss Collins, about this matter?'

'You mean — '

'I mean no ideas as to who it was killed Dr Christow?'

She said flatly:

'I've absolutely no idea at all, Inspector.'

Grange said slowly:

'When the body was found, Mrs Christow was standing beside it with the revolver in her hand — '

214

He left it purposely as an unfinished sentence.

Her reaction came promptly. Not heated, cool and judicial.

'If you think Mrs Christow killed her husband, I am quite sure you are wrong. Mrs Christow is not at all a violent woman. She is very meek and submissive, and she was entirely under the doctor's thumb. It seems to me quite ridiculous that anyone could imagine for a moment that she shot him, however much appearances may be against her.'

'Then if she didn't, who did?' he asked sharply.

Beryl said slowly, 'I've no idea.'

The inspector moved to the door. Beryl asked:

'Do you want to see Mrs Christow before you go?'

'No — yes, perhaps I'd better.'

Again Beryl wondered; this was not the same man who had been questioning her before the telephone rang. What news had he got that had altered him so much?

Gerda came into the room nervously. She looked unhappy and bewildered. She said in a low, shaky voice:

'Have you found out any more about who killed John?'

'Not yet, Mrs Christow.'

'It's so impossible — so absolutely impossible.'

'But it happened, Mrs Christow.'

She nodded, looking down, screwing a handkerchief into a little ball.

He said quietly:

'Had your husband any enemies, Mrs Christow?'

'John? Oh, no. He was wonderful. Everyone adored him.'

'You can't think of anyone who had a grudge against him' — he paused — 'or against you?'

'Against me?' She seemed amazed. 'Oh, no, Inspector.'

Inspector Grange sighed.

'What about Miss Veronica Cray?'

'Veronica Cray? Oh, you mean the one who came that night to borrow matches?'

'Yes, that's the one. You knew her?'

Gerda shook her head.

'I'd never seen her before. John knew her years ago — or so she said.'

'I suppose she might have had a grudge against him that you didn't know about.'

Gerda said with dignity:

'I don't believe anybody could have had a grudge against John. He was the kindest and most unselfish — oh, and one of the noblest men.'

'H'm,' said the inspector. 'Yes. Quite so. Well, good morning, Mrs Christow. You understand about the inquest? Eleven o'clock Wednesday in Market Depleach. It will be very simple — nothing to upset you — probably be adjourned for a week so that we can make further inquiries.'

'Oh, I see. Thank you.'

She stood there staring after him. He wondered whether, even now, she had grasped the fact that she was the principal suspect.

He hailed a taxi — justifiable expense in view of the piece of information he had just been given over the telephone. Just where that piece of information was leading him, he did not know. On the face of it, it seemed completely irrelevant — crazy. It simply did not make sense. Yet in some way he could not yet see, it must make sense.

The only inference to be drawn from it was that the case was not quite the simple, straightforward one that he had hitherto assumed it to be.

17

Sir Henry stared curiously at Inspector Grange.

He said slowly: 'I'm not quite sure that I understand you, Inspector.'

'It's quite simple, Sir Henry. I'm asking you to check over your collection of firearms. I presume they are catalogued and indexed?'

'Naturally. But I have already identified the revolver as part of my collection.'

'It isn't quite so simple as that, Sir Henry.' Grange paused a moment. His instincts were always against giving out any information, but his hand was being forced in this particular instance. Sir Henry was a person of importance. He would doubtless comply with the request that was being made to him, but he would also require a reason. The inspector decided that he had got to give him the reason.

He said quietly:

'Dr Christow was not shot with the revolver you identified.'

Sir Henry's eyebrows rose.

'Remarkable!' he said.

Grange felt vaguely comforted. Remarkable

was exactly what he felt himself. He was grateful to Sir Henry for saying so, and equally grateful for his not saying any more. It was as far as they could go at the moment. The thing was remarkable — and beyond that simply did not make sense.

Sir Henry asked:

'Have you any reason to believe that the weapon from which the fatal shot was fired comes from my collection?'

'No reason at all. But I have got to make sure, shall we say, that it doesn't.'

Sir Henry nodded his head in confirmation.

'I appreciate your point. Well, we will get to work. It will take a little time.'

He opened the desk and took out a leather-bound volume.

As he opened it he repeated:

'It will take a little time to check up — '

Grange's attention was held by something in his voice. He looked up sharply. Sir Henry's shoulders sagged a little — he seemed suddenly an older and more tired man.

Inspector Grange frowned.

He thought: 'Devil if I know what to make of these people down here.'

'Ah — '

Grange spun round. His eyes noted the

time by the clock, thirty minutes — twenty minutes — since Sir Henry had said, 'It will take a little time.'

Grange said sharply:

'Yes, sir?'

'A .38 Smith and Wesson is missing. It was in a brown leather holster and was at the end of the rack in this drawer.'

'Ah!' The inspector kept his voice calm, but he was excited. 'And when, sir, to your certain knowledge, did you last see it in its proper place?'

Sir Henry reflected for a moment or two.

'That is not very easy to say, Inspector. I last had this drawer open about a week ago and I think — I am almost certain — that if the revolver had been missing then I should have noticed the gap. But I should not like to swear definitely that I *saw* it there.'

Inspector Grange nodded his head.

'Thank you, sir, I quite understand. Well, I must be getting on with things.'

He left the room, a busy, purposeful man.

Sir Henry stood motionless for a while after the inspector had gone, then he went out slowly through the french windows on to the terrace. His wife was busy with a gardening basket and gloves. She was pruning some rare shrubs with a pair of secateurs.

She waved to him brightly.

'What did the inspector want? I hope he is not going to worry the servants again. You know, Henry, they *don't* like it. They can't see it as amusing or as a novelty like we do.'

'Do we see it like that?'

His tone attracted her attention. She smiled up at him sweetly.

'How tired you look, Henry. Must you let all this worry you so much?'

'Murder *is* worrying, Lucy.'

Lady Angkatell considered a moment, absently clipping off some branches, then her face clouded over.

'Oh, dear — that is the worst of secateurs, they are so fascinating — one can't stop and one always clips off more than one means. What was it you were saying — something about murder being worrying? But really, Henry, I have never seen *why*. I mean, if one has to die, it may be cancer, or tuberculosis in one of those dreadful bright sanatoriums, or a stroke — horrid, with one's face all on one side — or else one is shot or stabbed or strangled perhaps. But the whole thing comes to the same in the end. There one is, I mean, dead! Out of it all. And all the worry over. And the relations have all the difficulties — money quarrels and whether to wear black or not — and who was to have Aunt Selina's writing-desk — things like that!'

Sir Henry sat down on the stone coping. He said:

'This is all going to be more upsetting than we thought, Lucy.'

'Well, darling, we shall have to bear it. And when it's all over we might go away somewhere. Let's not bother about present troubles but look forward to the future. I really *am* happy about that. I've been wondering whether it would be nice to go to Ainswick for Christmas — or leave it until Easter. What do you think?'

'Plenty of time to make plans for Christmas.'

'Yes, but I like to see things in my mind. Easter, perhaps . . . yes.' Lucy smiled happily. 'She will certainly have got over it by then.'

'Who?' Sir Henry was startled.

Lady Angkatell said calmly:

'Henrietta. I think if they were to have the wedding in October — October of next year, I mean, then we could go and stop for *that* Christmas. I've been thinking, Henry — '

'I wish you wouldn't, my dear. You think too much.'

'You know the barn? It will make a perfect studio. And Henrietta will need a studio. She has real talent, you know. Edward, I am sure, will be immensely proud of her. Two boys and a girl would be nice — or two boys and two girls.'

'Lucy — Lucy! How you run on.'

'But, darling,' Lady Angkatell opened wide, beautiful eyes. 'Edward will never marry anyone but Henrietta. He is very, *very* obstinate. Rather like my father in that way. He gets an idea in his head! So of course Henrietta *must* marry him — and she *will* now that John Christow is out of the way. He was really the greatest misfortune that could possibly have happened to her.'

'Poor devil!'

'Why? Oh, you mean because he's dead? Oh, well, everyone has to die sometime. I never worry over people dying . . . '

He looked at her curiously.

'I always thought you liked Christow, Lucy?'

'I found him amusing. And he had charm. But I never think one ought to attach too much importance to *anybody*.'

And gently, with a smiling face, Lady Angkatell clipped remorselessly at a *Viburnum Carlesii*.

18

Hercule Poirot looked out of his window and saw Henrietta Savernake walking up the path to the front door. She was wearing the same green tweeds that she had worn on the day of the tragedy. There was a spaniel with her.

He hastened to the front door and opened it. She stood smiling at him.

'Can I come in and see your house? I like looking at people's houses. I'm just taking the dog for a walk.'

'But most certainly. How English it is to take the dog for a walk!'

'I know,' said Henrietta. 'I thought of that. Do you know that nice poem: 'The days passed slowly one by one. I fed the ducks, reproved my wife, played Handel's *Largo* on the fife and took the dog a run.' '

Again she smiled, a brilliant, insubstantial smile.

Poirot ushered her into his sitting-room. She looked round its neat and prim arrangement and nodded her head.

'Nice,' she said, 'two of everything. How you would hate my studio.'

'Why should I hate it?'

'Oh, a lot of clay sticking to things — and here and there just one thing that I happen to like and which would be ruined if there were two of them.'

'But I can understand that, Mademoiselle. You are an artist.'

'Aren't you an artist, too, M. Poirot?'

Poirot put his head on one side.

'It is a question, that. But on the whole I would say, no. I have known crimes that were artistic — they were, you understand, supreme exercises of imagination. But the solving of them — no, it is not the creative power that is needed. What is required is a passion for the truth.'

'A passion for the truth,' said Henrietta meditatively. 'Yes, I can see how dangerous that might make you. Would the truth satisfy you?'

He looked at her curiously.

'What do you mean, Miss Savernake?'

'I can understand that you would want to *know*. But would knowledge be enough? Would you have to go a step further and translate knowledge into action?'

He was interested in her approach.

'You are suggesting that if I knew the truth about Dr Christow's death — I might be satisfied to keep that knowledge to myself. Do *you* know the truth about his death?'

Henrietta shrugged her shoulders.

'The obvious answer seems to be Gerda. How cynical it is that a wife or a husband is always the first suspect.'

'But you do not agree?'

'I always like to keep an open mind.'

Poirot said quietly:

'Why did you come here, Miss Savernake?'

'I must admit that I haven't your passion for truth, M. Poirot. Taking the dog for a walk was such a nice English countryside excuse. But of course the Angkatells haven't got a dog — as you may have noticed the other day.'

'The fact had not escaped me.'

'So I borrowed the gardener's spaniel. I am not, you must understand, M. Poirot, very truthful.'

Again that brilliant brittle smile flashed out. He wondered why he should suddenly find it unendurably moving. He said quietly:

'No, but you have integrity.'

'Why on earth do you say that?'

She was startled — almost, he thought, dismayed.

'Because I believe it to be true.'

'Integrity,' Henrietta repeated thoughtfully. 'I wonder what that word really means.'

She sat very still, staring down at the carpet, then she raised her head and looked at him steadily.

'Don't you want to know why I did come?'

'You find a difficulty, perhaps, in putting it into words.'

'Yes, I think I do. The inquest, M. Poirot, is tomorrow. One has to make up one's mind just how much — '

She broke off. Getting up, she wandered across to the mantelpiece, displaced one or two of the ornaments and moved a vase of Michaelmas daisies from its position in the middle of a table to the extreme corner of the mantelpiece. She stepped back, eyeing the arrangement with her head on one side.

'How do you like that, M. Poirot?'

'Not at all, Mademoiselle.'

'I thought you wouldn't.' She laughed, moved everything quickly and deftly back to its original position. 'Well, if one wants to say a thing one has to say it! You are, somehow, the sort of person one can talk to. Here goes. Is it necessary, do you think, that the police should know that I was John Christow's mistress?'

Her voice was quite dry and unemotional. She was looking, not at him, but at the wall over his head. With one forefinger she was following the curve of the jar that held the purple flowers. He had an idea that in the touch of that finger was her emotional outlet.

Hercule Poirot said precisely and also without emotion:

'I see. You were lovers?'

'If you prefer to put it like that.'

He looked at her curiously.

'It was not how you put it, Mademoiselle.'

'No.'

'Why not?'

Henrietta shrugged her shoulders. She came and sat down by him on the sofa. She said slowly:

'One likes to describe things as — as accurately as possible.'

His interest in Henrietta Savernake grew stronger. He said:

'You had been Dr Christow's mistress — for how long?'

'About six months.'

'The police will have, I gather, no difficulty in discovering the fact?'

Henrietta considered.

'I imagine not. That is, if they are looking for something of that kind.'

'Oh, they will be looking, I can assure you of that.'

'Yes, I rather thought they would.' She paused, stretched out her fingers on her knee and looked at them, then gave him a swift, friendly glance. 'Well, M. Poirot, what does one do? Go to Inspector Grange and say

— what does one say to a moustache like that? It's such a domestic, family moustache.'

Poirot's hand crawled upwards to his own proudly borne adornment.

'Whereas mine, Mademoiselle?'

'Your moustache, M. Poirot, is an artistic triumph. It has no associations with anything but itself. It is, I am sure, unique.'

'Absolutely.'

'And it is probably the reason why I am talking to you as I am. Granted that the police have to know the truth about John and myself, will it necessarily have to be made public?'

'That depends,' said Poirot. 'If the police think it had no bearing on the case, they will be quite discreet. You — are very anxious on this point?'

Henrietta nodded. She stared down at her fingers for a moment or two, then suddenly lifted her head and spoke. Her voice was no longer dry and light.

'Why should things be made worse than they are for poor Gerda? She adored John and he's dead. She's lost him. Why should she have to bear an added burden?'

'It is for her that you mind?'

'Do you think that is hypocritical? I suppose you're thinking that if I cared at all about Gerda's peace of mind, I would never have become John's mistress. But you don't understand — it was not like that. I did not break up his married life. I was only one — of a procession.'

'Ah, it was like that?'

She turned on him sharply.

'No, no, *no*! Not what you are thinking. That's what I mind most of all! The false idea that everybody will have of what John was like. That's why I'm here talking to you — because I've got a vague, foggy hope that I can make you understand. Understand, I mean, the sort of person John was. I can see so well what will happen — the headlines in the papers — A Doctor's Love Life — Gerda, myself, Veronica Cray. John wasn't like that — he wasn't, actually, a man who thought much about women. It wasn't women who mattered to him most, it was his *work*. It was in his work that his interest and excitement — yes, and his sense of adventure — really lay. If John had been taken unawares at any moment and asked to name the woman who was most in his mind, do you know who he would have said? — Mrs Crabtree.'

'Mrs Crabtree?' Poirot was surprised. 'Who, then, is this Mrs Crabtree?'

There was something between tears and laughter in Henrietta's voice as she went on:

'She's an old woman — ugly, dirty,

wrinkled, quite indomitable. John thought the world of her. She's a patient in St Christopher's Hospital. She's got Ridgeway's Disease. That's a disease that's very rare, but if you get it you're bound to die — there just isn't any cure. But John was finding a cure — I can't explain technically — it was all very complicated — some question of hormone secretions. He'd been making experiments and Mrs Crabtree was his prize patient — you see, she's got *guts*, she *wants* to live — and she was fond of John. She and he were fighting on the same side. Ridgeway's Disease and Mrs Crabtree is what has been uppermost in John's mind for months — night and day — nothing else really counted. That's what being the kind of doctor John was really means — not all the Harley Street stuff and the rich, fat women, that's only a sideline. It's the intense scientific curiosity and the achievement. I — oh, I wish I could make you understand.'

Her hands flew out in a curiously despairing gesture, and Hercule Poirot thought how very lovely and sensitive those hands were.

He said:

'*You* seem to understand very well.'

'Oh, yes, I understood. John used to come and talk, do you see? Not quite to me

— partly, I think, to himself. He got things clear that way. Sometimes he was almost despairing — he couldn't see how to overcome the heightened toxicity — and then he'd get an idea for varying the treatment. I can't explain to you what it was like — it was like, yes, a *battle*. You can't imagine the — the fury of it and the concentration — and yes, sometimes the agony. And sometimes the sheer tiredness . . . '

She was silent for a minute or two, her eyes dark with remembrance.

Poirot said curiously:

'You must have a certain technical knowledge yourself?'

She shook her head.

'Not really. Only enough to understand what John was talking about. I got books and read about it.'

She was silent again, her face softened, her lips half-parted. She was, he thought, remembering.

With a sigh, her mind came back to the present. She looked at him wistfully.

'If I could only make you see — '

'But you have, Mademoiselle.'

'Really?'

'Yes. One recognizes authenticity when one hears it.'

'Thank you. But it won't be so easy to

explain to Inspector Grange.'

'Probably not. He will concentrate on the personal angle.'

Henrietta said vehemently:

'And that was so unimportant — so completely unimportant.'

Poirot's eyebrows rose slowly. She answered his unspoken protest.

'But it was! You see — after a while — I got between John and what he was thinking of. I affected him, as a woman. He couldn't concentrate as he wanted to concentrate — because of me. He began to be afraid that he was beginning to love me — he didn't want to love anyone. He — he made love to me because he didn't want to think about me too much. He wanted it to be light, easy, just an affair like other affairs that he had had.'

'And you — ' Poirot was watching her closely. 'You were content to have it — like that.'

Henrietta got up. She said, and once more it was her dry voice:

'No, I wasn't — content. After all, one is human . . .'

Poirot waited a minute then he said:

'Then why, Mademoiselle — '

'Why?' She whirled round on him. 'I wanted John to be satisfied, I wanted *John* to have what he wanted. I wanted him to be able

233

to go on with the thing he cared about — his work. If he didn't want to be hurt — to be vulnerable again — why — why, that was all right by me.'

Poirot rubbed his nose.

'Just now, Miss Savernake, you mentioned Veronica Cray. Was she also a friend of John Christow's?'

'Until last Saturday night, he hadn't seen her for fifteen years.'

'He knew her fifteen years ago?'

'They were engaged to be married.' Henrietta came back and sat down. 'I see I've got to make it all clearer. John loved Veronica desperately. Veronica was, and is, a bitch of the first water. She's the supreme egoist. Her terms were that John was to chuck everything he cared about and become Miss Veronica Cray's little tame husband. John broke up the whole thing — quite rightly. But he suffered like hell. His one idea was to marry someone as unlike Veronica as possible. He married Gerda, whom you might describe inelegantly as a first-class chump. That was all very nice and safe, but as anyone could have told him the day came when being married to a chump irritated him. He had various affairs — none of them important. Gerda, of course, never knew about them. But I think, myself, that for fifteen years there has been something wrong with John — something connected with Veronica. He never really got over her. And then, last Saturday, he met her again.'

After a long pause, Poirot recited dreamily:

'He went out with her that night to see her home and returned to The Hollow at 3 am.'

'How do you know?'

'A housemaid had the toothache.'

Henrietta said irrelevantly, 'Lucy has far too many servants.'

'But you yourself knew that, Mademoiselle.'

'Yes.'

'How did you know?'

Again there was an infinitesimal pause. Then Henrietta replied slowly:

'I was looking out of my window and saw him come back to the house.'

'The toothache, Mademoiselle?'

She smiled at him.

'Quite another kind of ache, M. Poirot.'

She got up and moved towards the door, and Poirot said:

'I will walk back with you, Mademoiselle.'

They crossed the lane and went through the gate into the chestnut plantation.

Henrietta said:

'We need not go past the pool. We can go up to the left and along the top path to the flower walk.'

A track led steeply uphill towards the woods. After a while they came to a broader path at right angles across the hillside above the chestnut trees. Presently they came to a bench and Henrietta sat down, Poirot beside her. The woods were above and behind them, and below were the closely planted chestnut groves. Just in front of the seat a curving path led downwards, to where just a glimmer of blue water could be seen.

Poirot watched Henrietta without speaking. Her face had relaxed, the tension had gone. It looked rounder and younger. He realized what she must have looked like as a young girl.

He said very gently at last:

'Of what are you thinking, Mademoiselle?'

'Of Ainswick.'

'What is Ainswick?'

'Ainswick? It's a place.' Almost dreamily, she described Ainswick to him. The white, graceful house, the big magnolia growing up it, the whole set in an amphitheatre of wooded hills.

'It was your home?'

'Not really. I lived in Ireland. It was where we came, all of us, for holidays. Edward and Midge and myself. It was Lucy's home actually. It belonged to her father. After his death it came to Edward.'

'Not to Sir Henry? But it is he who has the title.'

'Oh, that's a KCB,' she explained. 'Henry was only a distant cousin.'

'And after Edward Angkatell, to whom does it go, this Ainswick?'

'How odd, I've never really thought. If Edward doesn't marry — ' She paused. A shadow passed over her face. Hercule Poirot wondered exactly what thought was passing through her mind.

'I suppose,' said Henrietta slowly, 'it will go to David. So that's why — '

'Why what?'

'Why Lucy asked him here . . . David and Ainswick?' She shook her head. 'They don't fit somehow.'

Poirot pointed to the path in front of them.

'It is by that path, Mademoiselle, that you went down to the swimming pool yesterday?'

She gave a quick shiver.

'No, by the one nearer the house. It was Edward who came this way.' She turned on him suddenly. 'Must we talk about it any more? I hate the swimming pool. I even hate The Hollow.'

Poirot murmured:

'I hate the dreadful hollow behind the little wood;

237

Its lips in the field above are dabbled
  with blood-red heath,
The red-ribb'd ledges drip with a silent
  horror of blood
And Echo there, whatever is ask'd her,
  answers 'Death.''

Henrietta turned an astonished face on him.

'Tennyson,' said Hercule Poirot, nodding his head proudly. 'The poetry of your Lord Tennyson.'

Henrietta was repeating:

'*And Echo there, whatever is ask'd her* . . .' She went on, almost to herself, 'But of course — I see — that's what it is — Echo!'

'How do you mean, Echo?'

'This place — The Hollow itself! I almost saw it before — on Saturday when Edward and I walked up to the ridge. An echo of Ainswick. And that's what we are, we Angkatells. Echoes! We're not real — not real as John was real.' She turned to Poirot. 'I wish you had known him, M. Poirot. We're all shadows compared to John. John was really alive.'

'I knew that even when he was dying, Mademoiselle.'

'I know. One felt it . . . And John is dead,

and we, the echoes, are alive . . . It's like, you know, a very bad joke.'

The youth had gone from her face again. Her lips were twisted, bitter with sudden pain.

When Poirot spoke, asking a question, she did not, for a moment, take in what he was saying.

'I am sorry. What did you say, M. Poirot?'

'I was asking whether your aunt, Lady Angkatell, liked Dr Christow?'

'Lucy? She is a cousin, by the way, not an aunt. Yes, she liked him very much.'

'And your — also a cousin? — Mr Edward Angkatell — did he like Dr Christow?'

Her voice was, he thought, a little constrained, as she replied:

'Not particularly — but then he hardly knew him.'

'And your — yet another cousin? Mr David Angkatell?'

Henrietta smiled.

'David, I think, hates all of us. He spends his time immured in the library reading the *Encyclopædia Britannica*.'

'Ah, a serious temperament.'

'I am sorry for David. He has had a difficult home life. His mother was unbalanced — an invalid. Now his only way of protecting himself is to try to feel superior to

239

everyone. It's all right as long as it works, but now and then it breaks down and the vulnerable David peeps through.'

'Did he feel himself superior to Dr Christow?'

'He tried to — but I don't think it came off. I suspect that John Christow was just the kind of man that David would like to be. He disliked John in consequence.'

Poirot nodded his head thoughtfully.

'Yes — self-assurance, confidence, virility — all the intensive male qualities. It is interesting — very interesting.'

Henrietta did not answer.

Through the chestnuts, down by the pool, Hercule Poirot saw a man stooping, searching for something, or so it seemed.

He murmured: 'I wonder — '

'I beg your pardon?'

Poirot said: 'That is one of Inspector Grange's men. He seems to be looking for something.'

'Clues, I suppose. Don't policemen look for clues? Cigarette ash, footprints, burnt matches.'

Her voice held a kind of bitter mockery. Poirot answered seriously.

'Yes, they look for these things — and sometimes they find them. But the real clues, Miss Savernake, in a case like this, usually lie in the personal relationships of the people concerned.'

'I don't think I understand you.'

'Little things,' said Poirot, his head thrown back, his eyes half-closed. 'Not cigarette ash, or a rubber heel mark — but a gesture, a look, an unexpected action . . . '

Henrietta turned her head sharply to look at him. He felt her eyes, but he did not turn his head. She said:

'Are you thinking of — anything in particular?'

'I was thinking of how you stepped forward and took the revolver out of Mrs Christow's hand then dropped it in the pool.'

He felt the slight start she gave. But her voice was quite normal and calm.

'Gerda, M. Poirot, is rather a clumsy person. In the shock of the moment, and if the revolver had had another cartridge in it, she might have fired it and — and hurt someone.'

'But it was rather clumsy of *you*, was it not, to drop it in the pool?'

'Well, I had had a shock too.' She paused. 'What are you suggesting, M. Poirot?'

Poirot sat up, turned his head, and spoke in a brisk, matter-of-fact way.

'If there were fingerprints on that revolver, that is to say, fingerprints made *before Mrs*

241

Christow handled it, it would be interesting to know whose they were — and that we shall never know now.'

Henrietta said quietly but steadily:

'Meaning that you think they were *mine.* You are suggesting that I shot John and then left the revolver beside him so that Gerda could come along and pick it up and be left holding the baby. That is what you are suggesting, isn't it? But surely, if I did that, you will give me credit for enough intelligence to have wiped off my own fingerprints first!'

'But surely *you* are intelligent enough to see, Mademoiselle, that if you had done so and if the revolver had had *no fingerprints on it but Mrs Christow's, that* would have been very remarkable! For you were all shooting with that revolver the day before. Gerda Christow would hardly have wiped the revolver clean of fingerprints *before* using it — why should she?'

Henrietta said slowly:

'So you think I killed John?'

'When Dr Christow was dying, he said: '*Henrietta.*' '

'And you think that that was an accusation? It was not.'

'What was it then?'

Henrietta stretched out her foot and traced

242

a pattern with the toe. She said in a low voice:

'Aren't you forgetting — what I told you not very long ago? I mean — the terms we were on?'

'Ah, yes — he was your lover — and so, as he is dying, he says: '*Henrietta*'. That is very touching.'

She turned blazing eyes upon him.

'Must you sneer?'

'I am not sneering. But I do not like being lied to — and that, I think, is what you are trying to do.'

Henrietta said quietly:

'I have told you that I am not very truthful — but when John said: '*Henrietta*' he was not accusing me of having murdered him. Can't you understand that people of my kind, who *make* things, are quite incapable of taking life? I don't kill people, M. Poirot. I *couldn't* kill anyone. That's the plain stark truth. You suspect me simply because my name was murmured by a dying man who hardly knew what he was saying.'

'Dr Christow knew perfectly what he was saying. His voice was as alive and conscious as that of a doctor doing a vital operation who says sharply and urgently: 'Nurse, the forceps, please.' '

'But — ' She seemed at a loss, taken aback. Hercule Poirot went on rapidly:

'And it is not just on account of what Dr Christow said when he was dying. I do not believe for one moment that you are capable of premeditated murder — that, no. But you might have fired that shot in a sudden moment of fierce resentment — and if so — *if* so, Mademoiselle, you have the creative imagination and ability to cover your tracks.'

Henrietta got up. She stood for a moment, pale and shaken, looking at him. She said with a sudden, rueful smile:

'And I thought you liked me.'

Hercule Poirot sighed. He said sadly:

'That is what is so unfortunate for me. I do.'

19

When Henrietta had left him, Poirot sat on until he saw below him Inspector Grange walk past the pool with a resolute, easy stride and take the path on past the pavilion.

The inspector was walking in a purposeful way.

He must be going, therefore, either to Resthaven or to Dovecotes. Poirot wondered which.

He got up and retraced his steps along the way he had come. If Inspector Grange was coming to see him, he was interested to hear what the inspector had to say.

But when he got back to Resthaven there was no sign of a visitor. Poirot looked thoughtfully up the lane in the direction of Dovecotes. Veronica Cray had not, he knew, gone back to London.

He found his curiosity rising about Veronica Cray. The pale, shining fox furs, the heaped boxes of matches, that sudden imperfectly explained invasion on the Saturday night, and finally Henrietta Savernake's revelations about John Christow and Veronica.

It was, he thought, an interesting pattern. Yes, that was how he saw it: a pattern.

A design of intermingled emotions and the clash of personalities. A strange involved design, with dark threads of hate and desire running through it.

Had Gerda Christow shot her husband? Or was it not quite so simple as that?

He thought of his conversation with Henrietta and decided that it was not so simple.

Henrietta had jumped to the conclusion that he suspected her of the murder, but actually he had not gone nearly as far as that in his mind. No further indeed than the belief that Henrietta knew something. Knew something or was concealing something — which?

He shook his head, dissatisfied.

The scene by the pool. A set scene. A stage scene.

Staged by whom? Staged *for* whom?

The answer to the second question was, he strongly suspected, Hercule Poirot. He had thought so at the time. But he had thought then that it was an impertinence — a joke.

It was still an impertinence — but not a joke.

And the answer to the first question?

He shook his head. He did not know. He

had not the least idea.

But he half-closed his eyes and conjured them up — all of them — seeing them clearly in his mind's eye. Sir Henry, upright, responsible, trusted administrator of Empire. Lady Angkatell, shadowy, elusive, unexpectedly and bewilderingly charming, with that deadly power of inconsequent suggestion. Henrietta Savernake, who had loved John Christow better than she loved herself. The gentle and negative Edward Angkatell. The dark, positive girl called Midge Hardcastle. The dazed, bewildered face of Gerda Christow clasping a revolver in her hand. The offended adolescent personality of David Angkatell.

There they all were, caught and held in the meshes of the law. Bound together for a little while in the relentless aftermath of sudden and violent death. Each of them had their own tragedy and meaning, their own story.

And somewhere in that interplay of characters and emotions lay the truth.

To Hercule Poirot there was only one thing more fascinating than the study of human beings, and that was the pursuit of truth.

He meant to know the truth of John Christow's death.

II

'But of course, Inspector,' said Veronica. 'I'm only too anxious to help you.'

'Thank you, Miss Cray.'

Veronica Cray was not, somehow, at all what the inspector had imagined.

He had been prepared for glamour, for artificiality, even possibly for heroics. He would not have been at all surprised if she had put on an act of some kind.

In fact, she was, he shrewdly suspected, putting on an act. But it was not the kind of act he had expected.

There was no overdone feminine charm — glamour was not stressed.

Instead he felt that he was sitting opposite to an exceedingly good-looking and expensively dressed woman who was also a good business woman. Veronica Cray, he thought, was no fool.

'We just want a clear statement, Miss Cray. You came over to The Hollow on Saturday evening?'

'Yes, I'd run out of matches. One forgets how important these things are in the country.'

'You went all the way to The Hollow? Why not to your next-door neighbour, M. Poirot?'

She smiled — a superb, confident camera smile.

'I didn't know who my next-door neighbour was — otherwise I should have. I just thought he was some little foreigner and I thought, you know, he might become a bore — living so near.'

'Yes,' thought Grange, 'quite plausible.' She'd worked that one out ready for the occasion.

'You got your matches,' he said. 'And you recognized an old friend in Dr Christow, I understand?'

She nodded.

'Poor John. Yes, I hadn't seen him for fifteen years.'

'Really?' There was polite disbelief in the inspector's tone.

'Really.' Her tone was firmly assertive.

'You were pleased to see him?'

'Very pleased. It's always delightful, don't you think, Inspector, to come across an old friend?'

'It can be on some occasions.'

Veronica Cray went on without waiting for further questioning:

'John saw me home. You'll want to know if he said anything that could have a bearing on the tragedy, and I've been thinking over our conversation very carefully — but really there wasn't a pointer of any kind.'

'What did you talk about, Miss Cray?'

'Old days. 'Do you remember this, that and the other?' ' She smiled pensively. 'We had known each other in the South of France. John had really changed very little — older, of course, and more assured. I gather he was quite well known in his profession. He didn't talk about his personal life at all. I just got the impression that his married life wasn't perhaps frightfully happy — but it was only the vaguest impression. I suppose his wife, poor thing, was one of those dim, jealous women — probably always making a fuss about his better-looking lady patients.'

'No,' said Grange. 'She doesn't really seem to have been that way.'

Veronica said quickly:

'You mean — it was all *underneath*? Yes — yes, I can see that that would be far more dangerous.'

'I see you think Mrs Christow shot him, Miss Cray?'

'I oughtn't to have said that. One mustn't comment — is that it — before a trial? I'm extremely sorry, Inspector. It was just that my maid told me she'd been found actually standing over the body with the revolver still in her hand. You know how in these quiet country places everything gets so exaggerated and servants do pass things on.'

'Servants can be very useful sometimes, Miss Cray.'

'Yes, I suppose you get a lot of your information that way?'

Grange went on stolidly:

'It's a question, of course, of who had a motive — '

He paused. Veronica said with a faint, rueful smile:

'And a wife is always the first suspect? How cynical! But there's usually what's called 'the other woman'. I suppose *she* might be considered to have a motive too?'

'You think there was another woman in Dr Christow's life?'

'Well — yes, I did rather imagine there might be. One just gets an impression, you know.'

'Impressions can be very helpful sometimes,' said Grange.

'I rather imagined — from what he said — that that sculptress woman was, well, a very close friend. But I expect you know all about that already?'

'We have to look into all these things, of course.'

Inspector Grange's voice was strictly non-committal, but he saw, without appearing to see, a quick, spiteful flash of

251

satisfaction in those large blue eyes.

He said, making the question very official:

'Dr Christow saw you home, you say. What time was it when you said goodnight to him?'

'Do you know, I really can't remember! We talked for some time, I do know that. It must have been quite late.'

'He came in?'

'Yes, I gave him a drink.'

'I see. I imagined your conversation might have taken place in the — er — pavilion by the swimming pool.'

He saw her eyelids flicker. There was hardly a moment's hesitation before she said:

'You really *are* a detective, aren't you? Yes, we sat there and smoked and talked for some time. How did you know?'

Her face bore the pleased, eager expression of a child asking to be shown a clever trick.

'You left your furs behind there, Miss Cray.' He added just without emphasis: 'And the matches.'

'Yes, of course I did.'

'Dr Christow returned to The Hollow at 3 am,' announced the inspector, again without emphasis.

'Was it really as late as that?' Veronica sounded quite amazed.

'Yes, it was, Miss Cray.'

'Of course, we had so much to talk over

— not having seen each other for so many years.'

'Are you sure it was quite so long since you had seen Dr Christow?'

'I've just told you I hadn't seen him for fifteen years.'

'Are you quite sure you're not making a mistake? I've got the impression you might have been seeing quite a lot of him.'

'What on earth makes you think that?'

'Well, this note for one thing.' Inspector Grange took out a letter from his pocket, glanced down at it, cleared his throat and read:

Please come over this morning. I must see you. Veronica.

'Ye-es.' She smiled. 'It *is* a little peremptory, perhaps. I'm afraid Hollywood makes one — well, rather arrogant.'

'Dr Christow came over to your house the following morning in answer to that summons. You had a quarrel. Would you care to tell me, Miss Cray, what that quarrel was about?'

The inspector had unmasked his batteries. He was quick to seize the flash of anger, the ill-tempered tightening of the lips. She snapped out:

253

'We didn't quarrel.'

'Oh, yes, you did, Miss Cray. Your last words were: 'I think I hate you more than I believed I could hate anyone.' '

She was silent now. He could feel her thinking — thinking quickly and warily. Some women might have rushed into speech. But Veronica Cray was too clever for that.

She shrugged her shoulders and said lightly:

'I see. More servants' tales. My little maid has rather a lively imagination. There are different ways of saying things, you know. I can assure you that I wasn't being melodramatic. It was really a mildly flirtatious remark. We had been sparring together.'

'The words were not intended to be taken seriously?'

'Certainly not. And I can assure you, Inspector, that it was fifteen years since I had last seen John Christow. You can verify that for yourself.'

She was poised again, detached, sure of herself.

Grange did not argue or pursue the subject. He got up.

'That's all for the moment, Miss Cray,' he said pleasantly.

He went out of Dovecotes and down the lane, and turned in at the gate of Resthaven.

254

III

Hercule Poirot stared at the inspector in the utmost surprise. He repeated incredulously:

'The revolver that Gerda Christow was holding and which was subsequently dropped into the pool was not the revolver that fired the fatal shot? But that is extraordinary.'

'Exactly, M. Poirot. Put bluntly, it just doesn't make sense.'

Poirot murmured softly:

'No, it does not make sense. But all the same, Inspector, it has got to make sense, eh?'

The inspector sighed heavily: 'That's just it, M. Poirot. We've got to find some way that it does make sense — but at the moment I can't see it. The truth is that we shan't get much further until we've found the gun that *was* used. It came from Sir Henry's collection all right — at least, there's one missing — and that means that the whole thing is still tied up with The Hollow.'

'Yes,' murmured Poirot. 'It is still tied up with The Hollow.'

'It seemed a simple, straightforward business,' went on the inspector. 'Well, it isn't so simple or so straightforward.'

'No,' said Poirot, 'it is not simple.'

'We've got to admit the possibility that the thing was a frame-up — that's to say that it was all set to implicate Gerda Christow. But if that was so, why not leave the right revolver lying by the body for her to pick up?'

'She might not have picked it up.'

'That's true, but even if she didn't, so long as nobody else's fingerprints were on the gun — that's to say if it was wiped after use — she would probably have been suspected all right. And that's what the murderer wanted, wasn't it?'

'Was it?'

Grange stared.

'Well, if you'd done a murder, you'd want to plant it good and quick on someone else, wouldn't you? That would be a murderer's normal reaction.'

'Ye-es,' said Poirot. 'But then perhaps we have here a rather unusual type of murderer. It is possible that *that* is the solution of our problem.'

'What is the solution?'

Poirot said thoughtfully:

'An unusual type of murderer.'

Inspector Grange stared at him curiously. He said:

'But then — what *was* the murderer's idea? What was he or she getting at?'

Poirot spread out his hands with a sigh.

'I have no idea — I have no idea at all. But it seems to me — dimly — '

'Yes?'

'That the murderer is someone who wanted to kill John Christow but who did not want to implicate Gerda Christow.'

'H'h! Actually, we suspected her right away.'

'Ah, yes, but it was only a matter of time before the facts about the gun came to light, and that was bound to give a new angle. In the interval the murderer has had time — ' Poirot came to a full stop.

'Time to do what?'

'Ah, *mon ami*, there you have me. Again I have to say I do not know.'

Inspector Grange took a turn or two up and down the room. Then he stopped and came to a stand in front of Poirot.

'I've come to you this afternoon, M. Poirot, for two reasons. One is because I know — it's pretty well known in the Force — that you're a man of wide experience who's done some very tricky work on this type of problem. That's reason number one. But there's another reason. You were there. You were an eye-witness. You *saw* what happened.'

Poirot nodded.

'Yes, I *saw* what happened — but the eyes, Inspector Grange, are very unreliable witnesses.'

'What do you mean, M. Poirot?'

'The eyes see, sometimes, what they are *meant* to see.'

'You think that it was planned out beforehand?'

'I suspect it. It was exactly, you understand, like a stage scene. What I *saw* was clear enough. A man who had just been shot and the woman who had shot him holding in her hand the gun she had just used. That is what I *saw*, and already we know that in one particular the picture is wrong. That gun had *not* been used to shoot John Christow.'

'Hm!' The inspector pulled his drooping moustache firmly downwards. 'What you are getting at is that some of the other particulars of the picture may be wrong too?'

Poirot nodded. He said:

'There were three other people present — three people who had *apparently* just arrived on the scene. But that may not be true either. The pool is surrounded by a thick grove of young chestnuts. From the pool five paths lead away, one to the house, one up to the woods, one up to the flower walk, one down from the pool to the farm and one to the lane here.

'Of those three people, each one came along a different path, Edward Angkatell from the woods above, Lady Angkatell up from the farm, and Henrietta Savernake from the

258

flower border above the house. Those three arrived upon the scene of the crime almost simultaneously, and a few minutes after Gerda Christow.

'But one of those three, Inspector, could have been at the pool *before* Gerda Christow arrived, could have shot John Christow, and could have retreated up or down one of the paths and then, turning round, could have arrived at the same time as the others.'

Inspector Grange said:

'Yes, it's possible.'

'And another possibility, not envisaged at the time. Someone could have come along the path from the lane, could have shot John Christow, and could have gone back the same way, unseen.'

Grange said: 'You're dead right. There are two other possible suspects besides Gerda Christow. We've got the same motive — jealousy. It's definitely a *crime passionel*. There were two other women mixed up with John Christow.'

He paused and said:

'Christow went over to see Veronica Cray that morning. They had a row. She told him that she'd make him sorry for what he'd done, and she said she hated him more than she believed she could hate anyone.'

'Interesting,' murmured Poirot.

'She's straight from Hollywood — and by what I read in the papers they do a bit of shooting each other out there sometimes. She could have come along to get her furs, which she'd left in the pavilion the night before. They could have met — the whole thing could have flared up — she fired at him — and then, hearing someone coming, she could have dodged back the way she came.'

He paused a moment and added irritably:

'And now we come to the part where it all goes hay-wire. That damned gun! Unless,' his eyes brightened, 'she shot him with her own gun and dropped one that she'd pinched from Sir Henry's study so as to throw suspicion on the crowd at The Hollow. She mightn't know about our being able to identify the gun used from the marks on the rifling.'

'How many people do know that, I wonder?'

'I put the point to Sir Henry. He said he thought quite a lot of people would know — on account of all the detective stories that are written. Quoted a new one, *The Clue of the Dripping Fountain*, which he said John Christow himself had been reading on Saturday and which emphasized that particular point.'

'But Veronica Cray would have had to have got the gun somehow from Sir Henry's study.'

'Yes, it would mean premeditation.' The inspector took another tug at his moustache, then he looked at Poirot. 'But you've hinted yourself at another possibility, M. Poirot. There's Miss Savernake. And here's where your eye-witness stuff, or rather I should say, ear-witness stuff, comes in again. Dr Christow said: *'Henrietta'* when he was dying. You heard him — they all heard him, though Mr Angkatell doesn't seem to have caught what he said.'

'Edward Angkatell did not hear? That is interesting.'

'But the others did. Miss Savernake herself says he tried to speak to her. Lady Angkatell says he opened his eyes, saw Miss Savernake, and said: *'Henrietta'* She doesn't, I think, attach any importance to it.'

Poirot smiled. 'No — she would not attach importance to it.'

'Now, M. Poirot, what about you? You were there — you saw — you heard. Was Dr Christow trying to tell you all that it was Henrietta who had shot him? In short, was that word an *accusation?*'

Poirot said slowly:

'I did not think so at the time.'

'But now, M. Poirot? What do you think now?'

Poirot sighed. Then he said slowly:

'It may have been so. I cannot say more than that. It is an impression only for which you are asking me, and when the moment is past there is a temptation to read into things a meaning which was not there at the time.'

Grange said hastily:

'Of course, this is all off the record. What M. Poirot thought isn't evidence — I know that. It's only a pointer I'm trying to get.'

'Oh, I understand you very well — and an impression from an eye-witness can be a very useful thing. But I am humiliated to have to say that my impressions are valueless. I was under the misconception, induced by the visual evidence, that Mrs Christow had just shot her husband; so that when Dr Christow opened his eyes and said '*Henrietta*' I never thought of it as being an accusation. It is tempting now, looking back, to read into that scene something that was not there.'

'I know what you mean,' said Grange. 'But it seems to me that since '*Henrietta*' was the last word Christow spoke, it must have meant one of two things. It was either an accusation of murder or else it was — well, purely emotional. She's the woman he's in love with and he's dying. Now, bearing everything in mind, which of the two did it sound like to you?'

Poirot sighed, stirred, closed his eyes, opened them again, stretched out his hands in acute vexation. He said:

'His voice was urgent — that is all I can say — urgent. It seemed to me neither accusing nor emotional — but urgent, yes! And of one thing I am sure. He was in full possession of his faculties. He spoke — yes, he spoke like a doctor — a doctor who has, say, a sudden surgical emergency on his hands — a patient who is bleeding to death, perhaps.' Poirot shrugged his shoulders. 'That is the best I can do for you.'

'Medical, eh?' said the inspector. 'Well, yes, that *is* a third way of looking at it. He was shot, he suspected he was dying, he wanted something done for him quickly. And if, as Lady Angkatell says, Miss Savernake was the first person he saw when his eyes opened, then he would appeal to her. It's not very satisfactory, though.'

'Nothing about this case is satisfactory,' said Poirot with some bitterness.

A murder scene, set and staged to deceive Hercule Poirot — and which *had* deceived him! No, it was not satisfactory.

Inspector Grange was looking out of the window.

'Hallo,' he said, 'here's Clark, my sergeant. Looks as though he's got something. He's been working on the servants — the friendly touch. He's a nice-looking chap, got a way with women.'

Sergeant Clark came in a little breathlessly. He was clearly pleased with himself, though subduing the fact under a respectful official manner.

'Thought I'd better come and report, sir, since I knew where you'd gone.'

He hesitated, shooting a doubtful glance at Poirot, whose exotic foreign appearance did not commend itself to his sense of official reticence.

'Out with it, my lad,' said Grange. 'Never mind M. Poirot here. He's forgotten more about this game than you'll know for many years to come.'

'Yes, sir. It's this way, sir. I got something out of the kitchenmaid — '

Grange interrupted. He turned to Poirot triumphantly.

'What did I tell you? There's always hope where there's a kitchenmaid. Heaven help us when domestic staffs are so reduced that nobody keeps a kitchenmaid any more. Kitchenmaids talk, kitchenmaids babble. They're so kept down and in their place by the cook and the upper servants that it's only human nature to talk about what they know to someone who wants to hear it. Go on, Clark.'

'This is what the girl says, sir. That on Sunday afternoon she saw Gudgeon, the butler, walking across the hall with a revolver in his hand.'

'Gudgeon?'

'Yes, sir.' Clark referred to a notebook. 'These are her own words. 'I don't know what to do, but I think I ought to say what I saw that day. I saw Mr Gudgeon, he was standing in the hall with a revolver in his hand. Mr Gudgeon looked very peculiar indeed.'

'I don't suppose,' said Clark, breaking off, 'that the part about looking peculiar means anything. She probably put that in out of her head. But I thought you ought to know about it at once, sir.'

Inspector Grange rose, with the satisfaction of a man who sees a task ahead of him which he is well fitted to perform.

'*Gudgeon?*' he said. 'I'll have a word with Mr Gudgeon right away.'

20

Sitting once more in Sir Henry's study, Inspector Grange stared at the impassive face of the man in front of him.

So far, the honours lay with Gudgeon.

'I am very sorry, sir,' he repeated. 'I suppose I ought to have mentioned the occurrence, but it had slipped my memory.'

He looked apologetically from the inspector to Sir Henry.

'It was about 5.30 if I remember rightly, sir. I was crossing the hall to see if there were any letters for the post when I noticed a revolver lying on the hall table. I presumed it was from the master's collection, so I picked it up and brought it in here. There was a gap on the shelf by the mantelpiece where it had come from, so I replaced it where it belonged.'

'Point it out to me,' said Grange.

Gudgeon rose and went to the shelf in question, the inspector close behind him.

'It was this one, sir.' Gudgeon's finger indicated a small Mauser pistol at the end of the row.

It was a .25 — quite a small weapon. It was

certainly not the gun that had killed John Christow.

Grange, with his eyes on Gudgeon's face, said:

'That's an automatic pistol, not a revolver.'

Gudgeon coughed.

'Indeed, sir? I'm afraid that I am not at all well up in firearms. I may have used the term revolver rather loosely, sir.'

'But you are quite sure that that is the gun you found in the hall and brought in here?'

'Oh, yes, sir, there can be no possible doubt about that.'

Grange stopped him as he was about to stretch out a hand.

'Don't touch it, please. I must examine it for fingerprints and to see if it is loaded.'

'I don't think it is loaded, sir. None of Sir Henry's collection is kept loaded. And, as for fingerprints, I polished it over with my handkerchief before replacing it, sir, so there will only be my fingerprints on it.'

'Why did you do that?' asked Grange sharply.

But Gudgeon's apologetic smile did not waver.

'I fancied it might be dusty, sir.'

The door opened and Lady Angkatell came in. She smiled at the inspector.

'How nice to see you, Inspector Grange!

What is all this about a revolver and Gudgeon? That child in the kitchen is in floods of tears. Mrs Medway has been bullying her — but of course the girl was quite right to say what she saw if she thought she ought to do so. I always find right and wrong so bewildering myself — easy, you know, if right is unpleasant and wrong is agreeable, because then one knows where one is — but confusing when it is the other way about — and I think, don't you, Inspector, that everyone must do what they think right themselves. What have you been telling them about that pistol, Gudgeon?'

Gudgeon said with respectful emphasis:

'The pistol was in the hall, my lady, on the centre table. I have no idea where it came from. I brought it in here and put it away in its proper place. That is what I have just told the inspector and he quite understands.'

Lady Angkatell shook her head. She said gently:

'You really shouldn't have said that, Gudgeon. I'll talk to the inspector myself.'

Gudgeon made a slight movement, and Lady Angkatell said very charmingly:

'I do appreciate your motives, Gudgeon. I know how you always try to save us trouble and annoyance.' She added in gentle dismissal: 'That will be all now.'

Gudgeon hesitated, threw a fleeting glance towards Sir Henry and then at the inspector, then bowed and moved towards the door.

Grange made a motion as though to stop him, but for some reason he was not able to define to himself, he let his arm fall again. Gudgeon went out and closed the door.

Lady Angkatell dropped into a chair and smiled at the two men. She said conversationally:

'You know, I really do think that was very charming of Gudgeon. Quite feudal, if you know what I mean. Yes, feudal is the right word.'

Grange said stiffly:

'Am I to understand, Lady Angkatell, that you yourself have some further knowledge about the matter?'

'Of course. Gudgeon didn't find it in the hall at all. He found it when he took the eggs out.'

'The eggs?' Inspector Grange stared at her.

'Out of the basket,' said Lady Angkatell.

She seemed to think that everything was now quite clear. Sir Henry said gently:

'You must tell us a little more, my dear. Inspector Grange and I are still at sea.'

'Oh.' Lady Angkatell set herself to be explicit. 'The pistol, you see, was *in* the basket, *under* the eggs.'

'What basket and what eggs, Lady Angkatell?'

'The basket I took down to the farm. The pistol was in it, and then I put the eggs in on top of the pistol and forgot all about it. And when we found poor John Christow dead by the pool, it was such a shock I let go of the basket and Gudgeon just caught it in time (because of the eggs, I mean. If I'd dropped it they would have been broken). And he brought it back to the house. And later I asked him about writing the date on the eggs — a thing I always do — otherwise one eats the fresher eggs sometimes before the older ones — and he said all that had been attended to — and now that I remember, he was rather emphatic about it. And that is what I mean by being feudal. He found the pistol and put it back in here — I suppose really because there were police in the house. Servants are always so worried by police, I find. Very nice and loyal — but also quite stupid, because of course, Inspector, it's the truth you want to hear, isn't it?'

And Lady Angkatell finished up by giving the inspector a beaming smile.

'The truth is what I mean to get,' said Grange rather grimly.

Lady Angkatell sighed.

'It all seems such a fuss, doesn't it?' she

said. 'I mean, all this hounding people down. I don't suppose whoever it was who shot John Christow really meant to shoot him — not seriously, I mean. If it was Gerda, I'm sure she didn't. In fact, I'm really surprised that she didn't miss — it's the sort of thing that one would expect of Gerda. And she's really a very nice kind creature. And if you go and put her in prison and hang her, what on earth is going to happen to the children? If she did shoot John, she's probably dreadfully sorry about it now. It's bad enough for children to have a father who's been murdered — but it will make it infinitely worse for them to have their mother hanged for it. Sometimes I don't think you policemen *think* of these things.'

'We are not contemplating arresting anyone at present, Lady Angkatell.'

'Well, that's sensible at any rate. But I have thought all along, Inspector Grange, that you were a very sensible sort of man.'

Again that charming, almost dazzling smile.

Inspector Grange blinked a little. He could not help it, but he came firmly to the point at issue.

'As you said just now, Lady Angkatell, it's the truth I want to get at. You took the pistol from here — which gun was it, by the way?'

Lady Angkatell nodded her head towards

the shelf by the mantelpiece. 'The second from the end. The Mauser .25.' Something in the crisp, technical way she spoke jarred on Grange. He had not, somehow, expected Lady Angkatell, whom up to now he had labelled in his own mind as 'vague' and 'just a bit batty', to describe a firearm with such technical precision.

'You took the pistol from here and put it in your basket. Why?'

'I knew you'd ask me that,' said Lady Angkatell. Her tone, unexpectedly, was almost triumphant. 'And of course there must be some reason. Don't you think so, Henry?' She turned to her husband. 'Don't you think I must have had a reason for taking a pistol out that morning?'

'I should certainly have thought so, my dear,' said Sir Henry stiffly.

'One does things,' said Lady Angkatell, gazing thoughtfully in front of her, 'and then one doesn't remember why one has done them. But I think, you know, Inspector, that there always is a reason if one can only get at it. I must have had *some* idea in my head when I put the Mauser into my egg basket.' She appealed to him. 'What do you think it can have been?'

Grange stared at her. She displayed no embarrassment — just a childlike eagerness.

It beat him. He had never yet met anyone like Lucy Angkatell, and just for the moment he didn't know what to do about it.

'My wife,' said Sir Henry, 'is extremely absent-minded, Inspector.'

'So it seems, sir,' said Grange. He did not say it very nicely.

'Why *do* you think I took that pistol?' Lady Angkatell asked him confidentially.

'I have no idea, Lady Angkatell.'

'I came in here,' mused Lady Angkatell. 'I had been talking to Simmons about the pillow-cases — and I remember dimly crossing over to the fireplace — and thinking we must get a new poker — the curate, not the rector — '

Inspector Grange stared. He felt his head going round.

'And I remember picking up the Mauser — it was a nice handy little gun, I've always liked it — and dropping it into the basket — I'd just got the basket from the flower-room. But there were so many things in my head — Simmons, you know, and the bindweed in the Michaelmas daisies — and hoping Mrs Medway would make a really *rich* Nigger in his Shirt — '

'A Nigger in his shirt?' Inspector Grange had to break in.

'Chocolate, you know, and eggs — and

then covered with whipped cream. Just the sort of sweet a foreigner would like for lunch.'

Inspector Grange spoke fiercely and brusquely, feeling like a man who brushes away fine spiders' webs which are impairing his vision.

'Did you load the pistol?'

He had hoped to startle her — perhaps even to frighten her a little, but Lady Angkatell only considered the question with a kind of desperate thoughtfulness.

'Now did I? That's so stupid. I can't remember. But I should think I must have, don't you, Inspector? I mean, what's the good of a pistol without ammunition? I wish I could remember exactly what was in my head at the time.'

'My dear Lucy,' said Sir Henry. 'What goes on or does not go on in your head has been the despair of everyone who knows you well for years.'

She flashed him a very sweet smile.

'I *am* trying to remember, Henry dear. One does such curious things. I picked up the telephone receiver the other morning and found myself looking down at it quite bewildered. I couldn't imagine what I wanted with it.'

'Presumably you were going to ring someone up,' said the inspector coldly.

'No, funnily enough, I wasn't. I remembered afterwards — I'd been wondering why Mrs Mears, the gardener's wife, held her baby in such an odd way, and I picked up the telephone receiver to try, you know, just how one would hold a baby, and of course I realized that it had looked odd because Mrs Mears was left-handed and had its head the other way round.'

She looked triumphantly from one to the other of the two men.

'Well,' thought the inspector, 'I suppose it's possible that there are people like this.'

But he did not feel very sure about it.

The whole thing, he realized, might be a tissue of lies. The kitchenmaid, for instance, had distinctly stated that it was a revolver Gudgeon had been holding. Still, you couldn't set much store by that. The girl knew nothing of firearms. She had heard a revolver talked about in connection with the crime, and revolver or pistol would be all one to her.

Both Gudgeon and Lady Angkatell had specified the Mauser pistol — but there was nothing to prove their statement. It might actually have been the missing revolver that Gudgeon had been handling and he might have returned it, not to the study, but to Lady Angkatell herself. The servants all seemed absolutely besotted about the damned woman.

Supposing it was actually she who had shot John Christow? (But why should she? He couldn't see why.) Would they still back her up and tell lies for her? He had an uncomfortable feeling that that was just what they would do.

And now this fantastic story of hers about not being able to remember — surely she could think up something better than that. And looking so natural about it — not in the least embarrassed or apprehensive. Damn it all, she gave you the impression that she was speaking the literal truth.

He got up.

'When you remember a little more, perhaps you'll tell me, Lady Angkatell,' he said dryly.

She answered: 'Of course I will, Inspector. Things come to one quite suddenly sometimes.'

Grange went out of the study. In the hall he put a finger round the inside of a collar and drew a deep breath.

He felt all tangled up in the thistledown. What he needed was his oldest and foulest pipe, a pint of ale and a good steak and chips. Something plain and objective.

21

In the study Lady Angkatell flitted about touching things here and there with a vague forefinger. Sir Henry sat back in his chair watching her. He said at last:

'Why did you take the pistol, Lucy?'

Lady Angkatell came back and sank down gracefully into a chair.

'I'm not really quite sure, Henry. I suppose I had some vague ideas of an accident.'

'Accident?'

'Yes. All those roots of trees, you know,' said Lady Angkatell vaguely, 'sticking out — so easy, just to trip over one. One might have had a few shots at the target and left one shot in the magazine — careless, of course — but then people *are* careless. I've always thought, you know, that accident would be the simplest way to do a thing of that kind. One would be dreadfully sorry, of course, and blame oneself . . . '

Her voice died away. Her husband sat very still without taking his eyes off her face. He spoke again in the same quiet, careful voice.

'Who was to have had — the accident?'

Lucy turned her head a little, looking at him in surprise.

'John Christow, of course.'

'Good God, Lucy — ' He broke off.

She said earnestly:

'Oh, Henry, I've been so dreadfully worried. About Ainswick.'

'I see. It's Ainswick. You've always cared too much about Ainswick, Lucy. Sometimes I think it's the only thing you do care for.'

'Edward and David are the last — the last of the Angkatells. And David won't do, Henry. He'll never marry — because of his mother and all that. He'll get the place when Edward dies, and he won't marry, and you and I will be dead long before he's even middle-aged. He'll be the last of the Angkatells and the whole thing will die out.'

'Does it matter so much, Lucy?'

'Of course it matters! *Ainswick!*'

'You should have been a boy, Lucy.'

But he smiled a little — for he could not imagine Lucy being anything but feminine.

'It all depends on Edward's marrying — and Edward's so obstinate — that long head of his, like my father's. I hoped he'd get over Henrietta and marry some nice girl — but I see now that that's hopeless. Then I thought that Henrietta's affair with John would run the usual course. John's affairs were never, I imagine, very permanent. But I saw him looking at her the other evening. He really *cared* about her. If only John were out of the way I felt that Henrietta would marry Edward. She's not the kind of person to cherish a memory and live in the past. So, you see, it all came to that — get rid of John Christow.'

'Lucy. You didn't — What did you do, Lucy?'

Lady Angkatell got up again. She took two dead flowers out of a vase.

'Darling,' she said. 'You don't imagine for a moment, do you, that *I* shot John Christow? I did have that silly idea about an accident. But then, you know, I remembered that we'd *asked* John Christow here — it's not as though he proposed himself. One can't ask someone to be your guest and then arrange accidents. Even Arabs are most particular about hospitality. So don't worry, will you, Henry?'

She stood looking at him with a brilliant, affectionate smile. He said heavily:

'I always worry about you, Lucy.'

'There's no need, darling. And you see, everything has actually turned out all right. John has been got rid of without our doing anything about it. It reminds me,' said Lady Angkatell reminiscently, 'of that man in

Bombay who was so frightfully rude to me. He was run over by a tram three days later.'

She unbolted the french windows and went out into the garden.

Sir Henry sat still, watching her tall, slender figure wander down the path. He looked old and tired, and his face was the face of a man who lives at close quarters with fear.

In the kitchen a tearful Doris Emmott was wilting under the stern reproof of Mr Gudgeon. Mrs Medway and Miss Simmons acted as a kind of Greek chorus.

'Putting yourself forward and jumping to conclusions in a way only an inexperienced girl would do.'

'That's right,' said Mrs Medway.

'If you see me with a pistol in my hand, the proper thing to do is to come to me and say: 'Mr Gudgeon, will you be so kind as to give me an explanation?' '

'Or you could have come to me,' put in Mrs Medway. '*I'm* always willing to tell a young girl what doesn't know the world what she ought to think.'

'What you should *not* have done,' said Gudgeon severely, 'is to go babbling off to a policeman — and only a sergeant at that! Never get mixed up with the police more than you can help. It's painful enough having them in the house at all.'

'Inexpressibly painful,' murmured Miss Simmons.

'Such a thing never happened to *me* before.'

'We all know,' went on Gudgeon, 'what her ladyship is like. Nothing her ladyship does would ever surprise me — but the police don't know her ladyship the way we do, and it's not to be thought of that her ladyship should be worried with silly questions and suspicions just because she wanders about with firearms. It's the sort of thing she would do, but the police have the kind of mind that just sees murder and nasty things like that. Her ladyship is the kind of absent-minded lady who wouldn't hurt a fly, but there's no denying that she puts things in funny places. I shall never forget,' added Gudgeon with feeling, 'when she brought back a live lobster and put it in the card tray in the hall. Thought I was seeing things!'

'That must have been before my time,' said Simmons with curiosity.

Mrs Medway checked these revelations with a glance at the erring Doris.

'Some other time,' she said. 'Now then, Doris, we've only been speaking to you for your own good. It's *common* to be mixed up with the police, and don't you forget it. You can get on with the vegetables now, and be more careful with the runner-beans than you were last night.'

Doris sniffed.

'Yes, Mrs Medway,' she said, and shuffled over to the sink.

Mrs Medway said forebodingly:

'I don't feel as I'm going to have a light hand with my pastry. That nasty inquest tomorrow. Gives me a turn every time I think of it. A thing like that — happening to *us*.'

22

The latch of the gate clicked and Poirot looked out of the window in time to see the visitor who was coming up the path to the front door. He knew at once who she was. He wondered very much what brought Veronica Cray to see him.

She brought a delicious faint scent into the room with her, a scent that Poirot recognized. She wore tweeds and brogues as Henrietta had done — but she was, he decided, very different from Henrietta.

'M. Poirot.' Her tone was delightful, a little thrilled. 'I've only just discovered who my neighbour is. And I've always wanted to know you so much.'

He took her outstretched hands, bowed over them.

'Enchanted, Madame.'

She accepted the homage smilingly, refused his offer of tea, coffee or cocktail.

'No, I've just come to talk to you. To talk seriously. I'm worried.'

'You are worried? I am sorry to hear that.'

Veronica sat down and sighed.

'It's about John Christow's death. The

283

inquest's tomorrow. You know that?'

'Yes, yes, I know.'

'And the whole thing has really been so extraordinary — '

She broke off.

'Most people really wouldn't believe it. But you would, I think, because you know something about human nature.'

'I know a little about human nature,' admitted Poirot.

'Inspector Grange came to see me. He'd got it into his head that I'd quarrelled with John — which is true in a way though not in the way he meant. I told him that I hadn't seen John for fifteen years — and he simply didn't believe me. But it's true, M. Poirot.'

Poirot said: 'Since it is true, it can easily be proved, so why worry?'

She returned his smile in the friendliest fashion.

'The real truth is that I simply haven't dared to tell the inspector what actually happened on Saturday evening. It's so absolutely fantastic that he certainly wouldn't believe it. But I felt I must tell someone. That's why I have come to you.'

Poirot said quietly: 'I am flattered.'

That fact, he noted, she took for granted. She was a woman, he thought, who was very sure of the effect she was producing. So sure that she might, occasionally, make a mistake.

'John and I were engaged to be married fifteen years ago. He was very much in love with me — so much so that it rather alarmed me sometimes. He wanted me to give up acting — to give up having any mind or life of my own. He was so possessive and masterful that I felt I couldn't go through with it, and I broke off the engagement. I'm afraid he took that very hard.'

Poirot clicked a discreet and sympathetic tongue.

'I didn't see him again until last Saturday night. He walked home with me. I told the inspector that we talked about old times — that's true in a way. But there was far more than that.'

'Yes?'

'John went mad — quite mad. He wanted to leave his wife and children, he wanted me to get a divorce from my husband and marry him. He said he'd never forgotten me — that the moment he saw me time stood still.'

She closed her eyes, she swallowed. Under her makeup her face was very pale.

She opened her eyes again and smiled almost timidly at Poirot.

'Can you believe that a — a feeling like that is possible?' she asked.

'I think it is possible, yes,' said Poirot.

'Never to forget — to go on waiting — planning — hoping. To determine with all one's heart and mind to get what one wants in the end. There are men like that, M. Poirot.'

'Yes — and women.'

She gave him a hard stare.

'I'm talking about men — about John Christow. Well, that's how it was. I protested at first, laughed, refused to take him seriously. Then I told him he was mad. It was quite late when he went back to the house. We'd argued and argued. He was still — just as determined.'

She swallowed again.

'That's why I sent him a note the next morning. I couldn't leave things like that. I had to make him realize that what he wanted was — impossible.'

'It *was* impossible?'

'Of course it was impossible! He came over. He wouldn't listen to what I had to say. He was just as insistent. I told him that it was no good, that I didn't love him, that I hated him . . . ' She paused, breathing hard. 'I had to be brutal about it. So we parted in anger . . . And now — he's dead.'

He saw her hands creep together, saw the twisted fingers and the knuckles stand out. They were large, rather cruel hands.

The strong emotion that she was feeling communicated itself to him. It was not sorrow, not grief — no, it was anger. The anger, he thought, of a baffled egoist.

'Well, M. Poirot?' Her voice was controlled and smooth again. 'What am I to do? Tell the story, or keep it to myself? It's what happened — but it takes a bit of believing.'

Poirot looked at her, a long, considering gaze.

He did not think that Veronica Cray was telling the truth, and yet there was an undeniable under-current of sincerity. It happened, he thought, but it did not happen like that.

And suddenly he got it. It was a true story, inverted. It was she who had been unable to forget John Christow. It was she who had been baffled and repulsed. And now, unable to bear in silence the furious anger of a tigress deprived of what she considered her legitimate prey, she had invented a version of the truth that should satisfy her wounded pride and feed a little the aching hunger for a man who had gone beyond the reach of her clutching hands. Impossible to admit that she, Veronica Cray, could not have what she wanted! So she had changed it all round.

Poirot drew a deep breath and spoke.

'If all this had any bearing on John

Christow's death, you would have to speak out, but if it has not — and I cannot see why it should have — then I think you are quite justified in keeping it to yourself.'

He wondered if she was disappointed. He had a fancy that in her present mood she would like to hurl her story into the printed page of a newspaper. She had come to him — why? To try out her story? To test his reactions? Or to use him — to induce him to pass the story on?

If his mild response disappointed her, she did not show it. She got up and gave him one of those long, well-manicured hands.

'Thank you, M. Poirot. What you say seems eminently sensible. I'm so glad I came to you. I — I felt I wanted somebody to know.'

'I shall respect your confidence, Madame.'

When she had gone, he opened the windows a little. Scents affected him. He did not like Veronica's scent. It was expensive but cloying, overpowering like her personality.

He wondered, as he flapped the curtains, whether Veronica Cray had killed John Christow.

She would have been willing to kill him — he believed that. She would have enjoyed pressing the trigger — would have enjoyed seeing him stagger and fall.

But behind that vindictive anger was

something cold and shrewd, something that appraised chances, a cool, calculating intelligence. However much Veronica Cray wished to kill John Christow, he doubted whether she would have taken the risk.

23

The inquest was over. It had been the merest formality of an affair, and though warned of this beforehand, yet nearly everyone had a resentful sense of anti-climax.

Adjourned for a fortnight at the request of the police.

Gerda had driven down with Mrs Patterson from London in a hired Daimler. She had on a black dress and an unbecoming hat, and looked nervous and bewildered.

Preparatory to stepping back into the Daimler, she paused as Lady Angkatell came up to her.

'How are you, Gerda dear? Not sleeping too badly, I hope. I think it went off as well as we could hope for, don't you? So sorry we haven't got you with us at The Hollow, but I quite understand how distressing that would be.'

Mrs Patterson said in her bright voice, glancing reproachfully at her sister for not introducing her properly:

'This was Miss Collins's idea — to drive straight down and back. Expensive, of course, but we thought it was worth it.'

'Oh, I do so agree with you.'

Mrs Patterson lowered her voice.

'I am taking Gerda and the children straight down to Bexhill. What she needs is rest and quiet. The reporters! You've no idea! Simply swarming round Harley Street.'

A young man snapped off a camera, and Elsie Patterson pushed her sister into the car and they drove off.

The others had a momentary view of Gerda's face beneath the unbecoming hat brim. It was vacant, lost — she looked for the moment like a half-witted child.

Midge Hardcastle muttered under her breath: 'Poor devil.'

Edward said irritably:

'What did everybody see in Christow? That wretched woman looks completely heartbroken.'

'She was absolutely wrapped up in him,' said Midge.

'But why? He was a selfish sort of fellow, good company in a way, but — ' He broke off. Then he asked: 'What did you think of him, Midge?'

'I?' Midge reflected. She said at last, rather surprised at her own words: 'I think I respected him.'

'Respected him? For what?'

'Well, he knew his job.'

291

'You're thinking of him as a doctor?'

'Yes.'

There was no time for more.

Henrietta was driving Midge back to London in her car. Edward was returning to lunch at The Hollow and going up by the afternoon train with David. He said vaguely to Midge: 'You must come out and lunch one day,' and Midge said that that would be very nice but that she couldn't take more than an hour off. Edward gave her his charming smile and said:

'Oh, it's a special occasion. I'm sure they'll understand.'

Then he moved towards Henrietta. 'I'll ring you up, Henrietta.'

'Yes, do, Edward. But I may be out a good deal.'

'Out?'

She gave him a quick, mocking smile.

'Drowning my sorrow. You don't expect me to sit at home and mope, do you?'

He said slowly: 'I don't understand you nowadays, Henrietta. You are quite different.'

Her face softened. She said unexpectedly: 'Darling Edward,' and gave his arm a quick squeeze.

Then she turned to Lucy Angkatell. 'I can come back if I want to, can't I, Lucy?'

Lady Angkatell said: 'Of course, darling.

And anyway there will be the inquest again in a fortnight.'

Henrietta went to where she had parked the car in the market square. Her suitcases and Midge's were already inside.

They got in and drove off.

The car climbed the long hill and came out on the road over the ridge. Below them the brown and golden leaves shivered a little in the chill of a grey autumn day.

Midge said suddenly: 'I'm glad to get away — even from Lucy. Darling as she is, she gives me the creeps sometimes.'

Henrietta was looking intently into the small driving-mirror.

She said rather inattentively:

'Lucy has to give the coloratura touch — even to murder.'

'You know, I'd never thought about murder before.'

'Why should you? It isn't a thing one thinks about. It's a six-letter word in a crossword, or a pleasant entertainment between the covers of a book. But the real thing — '

She paused. Midge finished:

'*Is* real. That is what startles one.'

Henrietta said:

'It needn't be startling to you. *You* are outside it. Perhaps the only one of us who is.'

Midge said:

293

'We're all outside it now. We've got away.'

Henrietta murmured: 'Have we?'

She was looking in the driving-mirror again. Suddenly she put her foot down on the accelerator. The car responded. She glanced at the speedometer. They were doing over fifty. Presently the needle reached sixty.

Midge looked sideways at Henrietta's profile. It was not like Henrietta to drive recklessly. She liked speed, but the winding road hardly justified the pace they were going. There was a grim smile hovering round Henrietta's mouth.

She said: 'Look over your shoulder, Midge. See that car way back there?'

'Yes?'

'It's a Ventnor 10.'

'Is it?' Midge was not particularly interested.

'They're useful little cars, low petrol consumption, keep the road well, but they're not fast.'

'No?'

Curious, thought Midge, how fascinated Henrietta always was by cars and their performance.

'As I say, they're not fast — but that car, Midge, has managed to keep its distance although we've been going over sixty.'

Midge turned a startled face to her.

'Do you mean that — '

Henrietta nodded. 'The police, I believe, have special engines in very ordinary-looking cars.'

Midge said:

'You mean they're still keeping an eye on us all?'

'It seems rather obvious.'

Midge shivered.

'Henrietta, can you understand the meaning of this second gun business?'

'No, it lets Gerda out. But beyond that it just doesn't seem to add up to anything.'

'But, if it was one of Henry's guns — '

'We don't know that it was. It hasn't been found yet, remember.'

'No, that's true. It could be someone outside altogether. Do you know who I'd like to think killed John, Henrietta? That woman.'

'Veronica Cray?'

'Yes.'

Henrietta said nothing. She drove on with her eyes fixed sternly on the road ahead of her.

'Don't you think it's possible?' persisted Midge.

'*Possible*, yes,' said Henrietta slowly.

'Then you don't think — '

'It's no good thinking a thing because you *want* to think it. It's the perfect solution

— letting all of us out!'

'Us? But — '

'We're in it — all of us. Even you, Midge darling — though they'd be hard put to it to find a motive for your shooting John. Of course I'd *like* it to be Veronica. Nothing would please me better than to see her giving a lovely performance, as Lucy would put it, in the dock!'

Midge shot a quick look at her.

'Tell me, Henrietta, does it all make you feel vindictive?'

'You mean' — Henrietta paused a moment — 'because I loved John?'

'Yes.'

As she spoke, Midge realized with a slight sense of shock that this was the first time the bald fact had been put into words. It had been accepted by them all, by Lucy and Henry, by Midge, by Edward even, that Henrietta loved John Christow, but nobody had ever so much as hinted at the fact in words before.

There was a pause whilst Henrietta seemed to be thinking. Then she said in a thoughtful voice:

'I can't explain to you what I feel. Perhaps I don't know myself.'

They were driving now over Albert Bridge. Henrietta said:

'You'd better come to the studio, Midge. We'll have tea, and I'll drive you to your digs afterwards.'

Here in London the short afternoon light was already fading. They drew up at the studio door and Henrietta put her key into the door. She went in and switched on the light.

'It's chilly,' she said. 'We'd better light the gas fire. Oh, bother — I meant to get some matches on the way.'

'Won't a lighter do?'

'Mine's no good, and anyway it's difficult to light a gas fire with one. Make yourself at home. There's an old blind man stands on the corner. I usually get my matches off him. I shan't be a minute or two.'

Left alone in the studio, Midge wandered round looking at Henrietta's work. It gave her an eerie feeling to be sharing the empty studio with these creations of wood and bronze.

There was a bronze head with high cheek-bones and a tin hat, possibly a Red Army soldier, and there was an airy structure of twisted ribbon-like aluminium which intrigued her a good deal. There was a vast static frog in pinkish granite, and at the end of the studio she came to an almost life-sized wooden figure.

She was staring at it when Henrietta's key turned in the door and Henrietta herself came in slightly breathless.

Midge turned.

'What's this, Henrietta? It's rather frightening.'

'That? That's The Worshipper. It's going to the International Group.'

Midge repeated, staring at it:

'It's frightening.'

Kneeling to light the gas fire, Henrietta said over her shoulder:

'It's interesting your saying that. Why do you find it frightening?'

'I think — because it hasn't any face.'

'How right you are, Midge.'

'It's very good, Henrietta.'

Henrietta said lightly:

'It's a nice bit of pearwood.'

She rose from her knees. She tossed her big satchel bag and her furs on to the divan, and threw down a couple of boxes of matches on the table.

Midge was struck by the expression on her face — it had a sudden quite inexplicable exultation.

'Now for tea,' said Henrietta, and in her voice was the same warm jubilation that Midge had already glimpsed in her face.

It struck an almost jarring note — but

Midge forgot it in a train of thought aroused by the sight of the two boxes of matches.

'You remember those matches Veronica Cray took away with her?'

'When Lucy insisted on foisting a whole half-dozen on her? Yes.'

'Did anyone ever find out whether she had matches in her cottage all the time?'

'I expect the police did. They're very thorough.'

A faintly triumphant smile was curving Henrietta's lips. Midge felt puzzled and almost repelled.

She thought: 'Can Henrietta really have cared for John? Can she? Surely not.'

And a faint desolate chill struck through her as she reflected:

'Edward will not have to wait very long . . . '

Ungenerous of her not to let that thought bring warmth. She wanted Edward to be happy, didn't she? It wasn't as though she could have Edward herself. To Edward she would be always 'little Midge'. Never more than that. Never a woman to be loved.

Edward, unfortunately, was the faithful kind. Well, the faithful kind usually got what they wanted in the end.

Edward and Henrietta at Ainswick . . . that was the proper ending to the story. Edward and Henrietta living happy ever afterwards.

She could see it all very clearly.

'Cheer up, Midge,' said Henrietta. 'You mustn't let murder get you down. Shall we go out later and have a spot of dinner together?'

But Midge said quickly that she must get back to her rooms. She had things to do — letters to write. In fact, she'd better go as soon as she'd finished her cup of tea.

'All right. I'll drive you there.'

'I could get a taxi.'

'Nonsense. Let's use the car, as it's there.'

They went out into damp evening air. As they drove past the end of the Mews Henrietta pointed out a car drawn in to the side.

'A Ventnor 10. Our shadow. You'll see. He'll follow us.'

'How beastly it all is!'

'Do you think so? I don't really mind.'

Henrietta dropped Midge at her rooms and came back to the Mews and put her car away in the garage.

Then she let herself into the studio once more.

For some minutes she stood abstractedly drumming with her fingers on the mantelpiece. Then she sighed and murmured to herself:

'Well — to work. Better not waste time.'

She threw off her tweeds and got into her overall.

An hour and a half later she drew back and studied what she had done. There were dabs of clay on her cheek and her hair was dishevelled, but she nodded approval at the model on the stand.

It was the rough similitude of a horse. The clay had been slapped on in great irregular lumps. It was the kind of horse that would have given the colonel of a cavalry regiment apoplexy, so unlike was it to any flesh and blood horse that had ever been foaled. It would also have distressed Henrietta's Irish hunting forebears. Nevertheless it was a horse — a horse conceived in the abstract.

Henrietta wondered what Inspector Grange would think of it if he ever saw it, and her mouth widened a little in amusement as she pictured his face.

24

Edward Angkatell stood hesitantly in the swirl of foot traffic in Shaftesbury Avenue. He was nerving himself to enter the establishment which bore the gold-lettered sign: 'Madame Alfrege'.

Some obscure instinct had prevented him from merely ringing up and asking Midge to come out and lunch. That fragment of telephone conversation at The Hollow had disturbed him — more, had shocked him. There had been in Midge's voice a submission, a subservience that had outraged all his feelings.

For Midge, the free, the cheerful, the outspoken, to have to adopt that attitude. To have to submit, as she clearly was submitting, to rudeness and insolence on the other end of the wire. It was all wrong — the whole thing was wrong! And then, when he had shown his concern, she had met him point-blank with the unpalatable truth that one had to keep one's job, that jobs weren't easy to get, and that the holding down of jobs entailed more unpleasantness than the mere performing of a stipulated task.

Up till then Edward had vaguely accepted the fact that a great many young women had 'jobs' nowadays. If he had thought about it at all, he had thought that on the whole they had jobs because they liked jobs — that it flattered their sense of independence and gave them an interest of their own in life.

The fact that a working day of nine to six, with an hour off for lunch, cut a girl off from most of the pleasures and relaxations of a leisured class had simply not occurred to Edward. That Midge, unless she sacrificed her lunch hour, could not drop into a picture gallery, that she could not go to an afternoon concert, drive out of town on a fine summer's day, lunch in a leisurely way at a distant restaurant, but had instead to relegate her excursions into the country to Saturday afternoons and Sundays, and to snatch her lunch in a crowded Lyons or a snack bar, was a new and unwelcome discovery. He was very fond of Midge. Little Midge — that was how he thought of her. Arriving shy and wide-eyed at Ainswick for the holidays, tongue-tied at first, then opening up into enthusiasm and affection.

Edward's tendency to live exclusively in the past, and to accept the present dubiously as something yet untested, had delayed his recognition of Midge as a wage-earning adult.

It was on that evening at The Hollow when he had come in cold and shivering from that strange, upsetting clash with Henrietta, and when Midge had knelt to build up the fire, that he had been first aware of a Midge who was not an affectionate child but a woman. It had been an upsetting vision — he had felt for a moment that he had lost something — something that was a precious part of Ainswick. And he had said impulsively, speaking out of that suddenly aroused feeling, 'I wish I saw more of you, little Midge . . . '

Standing outside in the moonlight, speaking to a Henrietta who was no longer startlingly the familiar Henrietta he had loved for so long — he had known sudden panic. And he had come in to a further disturbance of the set pattern which was his life. Little Midge was also a part of Ainswick — and this was no longer little Midge, but a courageous and sad-eyed adult whom he did not know.

Ever since then he had been troubled in his mind, and had indulged in a good deal of self-reproach for the unthinking way in which he had never bothered about Midge's happiness or comfort. The idea of her uncongenial job at Madame Alfrege's had worried him more and more, and he had determined at last to see for himself just what this dress shop of hers was like.

Edward peered suspiciously into the show window at a little black dress with a narrow gold belt, some rakish-looking, skimpy jumper suits, and an evening gown of rather tawdry coloured lace.

Edward knew nothing about women's clothes except by instinct, but had a shrewd idea that all these exhibits were somehow of a meretricious order. No, he thought, this place was not worthy of her. Someone — Lady Angkatell, perhaps — must do something about it.

Overcoming his shyness with an effort, Edward straightened his slightly stooping shoulders and walked in.

He was instantly paralysed with embarrassment. Two platinum blonde little minxes with shrill voices were examining dresses in a show-case, with a dark saleswoman in attendance. At the back of the shop a small woman with a thick nose, henna red hair and a disagreeable voice was arguing with a stout and bewildered customer over some alterations to an evening gown. From an adjacent cubicle a woman's fretful voice was raised.

'Frightful — perfectly frightful — can't you bring me anything *decent* to try?'

In response he heard the soft murmur of Midge's voice — a deferential, persuasive voice.

'This wine model is really very smart. And I think it would suit you. If you'd just slip it on —'

'I'm not going to waste my time trying on things that I can see are no good. Do take a little trouble. I've told you I don't want reds. If you'd listen to what you are told —'

The colour surged up into Edward's neck. He hoped Midge would throw the dress in the odious woman's face. Instead she murmured:

'I'll have another look. You wouldn't care for green I suppose, Madam? Or this peach?'

'Dreadful — perfectly dreadful! No, I won't see anything more. Sheer waste of time —'

But now Madame Alfrege, detaching herself from the stout customer, had come down to Edward and was looking at him inquiringly.

He pulled himself together.

'Is — could I speak — is Miss Hardcastle here?'

Madame Alfrege's eyebrows went up, but she took in the Savile Row cut of Edward's clothes, and she produced a smile whose graciousness was rather more unpleasant than her bad temper would have been.

From inside the cubicle the fretful voice rose sharply.

'Do be careful! How clumsy you are.

You've torn my hairnet.'

And Midge, her voice unsteady:

'I'm very sorry, Madam.'

'Stupid clumsiness.' (The voice appeared muffled.) 'No, I'll do it myself. My belt, please.'

'Miss Hardcastle will be free in a minute,' said Madame Alfrege. Her smile was now a leer.

A sandy-haired, bad-tempered-looking woman emerged from the cubicle carrying several parcels and went out into the street. Midge, in a severe black dress, opened the door for her. She looked pale and unhappy.

'I've come to take you out to lunch,' said Edward without preamble.

Midge gave a harried glance up at the clock.

'I don't get off until quarter-past one,' she began.

It was ten past one.

Madame Alfrege said graciously:

'You can go off now if you like, Miss Hardcastle, as your *friend* has called for you.'

Midge murmured: 'Oh thank you, Madame Alfrege,' and to Edward: 'I'll be ready in a minute,' and disappeared into the back of the shop.

Edward, who had winced under the impact of Madame Alfrege's heavy emphasis on 'friend', stood helplessly waiting.

Madame Alfrege was just about to enter into arch conversation with him when the door opened and an opulent-looking woman with a Pekinese came in, and Madame Alfrege's business instincts took her forward to the newcomer.

Midge reappeared with her coat on, and taking her by the elbow, Edward steered her out of the shop into the street.

'My God,' he said, 'is that the sort of thing you have to put up with? I heard that damned woman talking to you behind the curtain. How can you stick it, Midge? Why didn't you throw the damned frocks at her head?'

'I'd soon lose my job if I did things like that.'

'But don't you want to fling things at a woman of that kind?'

Midge drew a deep breath.

'Of course I do. And there are times, especially at the end of a hot week during the summer sales, when I am afraid that one day I shall let go and just tell everyone exactly where they get off — instead of 'Yes, Madam,' 'No, Madam' — 'I'll see if we have anything else, Madam.' '

'Midge, dear little Midge, you can't put up with all this!'

Midge laughed a little shakily.

'Don't be upset, Edward. Why on earth did you have to come here? Why not ring up?'

'I wanted to see for myself. I've been worried.' He paused and then broke out, 'Why, Lucy wouldn't talk to a scullery maid the way that woman talked to you. It's all wrong that you should have to put up with insolence and rudeness. Good God, Midge, I'd like to take you right out of it all down to Ainswick. I'd like to hail a taxi, bundle you into it, and take you down to Ainswick now by the 2.15.'

Midge stopped. Her assumed nonchalance fell from her. She had had a long tiring morning with trying customers, and Madame at her most bullying. She turned on Edward with a sudden flare of resentment.

'Well, then, why don't you? There are plenty of taxis!'

He stared at her, taken aback by her sudden fury. She went on, her anger flaming up:

'Why do you have to come along and *say* these things? You don't mean them. Do you think it makes it any easier after I've had the hell of a morning to be reminded that there are places like Ainswick? Do you think I'm grateful to you for standing there and babbling about how much you'd like to take me out of it all? All very sweet and insincere.

You don't really mean a word of it. Don't you know that I'd sell my soul to catch the 2.15 to Ainswick and get away from everything? I can't bear even to *think* of Ainswick, do you understand? You mean well, Edward, but you're cruel! Saying things — just *saying* things . . . '

They faced each other, seriously incommoding the lunchtime crowd in Shaftesbury Avenue. Yet they were conscious of nothing but each other. Edward was staring at her like a man suddenly aroused from sleep.

He said: 'All right then, damn it. You're coming to Ainswick by the 2.15!'

He raised his stick and hailed a passing taxi. It drew into the kerb. Edward opened the door, and Midge, slightly dazed, got in. Edward said: 'Paddington Station' to the driver and followed her in.

They sat in silence. Midge's lips were set together. Her eyes were defiant and mutinous. Edward stared straight ahead of him.

As they waited for the traffic lights in Oxford Street, Midge said disagreeably:

'I seem to have called your bluff.'

Edward said shortly:

'It wasn't bluff.'

The taxi started forward again with a jerk.

It was not until the taxi turned left in Edgware Road into Cambridge Terrace that

Edward suddenly regained his normal attitude to life.

He said: 'We can't catch the 2.15,' and tapping on the glass he said to the driver: 'Go to the Berkeley.'

Midge said coldly: 'Why can't we catch the 2.15? It's only twenty-five past one now.'

Edward smiled at her.

'You haven't got any luggage, little Midge. No nightgowns or toothbrushes or country shoes. There's a 4.15, you know. We'll have some lunch now and talk things over.'

Midge sighed.

'That's so like you, Edward. To remember the practical side. Impulse doesn't carry you very far, does it? Oh, well, it was a nice dream while it lasted.'

She slipped her hand into his and gave him her old smile.

'I'm sorry I stood on the pavement and abused you like a fishwife,' she said. 'But you know, Edward, you *were* irritating.'

'Yes,' he said. 'I must have been.'

They went into the Berkeley happily side by side. They got a table by the window and Edward ordered an excellent lunch.

As they finished their chicken, Midge sighed and said: 'I ought to hurry back to the shop. My time's up.'

'You're going to take decent time over your

311

lunch today, even if I have to go back and buy half the clothes in the shop!'

'Dear Edward, you are really rather sweet.'

They ate Crêpes Suzette, and then the waiter brought them coffee. Edward stirred his sugar in with his spoon.

He said gently:

'You really do love Ainswick, don't you?'

'Must we talk about Ainswick? I've survived not catching the 2.15 — and I quite realize that there isn't any question of the 4.15 — but don't rub it in.'

Edward smiled. 'No, I'm not proposing that we catch the 4.15. But I am suggesting that you come to Ainswick, Midge. I'm suggesting that you come there for good — that is, if you can put up with me.'

She stared at him over the rim of her coffee cup — put it down with a hand that she managed to keep steady.

'What do you really mean, Edward?'

'I'm suggesting that you should marry me, Midge. I don't suppose that I'm a very romantic proposition. I'm a dull dog, I know that, and not much good at anything. I just read books and potter around. But although I'm not a very exciting person, we've known each other a long time and I think that Ainswick itself would — well, would compensate. I think you'd be happy at Ainswick,

Midge. Will you come?'

Midge swallowed once or twice, then she said:

'But I thought — Henrietta — ' and stopped.

Edward said, his voice level and unemotional:

'Yes, I've asked Henrietta to marry me three times. Each time she has refused. Henrietta knows what she doesn't want.'

There was a silence, and then Edward said:

'Well, Midge dear, what about it?'

Midge looked up at him. There was a catch in her voice. She said:

'It seems so extraordinary — to be offered heaven on a plate as it were, at the Berkeley!'

His face lighted up. He laid his hand over hers for a brief moment.

'Heaven on a plate,' he said. 'So you feel like that about Ainswick. Oh, Midge, I'm glad.'

They sat there happily. Edward paid the bill and added an enormous tip. The people in the restaurant were thinning out. Midge said with an effort:

'We'll have to go. I suppose I'd better go back to Madame Alfrege. After all, she's counting on me. I can't just walk out.'

'No, I suppose you'll have to go back and resign or hand in your notice or whatever you call it. You're not to go on working there, though. I won't have it. But first I thought we'd better go to one of those shops in Bond Street where they sell rings.'

'Rings?'

'It's usual, isn't it?'

Midge laughed.

★ ★ ★

In the dimmed lighting of the jeweller's shop, Midge and Edward bent over trays of sparkling engagement rings, whilst a discreet salesman watched them benignantly.

Edward said, pushing away a velvet-covered tray:

'Not emeralds.'

Henrietta in green tweeds — Henrietta in an evening dress like Chinese jade . . .

No, not emeralds.

Midge pushed away the tiny stabbing pain at her heart.

'Choose for me,' she said to Edward.

He bent over the tray before them. He picked out a ring with a single diamond. Not a very large stone, but a stone of beautiful colour and fire.

'I'd like this.'

Midge nodded. She loved this display of Edward's unerring and fastidious taste. She slipped it on her finger as Edward and the shopman drew aside.

Edward wrote out a cheque for three hundred and forty-two pounds and came back to Midge smiling.

He said: 'Let's go and be rude to Madame Alfrege.'

25

'But, darling, I *am* so delighted!'

Lady Angkatell stretched out a fragile hand to Edward and touched Midge softly with the other.

'You did quite right, Edward, to make her leave that horrid shop and bring her right down here. She'll stay here, of course, and be married from here. St George's, you know, three miles by the road, though only a mile through the woods, but then one doesn't go to a wedding through woods. And I suppose it will have to be the vicar — poor man, he has such dreadful colds in the head every autumn. The curate, now, has one of those high Anglican voices, and the whole thing would be far more impressive — and more religious, too, if you know what I mean. It is so hard to keep one's mind reverent when somebody is saying things through their noses.'

It was, Midge decided, a very Lucyish reception. It made her want to both laugh and cry.

'I'd love to be married from here, Lucy,' she said.

'Then that's settled, darling. Off-white satin, I think, and an ivory prayer-book — *not* a bouquet. Bridesmaids?'

'No. I don't want a fuss. Just a very quiet wedding.'

'I know what you mean, darling, and I think perhaps you are right. With an autumn wedding it's nearly always chrysanthemums — such an uninspiring flower, I always think. And unless one takes a lot of time to choose them carefully bridesmaids never *match* properly, and there's nearly always one terribly plain one who ruins the whole effect — but one has to have her because she's usually the bridegroom's sister. But of course — ' Lady Angkatell beamed, 'Edward hasn't got any sisters.'

'That seems to be one point in my favour,' said Edward, smiling.

'But children are really the worst at weddings,' went on Lady Angkatell, happily pursuing her own train of thought. 'Everyone says: 'How sweet!' but, my dear, the *anxiety*! They step on the train, or else they howl for Nannie, and quite often they're sick. I always wonder how a girl can go up the aisle in a proper frame of mind, while she's so uncertain about what is happening behind her.'

'There needn't be anything behind me,'

said Midge cheerfully. 'Not even a train. I can be married in a coat and skirt.'

'Oh, no, Midge, that's so like a widow. No, off-white satin and *not* from Madame Alfrege's.'

'Certainly not from Madame Alfrege's,' said Edward.

'I shall take you to Mireille,' said Lady Angkatell.

'My dear Lucy, I can't possibly afford Mireille.'

'Nonsense, Midge. Henry and I are going to give you your trousseau. And Henry, of course, will give you away. I do hope the band of his trousers won't be too tight. It's nearly two years since he last went to a wedding. And I shall wear — '

Lady Angkatell paused and closed her eyes.

'Yes, Lucy?'

'Hydrangea blue,' announced Lady Angkatell in a rapt voice. 'I suppose, Edward, you will have one of your own friends for best man, otherwise, of course, there is David. I cannot help feeling it would be frightfully good for David. It would give him poise, you know, and he would feel we all *liked* him. That, I am sure, is very important with David. It must be disheartening, you know, to feel you are clever and intellectual and yet nobody likes you any the better for it! But of course it would be rather a risk. He would probably lose the ring, or drop it at the last minute. I expect it would worry Edward too much. But it would be nice in a way to keep it to the same people we've had here for the murder.'

Lady Angkatell uttered the last few words in the most conversational of tones.

'Lady Angkatell has been entertaining a few friends for a murder this autumn,' Midge could not help saying.

'Yes,' said Lucy meditatively. 'I suppose it *did* sound like that. A party for the shooting. You know, when you come to think of it, that's just what it has been!'

Midge gave a faint shiver and said:

'Well, at any rate, it's over now.'

'It's not exactly over — the inquest was only adjourned. And that nice Inspector Grange has got men all over the place simply crashing through the chestnut woods and startling all the pheasants, and springing up like jacks in the box in the most unlikely places.'

'What are they looking for?' asked Edward. 'The revolver that Christow was shot with?'

'I imagine that must be it. They even came to the house with a search warrant. The inspector was most apologetic about it, quite *shy*, but of course I told him we should be delighted. It was really most interesting. They looked absolutely *everywhere*. I followed them round, you know, and I suggested one or two places which even they hadn't thought of. But they didn't find anything. It was most disappointing. Poor Inspector Grange, he is growing quite thin and he pulls and pulls at that moustache of his. His wife ought to give him specially nourishing meals with all this worry he is having — but I have a vague idea that she must be one of those women who care more about having the linoleum really well polished than in cooking a tasty little meal. Which reminds me, I must go and see Mrs Medway. Funny how servants cannot bear the police. Her cheese souffle last night was quite uneatable. Soufflés and pastry always show if one is off balance. If it weren't for Gudgeon keeping them all together I really believe half the servants would leave. Why don't you two go and have a nice walk and help the police look for the revolver?'

Hercule Poirot sat on the bench overlooking the chestnut groves above the pool. He had no sense of trespassing since Lady Angkatell had very sweetly begged him to wander where he would at any time. It was Lady Angkatell's sweetness which Hercule Poirot was considering at this moment.

From time to time he heard the cracking of twigs in the woods above or caught sight of a figure moving through the chestnut groves below him.

Presently Henrietta came along the path from the direction of the lane. She stopped for a moment when she saw Poirot, then she came and sat down by him.

'Good morning, M. Poirot. I have just been to call upon you. But you were out. You look very Olympian. Are you presiding over the hunt? The inspector seems very active. What are they looking for, the revolver?'

'Yes, Miss Savernake.'

'Will they find it, do you think?'

'I think so. Quite soon now, I should say.'

She looked at him inquiringly.

'Have you an idea, then, where it is?'

'No. But I *think* it will be found soon. It is *time* for it to be found.'

'You do say odd things, M. Poirot!'

'Odd things happen here. You have come back very soon from London, Mademoiselle.'

Her face hardened. She gave a short, bitter laugh.

'The murderer returns to the scene of the crime? That is the old superstition, isn't it? So you *do* think that I — did it! You don't believe me when I tell you that I wouldn't — that I *couldn't* kill anybody?'

Poirot did not answer at once. At last he said thoughtfully:

'It has seemed to me from the beginning that either this crime was very simple — so simple that it was difficult to believe its simplicity (and simplicity, Mademoiselle, can be strangely baffling) or else it was extremely complex. That is to say, we were contending against a mind capable of intricate and ingenious inventions, so that every time we seemed to be heading for the truth, we were actually being led on a trail that twisted away from the truth and led us to a point which — ended in nothingness. This apparent futility, this continual barrenness, is not *real* — it is artificial, it is *planned*. A very subtle and ingenious mind is plotting against us the whole time — and succeeding.'

'Well?' said Henrietta. 'What has that to do with me?'

'The mind that is plotting against us is a creative mind, Mademoiselle.'

'I see — that's where I come in?'

She was silent, her lips set together bitterly. From her jacket pocket she had taken a pencil and now she was idly drawing the outline of a fantastic tree on the white painted wood of the bench, frowning as she did so.

Poirot watched her. Something stirred in

his mind — standing in Lady Angkatell's drawing-room on the afternoon of the crime, looking down at a pile of bridge-markers, standing by a painted iron table in the pavilion the next morning, and a question that he had put to Gudgeon.

He said:

'That is what you drew on your bridge-marker — a tree.'

'Yes.' Henrietta seemed suddenly aware of what she was doing. 'Ygdrasil, M. Poirot.' She laughed.

'Why do you call it Ygdrasil?'

She explained the origin of Ygdrasil.

'And so, when you 'doodle' (that is the word, is it not?) it is always Ygdrasil you draw?'

'Yes. Doodling is a funny thing, isn't it?'

'Here on the seat — on the bridge-marker on Saturday evening — in the pavilion on Sunday morning . . . '

The hand that held the pencil stiffened and stopped. She said in a tone of careless amusement:

'In the pavilion?'

'Yes, on the round iron table there.'

'Oh, that must have been on — on Saturday afternoon.'

'It was not on Saturday afternoon. When Gudgeon brought the glasses out to the pavilion about twelve o'clock on Sunday morning, there was nothing drawn on the table. I asked him and he is quite definite about that.'

'Then it must have been' — she hesitated for just a moment — 'of course, on Sunday afternoon.'

But still smiling pleasantly, Hercule Poirot shook his head.

'I think not. Grange's men were at the pool all Sunday afternoon, photographing the body, getting the revolver out of the water. They did not leave until dusk. They would have seen anyone go into the pavilion.'

Henrietta said slowly:

'I remember now. I went along there quite late in the evening — after dinner.'

Poirot's voice came sharply:

'People do not 'doodle' in the dark, Miss Savernake. Are you telling me that you went into the pavilion at night and stood by a table and drew a tree without being able to see what you were drawing?'

Henrietta said calmly: 'I am telling you the truth. Naturally you don't believe it. You have your own ideas. What is your idea, by the way?'

'I am suggesting that you were in the pavilion on *Sunday morning after twelve o'clock* when Gudgeon brought the glasses out. That you stood by that table watching someone, or waiting for someone, and unconsciously took out a pencil and drew Ygdrasil without being fully aware of what you were doing.'

'I was not in the pavilion on Sunday morning. I sat out on the terrace for a while, then I got the gardening basket and went up to the dahlia border and cut off heads and tied up some of the Michaelmas daisies that were untidy. Then just on one o'clock I went along to the pool. I've been through it all with Inspector Grange. I never came near the pool until one o'clock, just after John had been shot.'

'That,' said Hercule Poirot, 'is your story. But Ygdrasil, Mademoiselle, testifies against you.'

'I was in the pavilion and I shot John, that's what you mean?'

'You were there and you shot Dr Christow, or you were there and you saw who shot Dr Christow — or someone else was there who knew about Ygdrasil and deliberately drew it on the table to put suspicion on *you*.'

Henrietta got up. She turned on him with her chin lifted.

'You still think that I shot John Christow. You think that you can prove I shot him. Well,

I will tell you this. You will never prove it. Never!'

'You think that you are cleverer than I am?'

'You will never prove it,' said Henrietta, and, turning, she walked away down the winding path that led to the swimming pool.

26

Grange came in to Resthaven to drink a cup of tea with Hercule Poirot. The tea was exactly what he had had apprehensions it might be — extremely weak and China tea at that.

'These foreigners,' thought Grange, 'don't know how to make tea. You can't teach 'em.' But he did not mind much. He was in a condition of pessimism when one more thing that was unsatisfactory actually afforded him a kind of grim satisfaction.

He said: 'The adjourned inquest's the day after tomorrow and where have we got? Nowhere at all. What the hell, that gun must be *somewhere*! It's this damned country — miles of woods. It would take an army to search them properly. Talk of a needle in a haystack. It may be anywhere. The fact is, we've got to face up to it — we may *never* find that gun.'

'You will find it,' said Poirot confidently.

'Well, it won't be for want of trying!'

'You will find it, sooner or later. And I should say sooner. Another cup of tea?'

'I don't mind if I do — no, no hot water.'

327

'Is it not too strong?'

'Oh, no, it's not too strong.' The inspector was conscious of understatement.

Gloomily he sipped at the pale, straw-coloured beverage.

'This case is making a monkey of me, M. Poirot — a monkey of me! I can't get the hang of these people. They *seem* helpful — but everything they tell you seems to lead you away on a wild-goose chase.'

'Away?' said Poirot. A startled look came into his eyes. 'Yes, I see. *Away* . . . '

The inspector was now developing his grievance.

'Take the gun now. Christow was shot — according to the medical evidence — only a minute or two before your arrival. Lady Angkatell had that egg basket, Miss Savernake had a gardening basket full of dead flower heads, and Edward Angkatell was wearing a loose shooting-coat with large pockets stuffed with cartridges. Any one of them could have carried the revolver away with them. It wasn't hidden anywhere near the pool — my men have raked the place, so that's definitely out.'

Poirot nodded. Grange went on:

'Gerda Christow was framed — but who by? That's where every clue I follow seems to vanish into thin air.'

'Their stories of how they spent the

morning are satisfactory?'

'The *stories* are all right. Miss Savernake was gardening. Lady Angkatell was collecting eggs. Edward Angkatell and Sir Henry were shooting and separated at the end of the morning — Sir Henry coming back to the house and Edward Angkatell coming down here through the woods. The young fellow was up in his bedroom reading. (Funny place to read on a nice day, but he's the indoor, bookish kind.) Miss Hardcastle took a book down to the orchard. All sounds very natural and likely, and there's no means of checking up on it. Gudgeon took a tray of glasses out to the pavilion about twelve o'clock. He can't say where any of the house party were or what they were doing. In a way, you know, there's something against almost all of them.'

'Really?'

'Of course the most obvious person is Veronica Cray. She had quarrelled with Christow, she hated his guts, she's quite *likely* to have shot him — but I can't find the least iota of proof that she *did* shoot him. No evidence as to her having had any opportunity to pinch the revolvers from Sir Henry's collection. No one who saw her going to or from the pool that day. And the missing revolver definitely isn't in her possession now.'

'Ah, you have made sure of that?'

'What do you think? The evidence would have justified a search warrant but there was no need. She was quite gracious about it. It's not anywhere in that tin-pot bungalow. After the inquest was adjourned we made a show of letting up on Miss Cray and Miss Savernake, and we've had a tail on them to see where they went and what they'd do. We've had a man on at the film studios watching Veronica — no sign of her trying to ditch the gun there.'

'And Henrietta Savernake?'

'Nothing there either. She went straight back to Chelsea and we've kept an eye on her ever since. The revolver isn't in her studio or in her possession. She was quite pleasant about the search — seemed amused. Some of her fancy stuff gave our man quite a turn. He said it beat him why people wanted to do that kind of thing — statues all lumps and swellings, bits of brass and aluminium twisted into fancy shapes, horses that you wouldn't know were horses.'

Poirot stirred a little.

'Horses, you say?'

'Well, a horse. If you'd call it a horse! If people want to model a horse, why don't they go and *look* at a horse!'

'A *horse*,' repeated Poirot.

Grange turned his head.

'What is there about that that interests you so, M. Poirot? I don't get it.'

'Association — a point of the psychology.'

'Word association? Horse and cart? Rocking-horse? Clothes horse. No, I don't get it. Anyway, after a day or two, Miss Savernake packs up and comes down here again. You know that?'

'Yes, I have talked with her and I have seen her walking in the woods.'

'Restless, yes. Well, she was having an affair with the doctor all right, and his saying: '*Henrietta*' as he died is pretty near to an accusation. But it's not quite near enough, M. Poirot.'

'No,' said Poirot thoughtfully, 'it is not near enough.'

Grange said heavily:

'There's something in the atmosphere here — it gets you all tangled up! It's as though they all *knew* something. Lady Angkatell now — she's never been able to put out a decent reason *why* she took out a gun with her that day. It's a crazy thing to do — sometimes I think she is crazy.'

Poirot shook his head very gently.

'No,' he said, 'she is not crazy.'

'Then there's Edward Angkatell. I thought I was getting something on *him*. Lady

Angkatell said — no, hinted — that he'd been in love with Miss Savernake for years. Well, that gives him a motive. And now I find it's the *other* girl — Miss Hardcastle — that he's engaged to. So bang goes the case against *him*.'

Poirot gave a sympathetic murmur.

'Then there's the young fellow,' pursued the inspector. 'Lady Angkatell let slip something about him. His mother, it seems, died in an asylum — persecution mania — thought everybody was conspiring to kill her. Well, you can see what that might mean. If the boy had inherited that particular strain of insanity, he might have got ideas into his head about Dr Christow — might have fancied the doctor was planning to certify him. Not that Christow was that kind of doctor. Nervous affections of the alimentary canal and diseases of the super — super something. That was Christow's line. But if the boy was a bit touched, he *might* imagine Christow was here to keep him under observation. He's got an extraordinary manner, that young fellow, nervous as a cat.'

Grange sat unhappily for a moment or two.

'You see what I mean? All vague suspicions, leading *nowhere*.'

Poirot stirred again. He murmured softly:

'*Away* — not *towards*. *From*, not *to*.

Nowhere instead of *somewhere* . . . Yes, of course, that *must* be it.'

Grange stared at him. He said:

'They're queer, all these Angkatells. I'd swear, sometimes, that they know all about it.'

Poirot said quietly:

'*They do.*'

'You mean, they know, all of them, who did it?' the inspector asked incredulously.

Poirot nodded.

'Yes, they know. I have thought so for some time. I am quite sure now.'

'I see.' The inspector's face was grim. 'And they're hiding it up between them? Well, I'll beat them yet. *I'm going to find that gun.*'

It was, Poirot reflected, quite the inspector's theme song.

Grange went on with rancour:

'I'd give anything to get even with them.'

'With — '

'All of them! Muddling me up! Suggesting things! Hinting! Helping my men — *helping* them! All gossamer and spiders' webs, nothing tangible. What I want is a good solid *fact!*'

Hercule Poirot had been staring out of the window for some moments. His eye had been attracted by an irregularity in the symmetry of his domain.

He said now:

'You want a solid fact? *Eh bien*, unless I am much mistaken, there is a solid fact in the hedge by my gate.'

They went down the garden path. Grange went down on his knees, coaxed the twigs apart till he disclosed more fully the thing that had been thrust between them. He drew a deep sigh as something black and steel was revealed.

He said: 'It's a revolver all right.'

Just for a moment his eye rested doubtfully on Poirot.

'No, no, my friend,' said Poirot. '*I* did not shoot Dr Christow and I did not put the revolver in my own hedge.'

'Of course you didn't, M. Poirot! Sorry! Well, we've got it. Looks like the one missing from Sir Henry's study. We can verify that as soon as we get the number. Then we'll see if it was the gun that shot Christow. Easy does it now.'

With infinite care and the use of a silk handkerchief he eased the gun out of the hedge.

'To give us a break, we want fingerprints. I've a feeling, you know, that our luck's changed at last.'

'Let me know.'

'Of course I will, M. Poirot. I'll ring you up.'

Poirot received two telephone calls. The first came through that same evening. The inspector was jubilant.

'That you, M. Poirot? Well, here's the dope. It's the gun all right. The gun missing from Sir Henry's collection *and* the gun that shot John Christow! That's definite. And there are a good set of prints on it. Thumb, first finger, part of middle finger. Didn't I tell you our luck had changed?'

'You have identified the fingerprints?'

'Not yet. They're certainly not Mrs Christow's. We took hers. They look more like a man's than a woman's for size. Tomorrow I'm going along to The Hollow to speak my little piece and get a sample from everyone. And then, M. Poirot, *we shall know where we are!*'

'I hope so, I am sure,' said Poirot politely.

The second telephone call came through on the following day and the voice that spoke was no longer jubilant. In tones of unmitigated gloom, Grange said:

'Want to hear the latest? Those fingerprints aren't the prints of anybody connected with the case! No, sir! They're not Edward Angkatell's, nor David's, nor Sir Henry's! They're not Gerda Christow's, nor the

Savernake's, nor our Veronica's, nor her ladyship's, nor the little dark girl's! They're not even the kitchenmaid's — let alone any of the other servants'!'

Poirot made consoling noises. The sad voice of Inspector Grange went on:

'So it looks as though, after all, it *was* an outside job. Someone, that is to say, who had a down on Dr Christow and who we don't know anything about. Someone invisible and inaudible who pinched the guns from the study, and who went away after the shooting by the path to the lane. Someone who put the gun in your hedge and then vanished into thin air!'

'Would you like *my* fingerprints, my friend?'

'I don't mind if I do! It strikes me, M. Poirot, that you were on the spot, and that taking it all round you're far and away the most suspicious character in the case!'

27

I

The coroner cleared his throat and looked expectantly at the foreman of the jury.

The latter looked down at the piece of paper he held in his hand. His Adam's apple wagged up and down excitedly. He read out in a careful voice:

'We find that the deceased came to his death by wilful murder by some person or persons unknown.'

Poirot nodded his head quietly in his corner by the wall. There could be no other possible verdict.

Outside the Angkatells stopped a moment to talk to Gerda and her sister. Gerda was wearing the same black clothes. Her face had the same dazed, unhappy expression. This time there was no Daimler. The train service, Elsie Patterson explained, was really very good. A fast train to Waterloo and they could easily catch the 1.20 to Bexhill.

Lady Angkatell, clasping Gerda's hand, murmured:

'You must keep in touch with us, my dear.

337

A little lunch, perhaps, one day in London? I expect you come up to do shopping occasionally.'

'I — I don't know,' said Gerda.

Elsie Patterson said:

'We must hurry, dear, our train,' and Gerda turned away with an expression of relief.

Midge said:

'Poor Gerda. The only thing John's death has done for her is to set her free from your terrifying hospitality, Lucy.'

'How unkind you are, Midge. Nobody could say I didn't try.'

'You are much worse when you try, Lucy.'

'Well, it's very nice to think it's all over, isn't it?' said Lady Angkatell, beaming at them. 'Except, of course, for poor Inspector Grange. I do feel so sorry for him. Would it cheer him up, do you think, if we asked him back to lunch? As a *friend*, I mean.'

'I should let well alone, Lucy,' said Sir Henry.

'Perhaps you are right,' said Lady Angkatell meditatively. 'And anyway it isn't the right kind of lunch today. Partridges au Choux — and that delicious Soufflé Surprise that Mrs Medway makes so well. Not at all Inspector Grange's kind of lunch. A really good steak, a little underdone, and a good old-fashioned apple tart with no nonsense about it — or perhaps apple dumplings — that's what I should order for Inspector Grange.'

338

'Your instincts about food are always very sound, Lucy. I think we had better get home to those partridges. They sound delicious.'

'Well, I thought we ought to have some celebration. It's wonderful, isn't it, how everything always seems to turn out for the best?'

'Ye-es.'

'I know what you're thinking, Henry, but don't worry. I shall attend to it this afternoon.'

'What are you up to now, Lucy?'

Lady Angkatell smiled at him.

'It's quite all right, darling. Just tucking in a loose end.'

Sir Henry looked at her doubtfully.

When they reached The Hollow, Gudgeon came out to open the door of the car.

'Everything went off very satisfactorily, Gudgeon,' said Lady Angkatell. 'Please tell Mrs Medway and the others. I know how unpleasant it has been for you all, and I should like to tell you now how much Sir Henry and I have appreciated the loyalty you have all shown.'

'We have been deeply concerned for you, my lady,' said Gudgeon.

'Very sweet of Gudgeon,' said Lucy as she went into the drawing-room, 'but really quite wasted. I have really almost enjoyed it all — so different, you know, from what one is accustomed to. Don't you feel, David, that an experience like this has broadened your mind? It must be so different from Cambridge.'

'I am at Oxford,' said David coldly.

Lady Angkatell said vaguely: 'The dear Boat Race. So English, don't you think?' and went towards the telephone.

She picked up the receiver and, holding it in her hand, she went on:

'I do hope, David, that you will come and stay with us again. It's so difficult, isn't it, to get to know people when there is a murder? And quite impossible to have any really intellectual conversation.'

'Thank you,' said David. 'But when I come down I am going to Athens — to the British School.'

Lady Angkatell turned to her husband.

'Who's got the Embassy now? Oh, of course. Hope-Remmington. No, I don't think David would like them. Those girls of theirs are so terribly hearty. They play hockey and cricket and the funny game where you catch the thing in a net.'

She broke off, looking down at the telephone receiver.

'Now, what am I doing with this thing?'

'Perhaps you were going to ring someone up,' said Edward.

'I don't think so.' She replaced it. 'Do you like telephones, David?'

It was the sort of question, David reflected irritably, that she would ask; one to which there could be no intelligent answer. He replied coldly that he supposed they were useful.

'You mean,' said Lady Angkatell, 'like mincing machines? Or elastic bands? All the same, one wouldn't — '

She broke off as Gudgeon appeared in the doorway to announce lunch.

'But you like partridges,' said Lady Angkatell to David anxiously.

David admitted that he liked partridges.

'Sometimes I think Lucy really is a bit touched,' said Midge as she and Edward strolled away from the house and up towards the woods.

The partridges and the Soufflé Surprise had been excellent, and with the inquest over a weight had lifted from the atmosphere.

Edward said thoughtfully:

'I always think Lucy has a brilliant mind that expresses itself like a missing word competition. To mix metaphors — the hammer jumps from nail to nail and never fails to hit each one squarely on the head.'

'All the same,' Midge said soberly, 'Lucy frightens me sometimes.' She added, with a tiny shiver: 'This place has frightened me lately.'

'The Hollow?'

Edward turned an astonished face to her.

'It always reminds me a little of Ainswick,' he said. 'It's not, of course, the real thing — '

Midge interrupted:

'That's just it, Edward. I'm frightened of things that aren't the real thing. You don't know, you see, what's *behind* them. It's like — oh, it's like a *mask*.'

'You mustn't be fanciful, little Midge.'

It was the old tone, the indulgent tone he had used years ago. She had liked it then, but now it disturbed her. She struggled to make her meaning clear — to show him that behind what he called fancy, was some shape of dimly apprehended reality.

'I got away from it in London, but now that I'm back here it all comes over me again. I feel that everyone knows who killed John Christow. That the only person who doesn't know — is *me*.'

Edward said irritably:

'Must we think and talk about John Christow? He's dead. Dead and gone.'

Midge murmured:

'*He is dead and gone, lady,
He is dead and gone.
At his head a grass green turf,
At his heels a stone.*'

She put her hand on Edward's arm. 'Who

did kill him, Edward? We thought it was Gerda — but it wasn't Gerda. Then who was it? Tell me what *you* think? Was it someone we've never heard of?'

He said irritably:

'All this speculation seems to me quite unprofitable. If the police can't find out, or can't get sufficient evidence, then the whole thing will have to be allowed to drop — and we shall be rid of it.'

'Yes — but it's the not knowing.'

'Why should we want to know? What has John Christow to do with us?'

With *us*, she thought, with Edward and me? Nothing! Comforting thought — she and Edward, linked, a dual entity. And yet — and yet — John Christow, for all that he had been laid in his grave and the words of the burial service read over him, was not buried deep enough. *He is dead and gone, lady* — But John Christow was not dead and gone — for all that Edward wished him to be. John Christow was still here at The Hollow.

Edward said: 'Where are we going?'

Something in his tone surprised her. She said:

'Let's walk up on to the top of the ridge. Shall we?'

'If you like.'

For some reason he was unwilling. She

343

wondered why. It was usually his favourite walk. He and Henrietta used nearly always — Her thought snapped and broke off. *He and Henrietta!* She said: 'Have you been this way yet this autumn?'

He said stiffly:

'Henrietta and I walked up here that first afternoon.' They went on in silence.

They came at last to the top and sat on the fallen tree.

Midge thought: '*He and Henrietta sat here, perhaps.*'

She turned the ring on her finger round and round. The diamond flashed coldly at her. ('*Not emeralds,*' he had said.)

She said with a slight effort:

'It will be lovely to be at Ainswick again for Christmas.'

He did not seem to hear her. He had gone far away.

She thought: 'He is thinking of Henrietta and of John Christow.'

Sitting here he had said something to Henrietta or she had said something to him. Henrietta might know what she didn't want, but he belonged to Henrietta still. He always would, Midge thought, belong to Henrietta . . .

Pain swooped down upon her. The happy bubble world in which she had lived for the last week quivered and broke.

She thought: 'I can't live like that — with Henrietta always there in his mind. I can't face it. I can't bear it.'

The wind sighed through the trees — the leaves were falling fast now — there was hardly any golden left, only brown.

She said: 'Edward!'

The urgency of her voice aroused him. He turned his head.

'Yes?'

'I'm sorry, Edward.' Her lips were trembling but she forced her voice to be quiet and self-controlled. 'I've got to tell you. It's no use. I can't marry you. It wouldn't work, Edward.'

He said: 'But, Midge — surely Ainswick — '

She interrupted:

'I can't marry you just for Ainswick, Edward. You — you must see that.'

He sighed then, a long gentle sigh. It was like an echo of the dead leaves slipping gently off the branches of the trees.

'I see what you mean,' he said. 'Yes, I suppose you are right.'

'It was dear of you to ask me, dear and sweet. But it wouldn't do, Edward. It wouldn't *work*.'

She had had a faint hope, perhaps, that he would argue with her, that he would try to persuade her, but he seemed, quite simply, to feel just as she did about it. Here, with the ghost of Henrietta close beside him, he too, apparently, saw that it couldn't work.

'No,' he said, echoing her words, 'it wouldn't work.'

She slipped the ring off her finger and held it out to him.

She would always love Edward and Edward would always love Henrietta and life was just plain unadulterated hell.

She said with a little catch in her voice:

'It's a lovely ring, Edward.'

'I wish you'd keep it, Midge. I'd like you to have it.'

She shook her head.

'I couldn't do that.'

He said with a faint, humorous twist of the lips:

'I shan't give it to anyone else, you know.'

It was all quite friendly. He didn't know — he would never know — just what she was feeling. Heaven on a plate — and the plate was broken and heaven had slipped between her fingers or had, perhaps, never been there.

II

That afternoon, Poirot received his third visitor.

He had been visited by Henrietta Savernake and Veronica Cray. This time it was

346

Lady Angkatell. She came floating up the path with her usual appearance of insubstantiality.

He opened the door and she stood smiling at him.

'I have come to see you,' she announced.

So might a fairy confer a favour on a mere mortal.

'I am enchanted, Madame.'

He led the way into the sitting-room. She sat down on the sofa and once more she smiled.

Hercule Poirot thought: 'She is old — her hair is grey — there are lines in her face. Yet she has magic — she will always have magic . . .'

Lady Angkatell said softly:

'I want you to do something for me.'

'Yes, Lady Angkatell?'

'To begin with, I must talk to you — about John Christow.'

'About Dr Christow?'

'Yes. It seems to me that the only thing to do is to put a full stop to the whole thing. You understand what I mean, don't you?'

'I am not sure that I do know what you mean, Lady Angkatell.'

She gave him her lovely dazzling smile again and she put one long white hand on his sleeve.

'Dear M. Poirot, you know perfectly. The police will have to hunt about for the owner of those fingerprints and they won't find him, and they'll have, in the end, to let the whole thing drop. But I'm afraid, you know, that *you* won't let it drop.'

'No, I shall not let it drop,' said Hercule Poirot.

'That is just what I thought. And that is why I came. It's the truth you want, isn't it?'

'Certainly I want the truth.'

'I see I haven't explained myself very well. I'm trying to find out just *why* you won't let things drop. It isn't because of your prestige — or because you want to hang a murderer (such an unpleasant kind of death, I've always thought — so *mediæval*). It's just, I think, that you want to *know*. You do see what I mean, don't you? If you were to know the truth — if you were to be *told* the truth, I think — I think perhaps that might satisfy you? Would it satisfy you, M. Poirot?'

'You are offering to tell me the truth, Lady Angkatell?'

She nodded.

'You yourself know the truth, then?'

Her eyes opened very wide.

'Oh, yes, I've known for a long time. I'd *like* to tell you. And then we could agree that — well, that it was all over and done with.'

348

She smiled at him.

'Is it a bargain, M. Poirot?'

It was quite an effort for Hercule Poirot to say:

'No, Madame, it is not a bargain.'

He wanted — he wanted, very badly, to let the whole thing drop, simply because Lady Angkatell asked him to do so.

Lady Angkatell sat very still for a moment. Then she raised her eyebrows.

'I wonder,' she said. 'I wonder if you really know what you are doing.'

28

Midge, lying dry-eyed and awake in the darkness, turned restlessly on her pillows. She heard a door unlatch, a footstep in the corridor outside passing her door. It was Edward's door and Edward's step. She switched on the lamp by her bed and looked at the clock that stood by the lamp on the table. It was ten minutes to three.

Edward passing her door and going down the stairs at this hour in the morning. It was odd.

They had all gone to bed early, at half-past ten. She herself had not slept, had lain there with burning eyelids and with a dry, aching misery racking her feverishly.

She had heard the clock strike downstairs — had heard owls hoot outside her bedroom window. Had felt that depression that reaches its nadir at 2 am. Had thought to herself: 'I can't bear it — I can't bear it. Tomorrow coming — another day. Day after day to be got through.'

Banished by her own act from Ainswick — from all the loveliness and dearness of

Ainswick which might have been her very own possession.

But better banishment, better loneliness, better a drab and uninteresting life, than life with Edward and Henrietta's ghost. Until that day in the wood she had not known her own capacity for bitter jealousy.

And after all, Edward had never told her that he loved her. Affection, kindliness, he had never pretended to more than that. She had accepted the limitation, and not until she had realized what it would mean to live at close quarters with an Edward whose mind and heart had Henrietta as a permanent guest, did she know that for her Edward's affection was not enough.

Edward walking past her door, down the front stairs. It was odd — very odd. Where was he going?

Uneasiness grew upon her. It was all part and parcel of the uneasiness that The Hollow gave her nowadays. What was Edward doing downstairs in the small hours of the morning? Had he gone out?

Inactivity at last became too much for her. She got up, slipped on her dressing-gown, and, taking a torch, she opened her door and came out into the passage.

It was quite dark, no light had been switched on. Midge turned to the left and came to the head of the staircase. Below all was dark too. She ran down the stairs and after a moment's hesitation switched on the light in the hall. Everything was silent. The front door was closed and locked. She tried the side door but that, too, was locked.

Edward, then, had not gone out. Where could he be?

And suddenly she raised her head and sniffed.

A whiff, a very faint whiff of gas.

The baize door to the kitchen quarters was just ajar. She went through it — a faint light was shining from the open kitchen door. The smell of gas was much stronger.

Midge ran along the passage and into the kitchen. Edward was lying on the floor with his head inside the gas oven, which was turned full on.

Midge was a quick, practical girl. Her first act was to swing open the shutters. She could not unlatch the window, and, winding a glass-cloth round her arm, she smashed it. Then, holding her breath, she stooped down and tugged and pulled Edward out of the gas oven and switched off the taps.

He was unconscious and breathing queerly, but she knew that he could not have been unconscious long. He could only just have gone under. The wind sweeping through from the window to the open door was fast dispelling the gas fumes. Midge dragged Edward to a spot near the window where the air would have full play. She sat down and gathered him into her strong young arms.

She said his name, first softly, then with increasing desperation. 'Edward, Edward, *Edward* . . . '

He stirred, groaned, opened his eyes and looked up at her. He said very faintly: 'Gas oven,' and his eyes went round to the gas stove.

'I know, darling, but why — *why?*'

He was shivering now, his hands were cold and lifeless. He said: 'Midge?' There was a kind of wondering surprise and pleasure in his voice.

She said: 'I heard you pass my door. I didn't know . . . I came down.'

He sighed, a very long sigh as though from very far away. 'Best way out,' he said. And then, inexplicably until she remembered Lucy's conversation on the night of the tragedy, '*News of the World.*'

'But, Edward, why, *why?*'

He looked up at her, and the blank, cold darkness of his stare frightened her.

'Because I know I've never been any good. Always a failure. Always ineffectual. It's men like Christow who do things. They get there and women admire them. I'm nothing — I'm not even quite alive. I inherited Ainswick and I've enough to live on — otherwise I'd have gone under. No good at a career — never much good as a writer. Henrietta didn't want me. No one wanted me. That day — at the Berkeley — I thought — but it was the same story. You couldn't care either, Midge. Even for Ainswick you couldn't put up with me. So I thought better get out altogether.'

Her words came with a rush. 'Darling, darling, you don't understand. It was because of Henrietta — because I thought you still loved Henrietta so much.'

'Henrietta?' He murmured it vaguely, as though speaking of someone infinitely remote. 'Yes, I loved her very much.'

And from even farther away she heard him murmur:

'It's so cold.'

'*Edward* — my darling.'

Her arms closed round him firmly. He smiled at her, murmuring:

'You're so warm, Midge — you're so warm.'

Yes, she thought, that was what despair was. A cold thing — a thing of infinite coldness and loneliness. She'd never understood until now that despair was a cold thing. She had thought of it as something hot and passionate, something violent, a hot-blooded desperation. But that was not so. *This* was despair — this utter outer darkness of coldness and loneliness. And the sin of despair, that priests talked of, was a cold sin, the sin of cutting oneself off from all warm and living human contacts.

Edward said again: 'You're so warm, Midge.' And suddenly with a glad, proud confidence she thought: 'But that's what he *wants* — that's what I can give him!' They were all cold, the Angkatells. Even Henrietta had something in her of the will-o'-the-wisp, of the elusive fairy coldness in the Angkatell blood. Let Edward love Henrietta as an intangible and unpossessable dream. It was warmth, permanence, stability that was his real need. It was daily companionship and love and laughter at Ainswick.

She thought: 'What Edward needs is someone to light a fire on his hearth — and *I* am the person to do that.'

Edward looked up. He saw Midge's face bending over him, the warm colouring of the skin, the generous mouth, the steady eyes and the dark hair that lay back from her forehead like two wings.

He saw Henrietta always as a projection from the past. In the grown woman he sought and wanted only to see the seventeen-year-old girl he had first loved. But now, looking up at Midge, he had a queer sense of seeing a continuous Midge. He saw the schoolgirl with her winged hair springing back into two pigtails, he saw its dark waves framing her face now, and he saw exactly how those wings would look when the hair was not dark any longer but grey.

'Midge,' he thought, 'is *real*. The only real thing I have ever known . . . ' He felt the warmth of her, and the strength — dark, positive, alive, *real*! 'Midge,' he thought, 'is the rock on which I can build my life.'

He said: 'Darling Midge, I love you so, never leave me again.'

She bent down to him and he felt the warmth of her lips on his, felt her love enveloping him, shielding him, and happiness flowered in that cold desert where he had lived alone so long.

Suddenly Midge said with a shaky laugh:

'Look, Edward, a blackbeetle has come out to look at us. Isn't he a *nice* blackbeetle? I never thought I could like a blackbeetle so much!'

She added dreamily: 'How odd life is. Here we are sitting on the floor in a kitchen that still smells of gas all amongst the black-beetles, and feeling that it's heaven.'

He murmured dreamily: 'I could stay here for ever.'

'We'd better go and get some sleep. It's four o'clock. How on earth are we to explain that broken window to Lucy?' Fortunately, Midge reflected, Lucy was an extraordinarily easy person to explain things to!

Taking a leaf out of Lucy's own book, Midge went into her room at six o'clock. She made a bald statement of fact.

'Edward went down and put his head in the gas oven in the night,' she said. 'Fortunately I heard him, and went down after him. I broke the window because I couldn't get it open quickly.'

Lucy, Midge had to admit, was wonderful.

She smiled sweetly with no sign of surprise.

'Dear Midge,' she said, 'you are always so practical. I'm sure you will always be the greatest comfort to Edward.'

After Midge had gone, Lady Angkatell lay thinking. Then she got up and went into her husband's room, which for once was unlocked.

'Henry.'

'My dear Lucy! It's not cockcrow yet.'

'No, but listen, Henry, this is really important. We must have electricity installed to cook by and get rid of that gas stove.'

'Why, it's quite satisfactory, isn't it?'

'Oh, yes, dear. But it's the sort of thing that gives people ideas, and everybody mightn't be as practical as dear Midge.'

She flitted elusively away. Sir Henry turned over with a grunt. Presently he awoke with a start just as he was dozing off. 'Did I dream it,' he murmured, 'or did Lucy come in and start talking about gas stoves?'

Outside in the passage, Lady Angkatell went into the bathroom and put a kettle on the gas ring. Sometimes, she knew, people liked an early cup of tea. Fired with self-approval, she returned to bed and lay back on her pillows, pleased with life and with herself.

Edward and Midge at Ainswick — the inquest over. She would go and talk to M. Poirot again. A nice little man . . .

Suddenly another idea flashed into her head. She sat upright in bed. 'I wonder now,' she speculated, 'if she has thought of *that*.'

She got out of bed and drifted along the passage to Henrietta's room, beginning her remarks as usual long before she was within earshot.

' — and it suddenly came to me, dear, that you *might* have overlooked that.'

Henrietta murmured sleepily: 'For heaven's sake, Lucy, the birds aren't up yet!'

'Oh, I know, dear, it *is* rather early, but it

seems to have been a very disturbed night — Edward and the gas stove and Midge and the kitchen window — and thinking of what to say to M. Poirot and everything — '

'I'm sorry, Lucy, but everything you say sounds like complete gibberish. Can't it wait?'

'It was only the holster, dear. I thought, you know, that you might not have thought about the holster.'

'Holster?' Henrietta sat up in bed. She was suddenly wide awake. 'What's this about a holster?'

'That revolver of Henry's was in a holster, you know. And the holster hasn't been found. And of course nobody may think of it — but on the other hand somebody might — '

Henrietta swung herself out of bed. She said:

'One always forgets something — that's what they say! And it's true!'

Lady Angkatell went back to her room.

She got into bed and quickly went fast asleep.

The kettle on the gas ring boiled and went on boiling.

29

Gerda rolled over to the side of the bed and sat up.

Her head felt a little better now but she was still glad that she hadn't gone with the others on the picnic. It was peaceful and almost comforting to be alone in the house for a bit.

Elsie, of course, had been very kind — very kind — especially at first. To begin with, Gerda had been urged to stay in bed for breakfast, trays had been brought up to her. Everybody urged her to sit in the most comfortable armchair, to put her feet up, not to do anything at all strenuous.

They were all so sorry for her about John. She had stayed cowering gratefully in that protective dim haze. She hadn't wanted to think, or to feel, or to remember.

But now, every day, she felt it coming nearer — she'd have to start living again, to decide what to do, where to live. Already Elsie was showing a shade of impatience in her manner. 'Oh, Gerda, don't be so *slow!*'

It was all the same as it had been — long ago, before John came and took her away. They all thought her slow and stupid. There was nobody to say, as John had said: 'I'll look after you.'

Her head ached and Gerda thought: 'I'll make myself some tea.'

She went down to the kitchen and put the kettle on. It was nearly boiling when she heard a ring at the front door.

The maids had been given the day out. Gerda went to the door and opened it. She was astonished to see Henrietta's rakish-looking car drawn up to the kerb and Henrietta herself standing on the doorstep.

'Why, Henrietta!' she exclaimed. She fell back a step or two. 'Come in. I'm afraid my sister and the children are out but — '

Henrietta cut her short. 'Good, I'm glad. I wanted to get you alone. Listen, Gerda, *what did you do with the holster?*'

Gerda stopped. Her eyes looked suddenly vacant and uncomprehending. She said: 'Holster?'

Then she opened a door on the right of the hall.

'You'd better come in here. I'm afraid it's rather dusty. You see, we haven't had much time this morning.'

Henrietta interrupted again urgently.

She said: 'Listen, Gerda, you've got to tell me. Apart from the holster everything's all right — absolutely watertight. There's

361

nothing to connect you with the business. I found the revolver where you'd shoved it into that thicket by the pool. I hid it in a place where you couldn't possibly have put it — and there are fingerprints on it which they'll never identify. So there's only the holster. I must know what you did with that?'

She paused, praying desperately that Gerda would react quickly.

She had no idea why she had this vital sense of urgency, but it was there. Her car had not been followed — she had made sure of that. She had started on the London road, had filled up at a garage and had mentioned that she was on her way to London. Then, a little farther on, she had swung across country until she had reached a main road leading south to the coast.

Gerda was still staring at her. The trouble with Gerda, thought Henrietta, was that she was so slow.

'If you've still got it, Gerda, you must give it to me. I'll get rid of it somehow. It's the only possible thing, you see, that can connect you now with John's death. *Have* you got it?'

There was a pause and then Gerda slowly nodded her head.

'Didn't you know it was madness to keep it?' Henrietta could hardly conceal her impatience.

'I forgot about it. It was up in my room.'

She added: 'When the police came up to Harley Street I cut it in pieces and put it in the bag with my leather work.'

Henrietta said: 'That was clever of you.'

Gerda said: 'I'm not quite so stupid as everybody thinks.' She put her hand up to her throat. She said: 'John — *John!*' Her voice broke.

Henrietta said: 'I know, my dear, I know.'

Gerda said: 'But you can't know . . . John wasn't — he wasn't — ' She stood there, dumb and strangely pathetic. She raised her eyes suddenly to Henrietta's face. 'It was all a lie — everything! All the things I thought he was. I saw his face when he followed that woman out that evening. Veronica Cray. I knew he'd cared for her, of course, years ago before he married me, but I thought it was all over.'

Henrietta said gently:

'But it *was* all over.'

Gerda shook her head.

'No. She came there and pretended that she hadn't seen John for years — but I saw John's face. He went out with her. I went up to bed. I lay there trying to read — I tried to read that detective story that John was reading. And John didn't come. And at last I went out . . . '

Her eyes seemed to be turning inwards, seeing the scene.

'It was moonlight. I went along the path to the swimming pool. There was a light in the pavilion. They were *there* — John and that woman.'

Henrietta made a faint sound.

Gerda's face had changed. It had none of its usual slightly vacant amiability. It was remorseless, implacable.

'I'd trusted John. I'd believed in him — as though he were God. I thought he was the noblest man in the world. I thought he was everything that was fine and noble. And it was all a *lie*! I was left with nothing at all. I — I'd *worshipped* John!'

Henrietta was gazing at her fascinated. For here, before her eyes, was what she had guessed at and brought to life, carving it out of wood. Here was The Worshipper. Blind devotion thrown back on itself, disillusioned, dangerous.

Gerda said: 'I couldn't bear it! I had to kill him! I *had* to — you do see that, Henrietta?'

She said it quite conversationally, in an almost friendly tone.

'And I knew I must be careful because the police are very clever. But then I'm not really as stupid as people think! If you're very slow and just stare, people think you don't take things in — and sometimes, underneath, you're laughing at them! I knew I could kill John and nobody would know because I'd read in that detective story about the police being able to tell which gun a bullet has been fired from. Sir Henry had shown me how to load and fire a revolver that afternoon. I'd take *two* revolvers. I'd shoot John with one and then hide it, and let people find me holding the other, and first they'd think *I'*d shot him and then they'd find he couldn't have been killed with that revolver and so they'd say I hadn't done it after all!'

She nodded her head triumphantly.

'But I forgot about the leather thing. It was in the drawer in my bedroom. What do you call it, a holster? Surely the police won't bother about that *now!*'

'They might,' said Henrietta. 'You'd better give it to me, and I'll take it away with me. Once it's out of your hands, you're quite safe.'

She sat down. She felt suddenly unutterably weary.

Gerda said: 'You don't look well. I was just making tea.'

She went out of the room. Presently she came back with a tray. On it was a teapot, milk jug and two cups. The milk jug had slopped over because it was over-full. Gerda put the tray down and poured out a cup of tea and handed it to Henrietta.

'Oh, dear,' she said, dismayed, 'I don't believe the kettle can have been boiling.'

'It's quite all right,' said Henrietta. 'Go and get that holster, Gerda.'

Gerda hesitated and then went out of the room. Henrietta leant forward and put her arms on the table and her head down on them. She was so tired, so dreadfully tired. But now it was nearly done. Gerda would be safe, as John had wanted her to be safe.

She sat up, pushed the hair off her forehead and drew the teacup towards her. Then at a sound in the doorway she looked up. Gerda had been quite quick for once.

But it was Hercule Poirot who stood in the doorway.

'The front door was open,' he remarked as he advanced to the table, 'so I took the liberty of walking in.'

'You!' said Henrietta. 'How did you get here?'

'When you left The Hollow so suddenly, naturally I knew where you would go. I hired a very fast car and came straight here.'

'I see.' Henrietta sighed. 'You would.'

'You should not drink that tea,' said Poirot, taking the cup from her and replacing it on the tray. 'Tea that has not been made with boiling water is not good to drink.'

'Does a little thing like boiling water really matter?'

Poirot said gently: 'Everything matters.'

There was a sound behind him and Gerda came into the room. She had a workbag in her hands. Her eyes went from Poirot's face to Henrietta's.

Henrietta said quickly:

'I'm afraid, Gerda, I'm rather a suspicious character. M. Poirot seems to have been shadowing me. He thinks that I killed John — but he can't prove it.'

She spoke slowly and deliberately. So long as Gerda did not give herself away.

Gerda said vaguely: 'I'm so sorry. Will you have some tea, M. Poirot?'

'No, thank you, Madame.'

Gerda sat down behind the tray. She began to talk in her apologetic, conversational way.

'I'm so sorry that everybody is out. My sister and the children have all gone for a picnic. I didn't feel very well, so they left me behind.'

'I am sorry, Madame.'

Gerda lifted a teacup and drank.

'It is all so very worrying. Everything is so worrying. You see, John always arranged *everything* and now John is gone . . . ' Her voice tailed off. 'Now John is gone.'

Her gaze, piteous, bewildered, went from one to the other.

'I don't know what to do without John. John looked after me. He took care of me. Now he is gone, everything is gone. And the children — they ask me questions and I can't answer them properly. I don't know what to say to Terry. He keeps saying: 'Why was Father killed?' Some day, of course, he will find out why. Terry always has to *know*. What puzzles me is that he always asks *why*, not *who*!'

Gerda leaned back in her chair. Her lips were very blue.

She said stiffly:

'I feel — not very well — if John — John — '

Poirot came round the table to her and eased her sideways down in the chair. Her head dropped forward. He bent and lifted her eyelid. Then he straightened up.

'An easy and comparatively painless death.'

Henrietta stared at him.

'Heart? No.' Her mind leaped forward. 'Something in the tea. Something she put there herself. She chose that way out?'

Poirot shook his head gently.

'Oh, no, it was meant for *you*. It was in *your* teacup.'

'For *me?*' Henrietta's voice was incredulous. 'But I was trying to help her.'

'That did not matter. Have you not seen a dog caught in a trap — it sets its teeth into anyone who touches it. She saw only that you knew her secret and so you, too, must die.'

Henrietta said slowly:

'And you made me put the cup back on the tray — you meant — you meant *her* — '

Poirot interrupted her quietly:

'No, no, Mademoiselle. I did not *know* that there was anything in your teacup. I only knew that there *might* be. And when the cup was on the tray it was an even chance if she drank from that or the other — if you call it chance. I say myself that an end such as this is merciful. For her — and for two innocent children.'

He said gently to Henrietta: 'You are very tired, are you not?'

She nodded. She asked him: 'When did you guess?'

'I do not know exactly. The scene was set; I felt that from the first. But I did not realize for a long time that it was set *by Gerda Christow* — that her attitude was stagey because she was, actually, acting a part. I was puzzled by the simplicity and at the same time the complexity. I recognized fairly soon that it was *your* ingenuity that I was fighting against, and that you were being aided and abetted by your relations as soon as they understood what you wanted done!' He paused and added: 'Why did *you* want it done?'

'Because John asked me to! That's what he meant when he said '*Henrietta.*' It was all there in that one word. He was asking me to protect Gerda. You see, he loved Gerda. I think he loved Gerda much better than he ever knew he did. Better than Veronica Cray. Better than me. Gerda *belonged* to him, and John liked things that belonged to him. He knew that if anyone could protect Gerda from the consequences of what she'd done, I could. And he knew that I would do anything he wanted, because I loved him.'

'And you started at once,' said Poirot grimly.

'Yes, the first thing I could think of was to get the revolver away from her and drop it in the pool. That would obscure the fingerprint business. When I discovered later that he had been shot with a different gun, I went out to look for it, and naturally found it at once because I knew just the sort of place Gerda would have put it. I was only a minute or two ahead of Inspector Grange's men.'

She paused and then went on: 'I kept it with me in that satchel bag of mine until I could take it up to London. Then I hid it in the studio until I could bring it back, and put it where the police would not find it.'

'The clay horse,' murmured Poirot.

'How did you know? Yes, I put it in a sponge bag and wired the armature round it, and then slapped up the clay model round it. After all, the police couldn't very well destroy an artist's masterpiece, could they? What made you know where it was?'

'The fact that you chose to model a horse. The horse of Troy was the unconscious association in your mind. But the fingerprints — how did you manage the fingerprints?'

'An old blind man who sells matches in the street. He didn't know what it was I asked him to hold for a moment while I got some money out!'

Poirot looked at her for a moment.

'*C'est formidable!*' he murmured. 'You are one of the best antagonists, Mademoiselle, that I have ever had.'

'It's been dreadfully tiring always trying to keep one move ahead of *you*!'

'I know. I began to realize the truth as soon as I saw that the pattern was always designed not to implicate any one person but to implicate *everyone* — other than Gerda Christow. Every indication always pointed *away* from her. You deliberately planted

371

Ygdrasil to catch my attention and bring yourself under suspicion. Lady Angkatell, who knew perfectly what you were doing, amused herself by leading poor Inspector Grange in one direction after another. David, Edward, herself.

'Yes, there is only one thing to do if you want to clear a person from suspicion who is actually guilty. You must suggest guilt elsewhere but never localize it. That is why every clue *looked* promising and then petered out and ended in nothing.'

Henrietta looked at the figure huddled pathetically in the chair. She said: 'Poor Gerda.'

'Is that what you have felt all along?'

'I think so. Gerda loved John terribly, but she didn't want to love him for what he was. She built up a pedestal for him and attributed every splendid and noble and unselfish characteristic to him. And if you cast down an idol, *there's nothing left.*' She paused and then went on: 'But John was something much finer than an idol on a pedestal. He was a real, living, vital human being. He was generous and warm and alive, and he was a great doctor — yes, a *great* doctor. And he's dead, and the world has lost a very great man. And I have lost the only man I shall ever love.'

Poirot put his hand gently on her shoulder. He said:

'But you are one of those who can live with a sword in their hearts — who can go on and smile — '

Henrietta looked up at him. Her lips twisted into a bitter smile.

'That's a little melodramatic, isn't it?'

'It is because I am a foreigner and I like to use fine words.'

Henrietta said suddenly:

'You have been very kind to me.'

'That is because I have admired you always very much.'

'M. Poirot, what are we going to do? About Gerda, I mean.'

Poirot drew the raffia workbag towards him. He turned out its contents, scraps of brown suède and other coloured leathers. There were some pieces of thick shiny brown leather. Poirot fitted them together.

'The holster. I take this. And poor Madame Christow, she was overwrought, her husband's death was too much for her. It will be brought in that she took her life whilst of unsound mind — '

Henrietta said slowly:

'And no one will ever know what really happened?'

'I think one person will know. Dr

Christow's son. I think that one day he will come to me and ask me for the truth.'

'But you won't tell him,' cried Henrietta.

'Yes. I shall tell him.'

'Oh, *no*!'

'You do not understand. To you it is unbearable that anyone should be hurt. But to some minds there is something more unbearable still — not to *know*. You heard the poor woman just a little while ago say: 'Terry always has to *know*.' To the scientific mind, truth comes first. Truth, however bitter, can be accepted, and woven into a design for living.'

Henrietta got up.

'Do you want me here, or had I better go?'

'It would be better if you went, I think.'

She nodded. Then she said, more to herself than to him:

'Where shall I go? What shall I do — without John?'

'You are speaking like Gerda Christow. You will know where to go and what to do.'

'Shall I? I'm so tired, M. Poirot, so tired.'

He said gently:

'Go, my child. Your place is with the living. I will stay here with the dead.'

30

As she drove towards London, the two phrases echoed through Henrietta's mind. 'What shall I do? Where shall I go?'

For the last few weeks she had been strung up, excited, never relaxing for a moment. She had had a task to perform — a task laid on her by John. But now that was over — she had failed — or succeeded? One could look at it either way. But however one looked at it, the task was over. And she experienced the terrible weariness of the reaction.

Her mind went back to the words she had spoken to Edward that night on the terrace — the night of John's death — the night when she had gone along to the pool and into the pavilion and had deliberately, by the light of a match, drawn Ygdrasil upon the iron table. Purposeful, planning — not yet able to sit down and mourn — mourn for her dead. 'I should like,' she had said to Edward, 'to grieve for John.'

But she had not dared to relax then — not dared to let sorrow take command over her.

But now she could grieve. Now she had all the time there was.

She said under her breath: 'John . . . John.'
Bitterness and black rebellion broke over her.

She thought: 'I wish I'd drunk that cup of tea.'

Driving the car soothed her, gave her strength for the moment. But soon she would be in London. Soon she would put the car in the garage and go along to the empty studio. Empty since John would never sit there again bullying her, being angry with her, loving her more than he wanted to love her, telling her eagerly about Ridgeway's Disease — about his triumphs and despairs, about Mrs Crabtree and St Christopher's.

And suddenly, with a lifting of the dark pall that lay over her mind, she thought:

'Of course. That's where I will go. To St Christopher's.'

Lying in her narrow hospital bed, old Mrs Crabtree peered up at her visitor out of rheumy, twinkling eyes.

She was exactly as John had described her, and Henrietta felt a sudden warmth, a lifting of the spirit. This was real — this would last! Here, for a little space, she had found John again.

'The pore doctor. Orful, ain't it?' Mrs Crabtree was saying. There was relish in her voice as well as regret, for Mrs Crabtree loved life; and sudden deaths, particularly murders or deaths in childbed, were the richest parts of the tapestry of life. 'Getting 'imself bumped off like that! Turned my stomach right over, it did, when I 'eard. I read all about it in the papers. Sister let me 'ave all she could get 'old of. Reely nice about it, she was. There was pictures and everythink. That swimming pool and all. 'Is wife leaving the inquest, pore thing, and that Lady Angkatell what the swimming pool belonged to. Lots of pictures. Real mystery the 'ole thing, weren't it?'

Henrietta was not repelled by her ghoulish enjoyment. She liked it because she knew that John himself would have liked it. If he had to die he would much prefer old Mrs Crabtree to get a kick out of it, than to sniff and shed tears.

'All I 'ope is that they catch 'ooever done it and 'ang 'im,' continued Mrs Crabtree vindictively. 'They don't 'ave 'angings in public like they used to once — more's the pity. I've always thought I'd like to go to an 'anging. And I'd go double quick, if you understand me, to see 'ooever killed the doctor 'anged! Real wicked, 'e must 'ave been. Why, the doctor was one in a thousand. Ever so clever, 'e was! And a nice way with 'im! Got you laughing whether you wanted to or not. The things 'e used to say sometimes! I'd 'ave done anythink for the doctor, I would!'

'Yes,' said Henrietta, 'he was a very clever man. He was a great man.'

'Think the world of 'im in the 'orspital, they do! All them nurses. *And* 'is patients! Always felt you were going to get well when 'e'd been along.'

'So you are going to get well,' said Henrietta.

The little shrewd eyes clouded for a moment.

'I'm not so sure about that, ducks. I've got that mealy-mouthed young fellow with the spectacles now. Quite different to Dr Christow. Never a laugh! 'E was a one, Dr Christow was — always up to his jokes! Given me some norful times, 'e 'as, with this treatment of 'is. 'I carn't stand any more of it, Doctor,' I'd say to him, and 'Yes, you can, Mrs Crabtree,' 'e'd say to me. 'You're tough, you are. You can take it. Going to make medical 'istory, you and I are.' And he'd jolly you along like. Do anything for the doctor, I would 'ave! Expected a lot of you, 'e did, but you felt you couldn't let him down, if you know what I mean.'

'I know,' said Henrietta.

The little sharp eyes peered at her.

'Excuse me, dearie, you're not the doctor's wife by any chance?'

'No,' said Henrietta, 'I'm just a friend.'

'*I* see,' said Mrs Crabtree.

Henrietta thought that she did see.

'What made you come along if you don't mind me asking?'

'The doctor used to talk to me a lot about you — and about his new treatment. I wanted to see how you were.'

'I'm slipping back — that's what I'm doing.'

Henrietta cried:

'But you mustn't slip back! You've got to get well.'

Mrs Crabtree grinned.

'*I* don't want to peg out, don't you think it!'

'Well, fight then! Dr Christow said you were a fighter.'

'Did 'e now?' Mrs Crabtree lay still a minute, then she said slowly:

''Ooever shot 'im it's a wicked shame! There aren't many of 'is sort.'

We shall not see his like again. The words passed through Henrietta's mind. Mrs Crabtree was regarding her keenly.

'Keep your pecker up, dearie,' she said. She added: ''E 'ad a nice funeral, I 'ope.'

'He had a lovely funeral,' said Henrietta obligingly.

'Ar! I wish I could of gorn to it!'

Mrs Crabtree sighed.

'Be going to me own funeral next, I expect.'

'No,' cried Henrietta. 'You mustn't let go. You said just now that Dr Christow told you that you and he were going to make medical history. Well, you've got to carry on by yourself. The treatment's just the same. You've got to have the guts for two — you've got to make medical history by yourself — for him.'

Mrs Crabtree looked at her for a moment or two.

'Sounds a bit grand! I'll do my best, ducks. Carn't say more than that.'

Henrietta got up and took her hand.

'Goodbye. I'll come and see you again if I may.'

'Yes, do. It'll do me good to talk about the doctor a bit.' The bawdy twinkle came into her eye again. 'Proper man in every kind of way, Dr Christow.'

'Yes,' said Henrietta. 'He was.'

The old woman said:

'Don't fret, ducks — what's gorn's gorn. You can't 'ave it back.'

Mrs Crabtree and Hercule Poirot, Henrietta thought, expressed the same idea in different language.

She drove back to Chelsea, put away the

car in the garage and walked slowly to the studio.

'Now,' she thought, 'it has come. The moment I have been dreading — the moment when I am alone.

'Now I can put it off no longer. Now grief is here with me.'

What had she said to Edward? 'I should like to grieve for John.'

She dropped down on a chair and pushed back the hair from her face.

Alone — empty — destitute. This awful emptiness.

The tears pricked at her eyes, flowed slowly down her cheeks.

Grief, she thought, grief for John. Oh, John — John.

Remembering, remembering — his voice, sharp with pain:

'*If I were dead, the first thing you'd do, with the tears streaming down your face, would be to start modelling some damn' mourning woman or some figure of grief.*'

She stirred uneasily. Why had that thought come into her head?

Grief — Grief . . . A veiled figure — its outline barely perceptible — its head cowled.

Alabaster.

She could see the lines of it — tall, elongated, its sorrow hidden, revealed only by the long, mournful lines of the drapery.

Sorrow, emerging from clear, transparent alabaster.

'*If I were dead* . . . '

And suddenly bitterness came over her full tide!

She thought: '*That's what I am*! John was right. I cannot love — I cannot mourn — not with the whole of me.

'It's Midge, it's people like Midge who are the salt of the earth.'

Midge and Edward at Ainswick.

That was reality — strength — warmth.

'But I,' she thought, 'am not a whole person. I belong not to myself, but to something outside me. I cannot grieve for my dead. Instead I must take my grief and make it into a figure of alabaster . . . '

Exhibit No. 58. 'Grief'. Alabaster. Miss Henrietta Savernake . . .

She said under her breath:

'John, forgive me, forgive me, for what I can't help doing.'

HERCULE POIROT'S CHRISTMAS
SAD CYPRESS
ONE, TWO, BUCKLE MY SHOE
EVIL UNDER THE SUN
FIVE LITTLE PIGS
THE HOLLOW
THE LABOURS OF HERCULES
TAKEN AT THE FLOOD
MRS McGINTY'S DEAD
AFTER THE FUNERAL
HICKORY DICKORY DOCK
DEAD MAN'S FOLLY
CAT AMONG THE PIGEONS
THE ADVENTURE OF
THE CHRISTMAS PUDDING
THE CLOCKS
THIRD GIRL
HALLOWE'EN PARTY
ELEPHANTS CAN REMEMBER
POIROT'S EARLY CASES
CURTAIN: POIROT'S LAST CASE

TOMMY & TUPPENCE
THE SECRET ADVERSARY
PARTNERS IN CRIME
N OR M?
BY THE PRICKING OF MY THUMBS
POSTERN OF FATE

We do hope that you have enjoyed reading this large print book.

Did you know that all of our titles are available for purchase?

We publish a wide range of high quality large print books including:
Romances, Mysteries, Classics
General Fiction
Non Fiction and Westerns

Special interest titles available in large print are:
The Little Oxford Dictionary
Music Book
Song Book
Hymn Book
Service Book

Also available from us courtesy of Oxford University Press:
Young Readers' Dictionary
(large print edition)
Young Readers' Thesaurus
(large print edition)

For further information or a free brochure, please contact us at:
Ulverscroft Large Print Books Ltd.,
The Green, Bradgate Road, Anstey,
Leicester, LE7 7FU, England.
Tel: (00 44) **0116 236 4325**
Fax: (00 44) **0116 234 0205**